Praise for the *Finding Fae* Trilogy

Finding Fae

"Un-put-downable."
~The Prairies Book Review

"*Finding Fae* melds the elements of coming-of-age and YA Fantasy to create an unforgettable reading experience."
~Christina Prescott, The Book Commentary

A Twist of Fae

"Not the one to be missed."
~BookView Review

"A real forward-driven, exciting adventure for young readers."
~Readers Favorite Review

Fate of the Fae

"Gripping, thrilling, and fantastical; A read-in-one-sitting kind of book."
~The Prairies Book Review

"A brilliant ending to a stunning series."
~BookView Review

FATE OF THE FAE

THE FINAL BOOK IN THE FINDING FAE TRILOGY

Also by
EL HOLLY

Finding Fae
A Twist of Fae

PHANTASMIC WARS
The Book of Imagination
The Quest for the Artifacts
The Waking of the Nightmares
The Hunt for the Five
The Return to Phantasmagoria

EL HOLLY

Fate of the Fae
Book Three in the Finding Fae Trilogy
By El Holly

Imprint: Ivy Wolf Publishing House

Book cover art designed by Mariia from Miblart

Interior content graphics by these artists found on Canva .com:
beandbloom.com
Graphixmania
@edvankun488445818
@angela-apostols-images
Ton Photographer 4289
@canvacreativestudio
SamuilLevich
TMvectorart

Th' occasion speaks thee, and
My strong imagination sees a crown
Dropping upon thy head.
~William Shakespeare, *The Tempest*

Contents

Quince

When I was young and adjusting to my new life among humans, I had a tough time controlling my emotions. My parents taught me how to refocus and calm my brain by creating a haiku to describe the situation. One would think, given my theater background, maybe I'd switch to coming up with sonnets instead of haiku as I grew older, but I like the simplicity of the haiku: five syllables, seven syllables, five syllables. A tiny blip of words which can show so much with so little. I should note, the only sonnet I've ever written was for a high school English class, and it was less than memorable.

After years of practicing haiku to make sense of the world around me, my brain automatically starts to form thoughts into haiku when I'm in confusing or, as of late, dangerous situations. For example, when I accidentally phased, or realm-hopped, as Eevee puts it, to Sweden instead of Minnesota at the age of fifteen, and found myself on top of a reindeer, I calmed myself by thinking:

Seated on a deer
Who knows where I'll go from here?
I'm falling–oh dear!

Nothing too memorable, either, I suppose. But unlike my English class sonnet, my reindeer haiku is forever associated in my brain with the pain of falling in a snowbank and the confusion of finding myself in Sweden. Plus, I like the wordplay of "deer" and "dear."

There is another haiku which has stuck with me, though this one is more recent. When I first saw Eevee walk into the office at Duluth High only three months ago now, she looked apprehensive, with a dash of rebellion coloring the edges of her profile. This alone would have interested me, but I had been shocked to see the shimmery aura of recently practiced magic around her, which let me know she was a fae like me. Another fae at Duluth High? I knew some fae lived in the human realm, like my family, but I hadn't come across any in Duluth, Minnesota.

Until Eevee.

At that moment, words left my brain like birds flocking to the skies. But I still managed to come up with this haiku:

> She walks in with sparks
> Ready to burst into flame
> Wish I knew her name.

So much has happened in the three months since we met. Right now the only words I can think of, as I listen to someone sobbing from a prison cell down the hall, are these:

> Today's my birthday
> Candles should be burning bright
> Instead, all is dark.

Fae By the Ice Machine

My bones buzz with adrenaline as I shut the door behind me and deadbolt it. On shaky legs, I step the ten feet or so to the bed and flop down. That was close. Too close. And it means we'll have to move yet again, whenever my birth father, Aspen, deigns to return from his nightly foray into the fae realm.

In my hands, which are cupped to my chest, I hear a protesting cheep.

Slowly, I lower them from my chest and spread them apart until a small, feathered head pokes through and chirps its protests at its captivity. In my mind, I sense its indignation, and though my heartbeat races like I'm mid-marathon, I grin down at the tiny creature.

I was supposed to stay in the motel room, safe

and sound, while Aspen was out. But when I sensed distress nearby, I couldn't ignore it. It had almost been a coyote's dinner in an attempt to get the coyote away from its nest. At least, that's what I assume she was doing, based on the motherly alarm coming off of her in waves.

"Your babies will want their mama back," I tell the bird, who chirps up at me and glares out of one beady eye as if to say *let me go this instant.* "I know they're not newly hatched, but they're young. They still need their mom."

I try not to cry. I sympathize with this bird's young ones. I want my mother, too—my adopted mother, Penny Acker. The woman who hugged me when I was sad, took care of me when I was sick, and defends her family as fiercely as a mama bear.

"Let's see if the coast is clear," I whisper to the bird. Closing my eyes helps me focus, so I close them, leaning my head against the cheap wooden headboard. One moment, then two. Yes. I sense the coyote's hunger, but it's farther away now.

Quietly, I walk over to the sliding glass door—thank goodness Aspen decided on a ground level room for this motel—and crack it open with an elbow.

The bird, sensing her freedom is imminent, struggles hard, her wings with their white stripes beating frantically against my fingers. Once the door is open wide enough, I reach my hands through the opening and release her, watching as she flies away, directly to a pine tree nearby where her young ones await, their worry and fear decreasing as soon as she lands in their nest.

I close and lock the door, then make sure the curtains are fully drawn shut before throwing myself back onto the bed closest to the sliding glass door. My bed for tonight.

I want nothing more than to disappear from this motel room in northern Iowa with its musty sheets, blankets dotted with cigarette holes, and a heater which clicks and buzzes as it coughs out tepid air.

What's keeping me here? That's a question I can't shake, and it's followed me from one dilapidated motel room to the next. I'd like to say what's keeping me here in the human realm is a sense of honor or duty, but I'm not that kind of a person.

I'm not even a person at all.

You're a coward, Eevee, I think, sinking miserably onto the lumpy pillow behind me. Not even wearing my dad's favorite flannel shirt has cheered me up today. Instead, it's made me miss my old life more than ever.

To distract myself, I unlock my phone and search for what kind of bird species the mama bird I saved is. It strikes me as unusual she has young ones in January versus in the spring. Maybe she's some kind of bird from Elfaeme who found her way to Earth?

But…no. I find a bird in my search which looks identical to her. A white-winged crossbill. Rare to find in Iowa, but not impossible.

I set down my phone and run my hands through my short-cropped brown hair. The last two weeks have been a blur. Could I have done anything differently at the Winter Solstice Festival or in the events leading up to it? Each scenario I play out in my head ends the same. Me on the run with my birth father. Cut off except through the occasional text and email from my best friends, Cam and Maggie, and my adopted family, the quintessentially Midwestern Ackers. Abandoning my not-quite-but-pretty-much boyfriend Quince with his parents, all imprisoned by the Unseelie King. My birth mother turned to stone.

This is my life now. Living on the run, cut off from the family I grew up with, and unable to return to the world I only recently found out I was from. Constantly being followed by fae wanting to collect on the bounty King Nightglade placed on me and Aspen.

And yes, saving the occasional wild animal.

I don't want to think about the fae I saw by the ice machine just now. It was reckless of me to go out and help the bird, I know, but in my defense, I also had not expected to see any other fae in the hall of a run-down motel in Iowa. The last few days we've stayed here, there have hardly been any humans, let alone fae, checking in or out.

Instead, I curl up in a ball and obsessively replay the events of the Winter Solstice Festival like they're a dream, one of those awesome dreams in which you can actually change what happens. I revise details here and there, so this time I don't fail. I save Quince and his parents, as successfully as I saved the mama bird tonight. I prevent my birth mother from getting turned to stone by Nightglade, and she and I get to have a long conversation. I even manage to incapacitate Nightglade in the process of saving my birth parents so someone, like one of Quince's cousins, Sean or Shannon, can swoop in and take the Unseelie crown, ending Nightglade's increasingly unstable reign of the Unseelie Court.

Rolling over, I pound a particularly knobbly part of my pillow. No matter how many times I might replay it in my head, the reality is I did fail. And now I'm dealing with the consequences of it: living life on the run in the human realm with a fae father I just met, who, I've come to realize, needs a lot of looking after.

Great job I'm doing of it, too. I don't know where he is right now, aside from somewhere in Elfaeme. Most nights he disappears to the fae realm despite the danger it poses to the both of us, but not before making me promise not to follow him. I think it's his way of trying to impose some kind of fatherly order with a daughter he's just met?

Whatever the reason, I'm eighteen, and fully capable of taking care of myself, which is why it annoys me every time he makes me promise to stay put. Who is he to swoop in and act like he has some kind of right to my wellbeing when he gave that up eighteen years ago?

A noise in the hall like shuffling feet sets my heart racing. I forget to breathe, and strain to hear over the loud heartbeats pounding in my ears. *Please don't stop by my door, please don't stop…*

The footsteps slow, and I hold my hands in

front of my mouth, stifling a silent scream. What if this is it? What if they find me when Aspen is out and I'm captured, possibly executed, before Aspen even returns in the morning?

After what seems like hours, the footsteps shuffle away. I slowly let out a breath, unwilling even now to make unnecessary noise.

It was an elderly guest, I'm sure.

Who has absolutely no connection at all to the pointy-eared fae I saw filling up one of those cheap plastic ice buckets at the ice machine while I snuck by them with a bird in my hands. At the time, it had made sense to bring the bird inside with me until the coyote lost interest and went somewhere else. Now, I'm wondering if the fae noticed me like I noticed them.

I'm not always a quick learner. That's more my friend Maggie, who is smart and insightful and overall a badass human being. But when a pattern starts to emerge (in this case, fae staying at every motel and hotel we've checked in to in the last week), maybe it's time to change our strategy.

For the first few nights on the run, I felt a guilty sense of relief whenever I promised Aspen, "I won't follow you tonight."

I felt safe in the mildewed motel rooms with their outdated wallpaper and threadbare blankets. I was anonymous, hidden. No different than any of the humans around me, so long as I had a winter hat to cover my pointed ears.

But then Aspen messed up. He won't admit it,

and we don't talk about it, but we both know it. He wasn't careful enough when realm-hopping from Earth, to Elfaeme, and back again. After he returned from Elfaeme last week, we've had to stay in a different motel almost every night. It's exhausting. I was relieved when he decided we could stay here another night, but I guess it was one night too many.

Despite this, each night without fail, he leaves to go back to Elfaeme anyway, like staying in a room with me too long will give him hives or uncomfortable things like feelings.

The only feelings he has room for right now are self-pity and grief. I don't think he saved any space in his heart for anything or anyone else, not even for his own daughter.

I bite the inside of my cheeks. If I don't stay awake and alert, I won't be able to warn Aspen about the newest spy on our trail. I don't know why I care so much, when he doesn't extend me the same caution and courtesy.

Maybe it's because my only other birth parent is now a statue. Aspen's all I have left for biological parents, whether either of us likes it or not.

And I guess I expected more. More…fatherly affection? More attentiveness? More of a connection, rather than this awkward back-and-forth we always do?

In a weak moment while driving from Minnesota to Iowa, I opened up to him about the clues Maeve had left for me throughout the fae realm. I'm not sure what I hoped for. Maybe a confession that he knew about the clues, even helped her with them. Part of me wanted him to give me a conspiratorial grin and say, "Ah, I wondered when you'd bring that up."

But instead, all he did was tilt his head and go extra quiet before saying, "So that's what she'd been up to."

We watched corn fields out the car windows in silence afterward. Conversation over.

That was five motels and eight nights ago, though. And, of the last five motels, this one, in some small town in Iowa, is my least favorite.

"This pillow is the worst." I groan and flop onto my back, stretching my body like a cat. It's quiet here, except for the heater. Too quiet. Which is exactly why we need to leave, before the ice machine spy figures out which room we're in. For half a second, I consider leaving without Aspen, just cutting my ties with him and his wooden, awkward attitude for good. Obviously, this isn't working between us. We're not meant to be a father-daughter duo.

Something keeps me on the bed waiting for him, though.

Outside, a car alarm blares then shuts off.

The clock on the wall, one of those old analog clocks, ticks away. My eyes grow heavy.

I can hear fine with my eyes closed. Right?

Between the lumpy pillow, musty sheets, and terror that any second a fae spy was going to knock on the door, I'm surprised when I find myself blinking at the watery sunlight shining through the gauzy motel curtains. To my left is the sound of a low, buzzing snore.

I lob my lumpy pillow at Aspen's sleeping form. Snort, snuffle. He rolls over.

Anger coats the inside of my mouth like oil.

"Get up." My voice is cold as the winter wind swirling outside.

Aspen mumbles incoherently and pulls the blankets over his head.

Rolling out of bed, I stomp the five feet to the end of his bed and yank the covers back.

Leaves and dirt rain to the floor. Always with the leaves and dirt. What does he do, roll on the ground under the trees of the Sweetbriar Wood every night?

I grimace, banishing the thought before it gives me any images I don't want in my head. Instead, I focus on the last leaf floating to the motel floor.

He won't tell me where he goes every night, but my best guess is he's returning to the wild fae, to his old home. It's what I'd want to do, if I could.

Homesickness washes over me for my house in Duluth. I wonder what everyone is doing, now that school's started up again? Spending the holidays with Aspen in a motel room, while I knew my family was doing their traditional cookie baking, hot chocolate drinking, and gift exchange, was like having my organs stabbed repeatedly with a serrated knife.

"We need to go." I run my fingers through my hair, partly out of necessity, because it's totally flat on one side but sticking up in random spikes on the other, but also because the memory of the terror I felt last night has returned, with an extra healthy dose of renewed trepidation.

Apparently unconcerned about his lack of blankets or my proclamation, Aspen turns over.

No. I poke him. He's still sleeping.

Seriously, he's still sleeping?

I lean in close to his ear. "There's another fae staying at this motel," I hiss. "I don't think that's a coincidence, do you?"

This gets him out of bed. With more grace than anyone should have before nine in the morning, he vaults off the mattress to the floor, narrowly missing hitting my chin as I scramble back in alarm at the sudden movement.

"You should've told me right when I got back," he grumbles as he stuffs clothes into his suitcase.

"I was asleep when you got back!"

He pauses, frowning. "We had a whole conversation, Eevee. About pickles. Remember?"

I groan, rubbing my face. "You were talking to sleep Eevee. I don't remember that conversation at all."

Sitting on the suitcase to help smash his hastily packed clothes down, he glances up at me. "Sleep Eevee, huh? That would explain the odd comment you made about flamingos. You said they liked dill pickles best, and I asked how you knew that, and you told me to consult the Head Flamingo."

"Right," I say shortly, not as amused by Sleep Eevee's imaginative conversation as Aspen apparently is. "You ready?"

Less than five minutes later we're out of the motel and on the road, choosing our direction at random. Southeast. I guess we're heading to Illinois next. Aspen adjusts the car temperature to a few degrees below sweltering. I think longingly of the first few days on the run together when he didn't know how to work anything in the car.

"I'm ravenous," Aspen groans as we pass another exit without stopping for food. I grit my teeth. He's worse than my little brothers, Greg and Charlie, when it comes to his appetite. I pull the car over on the side of the road, turn on the hazards, and look at my birth father, who stares back at me in confusion.

"Why did you stop? Is there a food truck?" He turns in his seat to look around at the empty highway, then sighs in disappointment. Since returning to the human realm for the first time in almost twenty years, Aspen has discovered new interests like food trucks, home improvement shows, and couponing.

"Every night, you go out." I cross my arms. "Every night, you make me promise not to follow you. I've done what you've asked for the last couple weeks because I thought, I don't know, you're older, you know how the fae realm works more than I do, obviously you can make better judgment calls when it comes to our current situation. But we're in Iowa, and a fae almost found us last night. Why exactly are we safer here?"

He swallows, and I narrow my eyes, hoping he buys my outward act of toughness. Really, truly? I'm scared and confused and I miss my family and friends so much it's like my lungs can never get enough oxygen. Not to mention I spend every night wracked with guilt over what happened to Maeve, and thinking about what kind of torture Quince and his family are being put through. But I can't tell all of this to Aspen, I hardly know him. I long to message Cam or Maggie, but they're in school today and we agreed it would be safer for them and me if we reduced our communication for now.

When he doesn't answer, I add, "I'm not stopping for food until you give me some kind of an explanation."

"There's no need to threaten me," he answers mildly, chuckling. "I was thinking about how to explain it."

"Mm-hmm."

"You know Nightglade is searching for a Queen now."

"I do?"

"Oh, right." He chuckles again and it makes me want to throttle him.

He's lucky I spent so many nights practicing self-control with Sean and Shannon last fall. Their lessons were meant to help me control my fae powers, but they're applicable in other ways, too. Like restraining myself from doing bodily harm to Aspen for laughing at me.

"I was talking to sleep Eevee last night. She knows." He winks, and acts totally oblivious to the murderous expression on my face.

"Nightglade is searching for a Queen?" I prompt stiffly. I don't care at all that Nightglade is looking for a Queen. Honestly, in a list of things I don't care about at all, it's probably somewhere near the bottom. He can hold a contest for Queen for all I care, if he'd only release Quince and his family and un-stonify Maeve (is there a word for bringing someone back to life after being turned to stone?). "Which has to do with us living in cheap motels in the Midwest because…?"

"His search for a Queen, our current living situation, it all comes back to the crowns." Aspen's voice is as vague as his words. He looks at me, his expression drooping into a frown. "It's because the Unseelie King's crown is in possession of Nightglade, not the other way around. He's forced to look for a Queen, now that Maeve…" He breaks off, his voice cracking.

Steer the conversation into safer waters, Eevee, or you're never going to get an explanation. Poor Aspen has been in a near-constant grief spiral these last few weeks at any mention of Maeve. "And the crown has something to do with why we're safer in the human realm?"

A moment passes while Aspen takes some steadying breaths. "Yes. Right. It all comes back to the crown. Which is why we're safer spending most of our time here. Nightglade's power is tied to the Unseelie crown, to the fae realm. He can't leave Elfaeme. None of the fae who wear one of the four crowns can leave."

"Like, at all?"

He puffs out his cheeks. "I'm not sure exactly how it works. I just know that once the crowns have claimed a new ruler, a King and a Queen for the Unseelie and Seelie, those rulers very rarely leave their own domains. They occasionally travel to other parts of Elfaeme, but it's rare. And they never travel to the human world."

"So, here we are," I whisper.

"So here we are," Aspen echoes. "Can we stop at the next exit?" He pulls a wad of cash out of his jacket.

"More emergency funds?" I ask lightly, merging onto the highway.

He won't tell me where he gets all the money. But I have my suspicions. I know it sounds crazy, but as soon as we realm-hopped from almost-caught-in-Nightglade's-clutches to the human world, Aspen started gathering as much plant matter as he could find. Leaves, acorns, twigs, you name it. This was no easy feat, given I brought us to Minnesota in the dead of winter, and there was no rational explanation I could think of. I thought he'd gone insane over seeing Maeve turn to stone and just snapped, gathering anything plantlike to himself like a squirrel storing up for winter. But ever since then, he's been able to pull cash out of his pocket whenever it's needed. Are the two connected? Perhaps. Or, I suppose, the less fun theory is he's being given cash by whatever fae he's seeing on his nightly forays into Sweetbriar Wood.

I pull onto the highway and contemplate what Aspen has now told both myself and my sleep self. Nightglade can't follow us to the human realm. His connection to the Unseelie King's crown ties him to the Unseelie territory, where his power is strongest.

All he can do is keep sending fae after us.

It isn't comforting, per se, but it does ease my worries enough that, when we stop for food, I buy myself an extra doughnut with the largest black coffee I can get at the gas station.

If Nightglade can't follow me anywhere in the human realm, then maybe going back home to Duluth for a quick visit would be okay.

I glance over at Aspen, who's munching on an apple, and keep that thought to myself.

A Failed Return

We are the choices we make. I read that phrase on a fortune cookie today after yet another takeout dinner. Usually the fortunes don't apply to me, but I enjoy reading them anyway. Today, I crumple the fortune and the cookie and throw it all in the tiny motel trash bin.

I feel like it's mocking me.

Has it really only been twenty days since the choice that turned my life upside-down? It feels like a lifetime.

Thank goodness for modern technology. I hate not seeing my human friends and family, but at least I know they're safe. I look at the texts I received earlier today from Cam and Maggie, the first I've heard from them in days.

C: *the protection charms are still holding!*
M: *so far.*
M: *miss you soooooo much, E!*
M: *Java Jive isn't the same*
M: *school isn't the same*
C: *nothing's the same*

I wish I could text Quince as easily as I can text Cam, Maggie, and my sister, Amelia. I have no idea what happened to him or his parents after I left them at the mercy of King Nightglade, a fae not exactly known for his mercy.

For all I know, they're dead.

But I can't go back to the Unseelie Court without being imprisoned myself.

Can one die from inaction? Because not doing anything is slowly leaching away at my soul.

Next to me, my birth father Aspen laughs quietly, his back propped on a pile of pillows on his motel bed. He hasn't laughed often in the last few weeks. But when he does, I find myself smiling, no matter what mood I'm in. Like right now. He's laughing at a commercial and I can feel the corners of my lips raise into a crooked smile of their own accord. His laugh is nice; kind of reedy, but full of amusement.

My smile fades as I frown down at my phone. What Aspen doesn't know is that tonight is the night

I'm going home to check on my adoptive family in person.

Texts and emails are great, and I appreciate Cam, Maggie, and Amelia for keeping me in the loop. But it isn't the same as seeing them in person. I miss them all so much it's like a constant stomach ache. Like I've done so often over the last few weeks, I open up the gallery on my phone and scroll through the pictures in my camera roll while Aspen flips through the channels to find something new to watch.

This is our usual evening activity. Trying to engage in conversation is like pulling teeth, so neither of us has attempted more than surface level topics recently.

I stop on a picture of my little brothers, Greg and Charlie, with their cheeks reddened from the snow and big smiles on their faces, standing next to the snow monster they made. Amelia sent me this picture only yesterday.

Scrolling a few more, my eyes tear up at a selfie of me and my sister Jess. We're snuggled under a fleece blanket on the couch, and Jess is sticking her tongue out at the camera. This picture usually makes me smile. I had forced her to take a picture with me when all she wanted to do was watch a documentary on chimpanzees. "Ugh, Eevee, another picture?" she'd asked right before making a goofy face. Tonight it makes me miss Jess even more.

There are so many pictures of me, Cam, and Maggie together. A lot of them at the Java Jive, where

Maggie works. My favorite is a picture of the three of us sitting at our table at the Java Jive. Maggie's wearing a black Java Jive apron, her brown eyes crinkled in a smile as she toasts the camera with a coffee mug decorated with dancing Santas. She has a coffee-colored headband keeping her Afro back from her face. Cam is slouched over one of their drawings. The left side of their head had been freshly shaved, and the right side, which they keep longer, is dyed stripes of red and orange like fire. Between them is me, grinning like a dork, wearing my usual sweatshirt and leggings.

I scroll some more. There are a lot of pictures of me and Amelia, too. Selfies of the two of us, even some pictures I had taken of her and shoulders guy (her boyfriend, Trent). She really does look radiantly happy wrapped up in his arms, her round face and doe eyes glowing as she looks up at him.

I only have one picture of me and Quince. It's the last picture I took before going to the Winter Solstice Festival. Most of our time together up until the winter solstice was spent in the fae realm, and technology doesn't mix well with Elfaeme. We spent part of a day together in Duluth the day of the winter solstice. I had taken the picture of us when we were shopping for the outfits we wore that night. We have smiles on our faces, but both of our eyes are pinched with stress. His are almost black compared to my light brown, but even though they're dark, they have a mischievous twinkle in them I can't help but love.

I glance over at Aspen. When will he fall asleep?

He looks tired, but then again, he always looks like he's behind on sleep. Without his brilliant green wings and butterfly markings on his arms, he looks like an overworked, exhausted office worker. An overworked, exhausted office worker with pointy-tipped ears.

He also looks too young to be my birth father, but then again, fae age differently than humans. Many times when we're out getting food or gas, people have assumed we're brother and sister. Though my face is nearly identical to my birth mother, Maeve's, I do have a striking resemblance to Aspen as well. Our similarities are more in our mannerisms. It's strange, knowing I've grown up my whole life with the Ackers, to find out I smile or tilt my head the same way as my birth father, who I've only recently reconnected with.

"Look at that place! It's a luxury resort, not a cabin," Aspen comments. His favorite way to relax in the evenings has been snacking on food while watching home renovation and home buying shows.

"Mmm," I reply, looking down at the picture of me and Quince. *Are you still alive? Did you make it to your birthday, on December 29th? I wish I could have celebrated with you.*

An hour passes. Aspen slides lower and lower on his pillows until I hear a soft snoring from his bed. I switch off the television, a thrill running through me. This is my chance. Aspen will wake up in an hour or two and head to Elfaeme, which doesn't give me a lot of time. But I don't care.

In less than a minute, I'll be able to see my

family again.

I shoot a guilty glance at Aspen, where he lays asleep beneath the white motel blanket. He's lectured me, almost daily, on the dangers of returning home or traveling to Elfaeme. I understand the danger. But I can't "be patient as this situation sorts itself out" any longer.

I slip out of my bed. The department-store clearance section sweatpants and sweatshirt I wear aren't warm enough for being outside in a Minnesota winter, but I don't plan to stay for long. Besides, thanks to my Unseelie blood, I can handle cold temperatures a little better than most humans. Growing up, I had thought it was the extra tough Midwestern in me. I ready myself, my heart hammering, then close my eyes and take a step.

Realm-hopping from the motel in Illinois, to the fae realm, to outside my house in Duluth, Minnesota in the space of thirty seconds on an empty stomach is not the best idea I've ever had. My house appears in front of me, and though my heart lifts at the sight of it, I clutch at my stomach and stagger in the icy driveway. That's the most realm-hopping I've done since fleeing the Winter Solstice Festival.

From behind one of the bushes below the living room window, I spy the slightest shiver of movement, and a flash of white-blond hair. Anger flares in my heart.

"Ilinor," I hiss under my breath. What is Nightglade's daughter doing here, so close to my family?

I barely make it two steps toward the bush when a small, green-skinned figure shoots out from behind the snow monster near the driveway and tackles me.

"It–isn't–safe!" croaks Folsom.

Before I can stop him, he touches his sticky-padded fingers to my hand and we vanish.

Folsom may be ancient and no match for me physically, but his magic is much stronger than mine. He pulls me along with him as if I'm no more substantial than a cloud, despite being almost double his size.

We materialize next to the Reflecting Pool in the In Between. The trees around us are in the final stages of autumn, only a few leaves clinging to the branches. Somewhere nearby an owl hoots and I see its shape as it flies in front of the moon. In an hour, the forest will reset into the first stages of spring. The pool's illuminated reflection shifts through the cycle, from bright greens to the warm colors of autumn.

I yank my hand away from Folsom's, which is cold against my skin. How long had he been hiding behind the snow monster my little brothers built at my childhood home? Why was he there?

He picks up his gnarled walking stick and leans on it, looking up at me. His brown robes hang loose on his body and the skin on his wide, froggy face sags. It gives him the appearance of a tiny old man wearing a loose-fitting frog costume.

"What did you do that for?" I demand in a whisper.

He blinks once, twice, with red-rimmed, bulbous yellow eyes. "It isn't safe at your house," he says in his croaky voice.

"Why not?" My heart races as I think of that flash of white-blond hair in the bushes. Did Ilinor see me? I should never have come here. It was stupid of me to risk everyone's safety just to see my family's faces.

He looks at me as if I'm insufferably dim-witted. "The house is being watched. You don't think King Nightglade would let you and Aspen escape without any consequences?"

"M-my family," I interrupt, stammering, then swallow. "You were at the house. They're okay?"

He inclines his head, revealing his green, spotted pate. "For now."

My knees feel watery. I crouch so I am looking eye-to-eye with Folsom. "I think it's time you and I have a chat."

"About what?" he asks dully.

I think back on what I know and don't know about Folsom. He was the fae I met in my first foray into Elfaeme. At the time, it had seemed like a chance encounter, until he showed up again, right before Quince and I traveled to Maeve and Aspen's cottage.

"'I never told him, remember that,'" I say aloud.

He starts in recognition.

"For the longest time, I couldn't figure out what you meant by that. Until the Winter Solstice Festival."

Covering his eyes, a ribbety moan escapes from him.

"You were talking about Nightglade, weren't you?" I press. He nods, still moaning and covering his eyes. "So…" I stand and pace in front of him, the Reflecting Pool to my back. "You knew about my birth parents. You even…helped them?"

He nods.

"I gotta know. Why are you and Scamp such enemies then?" When they saw each other, fighting ensued. If I hadn't stopped them, Folsom would be in a lot worse shape than he is today. Scamp's claws are sharp, and he was out to kill.

At the mention of Scamp, Folsom lowers his hands and shoots me a venomous look. "Don't talk to me about that opportunistic cat," he spits. "There doesn't have to be a deep reason behind everything. He's a cat, and I'm a frog fae. We just don't like each other."

I hold my hands up in a placating gesture. "Okay, I'm just trying to figure out what your role is in all of this. I thought you were trying to get your place back in the Unseelie Court."

His eyes widen and he quakes. "That—that is true. My lady wanted me to play the part of the embittered, cast out member of the Court." He's talking fast now, his words all running together. His eyes dart often toward our reflections in the pool behind me. "And so I did, though my true desire, as always, has been to serve her. It is my greatest honor." Tears tremble at the edges of his eyes.

I can't breathe. He's talking about my birth mother, something Aspen never does. The way Folsom threw himself at her feet after Nightglade turned her to stone…

I open my mouth to ask all the burning questions I have about Maeve. There are so many, and Aspen won't talk about her without breaking down.

Probably because Maeve is a statue now.

"You were loyal to Maeve all this time?"

He sits on a moss-covered stone at the edge of the Reflecting Pool, resting his knobbly walking stick on his knees and nods wearily.

"My lady did her best to prevent the curse of the revoked crown. But in the end, she couldn't escape it."

I rub my arms and gingerly sit next to Folsom. "So, what does that mean for you now?"

He raises his chin. "Nothing has changed. I still serve her. I will do my best to carry out her wishes, even if she is not…" His bulbous eyes close.

"What are you up to, Folsom?" I press. "Why were you watching my house?"

"I was watching for you," he snaps, his eyes opening to give me a scornful look. "I knew you'd be stupid enough to come back to your house eventually, E."

The first time I met Folsom, I had been wary. My admittedly rushed and patchy internet research had informed me not to tell any fae my full name. Now, it's the only thing he calls me and I'm not correcting him at this point.

Crossing my arms, I scowl at him. "You can't blame me. I wanted to check up on my family."

"You wanted to see them for your own benefit. Not for them."

His words cut deep. He's not wrong. They are safer if I keep my distance.

"Security around the Unseelie Court is tighter than I ever remember it being," he says in a croaky whisper. "Everyone's allegiance is in question, especially after…" He swallows. "Well. Regardless. One thing hasn't changed. Anyone with a known association with you is imprisoned, in hiding, or being watched, while Nightglade searches for a suitable fae to take up the title of Unseelie Queen."

Not wanting to be viewed as totally out of the loop, even by Folsom, I quickly say, "Aspen told me Nightglade's been looking for someone to wear the Unseelie Queen's crown."

I miss Folsom's response. If I'm being honest, I don't really care about Nightglade's search for a co-ruler right now. Folsom's words play on repeat in my head. *Imprisoned. In hiding. Being watched.* No mention of any deaths. I'm so relieved for Quince and his parents, I feel dizzy.

"No deaths," I breathe.

Folsom stutters to a stop mid-sentence and cocks his head.

"That's…good," I add, uneasy by his silence.

He regards me pensively.

"Right?"

The already thin line of his mouth presses together until it's almost nonexistent. "Being a prisoner in the Iron Prison is as good as a death sentence."

"Then I have to free Quince and his parents!" I jump up, ready to realm-hop straight to the Unseelie Court, dangers be damned.

Folsom tugs me down. "Don't be a fool," he says in a hoarse voice. "You'll get yourself captured, too, and then what good will you do?" There's a strange gleam in Folsom's eyes as he looks up at me, his hand on my arm. "Stay away from Elfaeme, E. And from your home in the human realm."

The fight drains out of me and my head drops into my hands. "I feel useless."

We sit next to the Reflecting Pool in silence.

No.

The woods aren't totally silent.

In the distance, so far away I can barely hear it, is the sound of whoops and howls.

"You need to go." Folsom props his weight on the gnarled walking stick and stands. He regards me warily. "Back to Aspen. For now."

"But Quince—my family—"

"You will be able to help them," he insists. "When the time is right."

"And how will I know when that is?" I demand, standing so that, even though I'm barely over five feet tall, I loom over him. The light from the Reflecting

Pool adds a glistening sheen to his moist skin.

"If you're smart, you'll figure it out. Now go!"

I hesitate, frowning down at him.

A baying call sounds nearby and Folsom startles, dropping his walking stick. He bends to pick it up, then brandishes it at me. "Go!"

There are so many things I want to do. Somehow break Quince and his parents out of the Iron Prison before it becomes their death sentence. See my family: my parents, my sisters Amelia and Jess, my brothers Greg and Charlie. Curl up in my bed with the family cat, Slinky.

But at the deadly serious look on Folsom's face, I know I can't.

"You promise I'll know when it's time to come back to Elfaeme?"

His chin dips. "You have my word, E."

I'm not sure how reliable Folsom's word is, but I do know he's loyal to my birth mother. And for now, that'll have to be good enough.

"Okay. I'll be waiting."

I step off the rock and use the last of my strength to realm-hop back to the motel room.

Aspen snorts and rolls over when I bang my shin on the corner of the bed upon arrival, but he doesn't wake up. I tuck myself under the covers, breathing in their musty smell, and worry pinches my stomach. By the time he wakes from his nap to go to Elfaeme without me, my stomach has twisted itself into braids, knots, you name it. He pauses next to my bed and I can sense him looking down at me, but I keep my eyes closed.

Then he's gone, and I'm left to my own thoughts and knotted stomach.

Send word soon, Folsom, I think.

Quince

Time appears to be at a standstill in the dark and damp, but I know better. I know it marches on and on, so I mark its passage by counting screams and whimpers of the other prisoners, other fae like me who Nightglade prefers to hide away from the Court.

But there's something else I have noticed. Since the Winter Solstice, since choosing to stay with my parents over the one I love, I have also heard the whispers.

Here in the dark, it is not so hard to confess my love for Eevee, to join my whispers with the ones I hear around me. All I have in this cell with me are my thoughts and feelings, everything I have said or left unsaid, felt or refused to acknowledge because the timing was not right. So I whisper it to the walls of my prison.

I keep away from the walls, though. It is called the Iron Prison for a reason. The floors are the only thing any fae can touch without experiencing agony and nausea.

On Earth, iron's effects on fae are minimal. A little upset stomach, occasionally, or a sense of unease, at the most. But in Elfaeme, iron is powerful enough to cause extreme disgust, revulsion, an immediate need to get as far away as possible or throw up.

Some prisoners throw themselves against their walls, against the iron bars of their cells, then shriek and shriek.

Then it's back to whispers.

Their words don't have meaning to me, not when I am mired in my own haze of self-doubt and despair.

But after a few agonizing weeks where seconds were centuries and hours were millenia, I huddle in the center of my cell and pause my own rambling.

The whispers around me have coalesced, and all I can hear from the other cells are the words, "A new moon is upon us."

I don't know what the meaning of that comment is. This is the first time they've said it since I was imprisoned.

Seconds, minutes, weeks pass, and the whispers coalesce again.

"A new moon is upon us."

It isn't until today, with those whispers floating along the hall for the second time since my imprisonment, that I wonder what it might mean to have another new moon? Aside from marking the passage of time.

I wrack my brain, trying to remember what I've learned of fae lore about the new moon. It's a time for darker magic, for Unseelie magic. While the Seelie are strongest with the full moon, Unseelie fae have the most power during a new moon. Fae like me, of both Seelie and Unseelie blood, are mixed. Some take after one parent or the other, and end up most powerful at the new or full moon, and some find their strength is greatest at the waxing or waning half-moons.

Is that why the prisoners are whispering, because of the greater power the Unseelie have during a new moon?

I study today's meal in the dim light cast by the torch across the hall. I have left it untouched on the ground next to the barred door of my cell. I say today's meal as if we get fed daily. We don't. But even on the days someone does bring us food, I find I cannot stomach all of it. The proximity of the iron messes with my stomach.

Instead, I pace my cell, listening to the whispers about the new moon and wondering what it could mean. Does Nightglade do something during the new moon, some kind of Unseelie ritual I don't know of?

As I pace, I train my ears to pick out my father's or mother's murmurs or, worse, screams, amongst the disembodied voices. Sometimes I think I can hear the timbre of my father's voice or the distinctive way my mother's sentences turn up at the end in a question. It was never, "Quince, you look tired." It was, "Quince, you look tired?"

Today, I don't hear anyone who sounds like them.

A thought occurred to me yesterday, or the day before, or last week. Maybe I am imagining their voices and it is all in my head. Maybe Nightglade killed them already and I chose to stay with them, be imprisoned, for nothing.

Admittedly, I had not planned what I would do after I stayed at the Winter Solstice and Eevee left with Aspen. I just knew I did not want to be, could not be separated from my parents when they were so obviously in pain.

Five steps, turn, five steps, turn. Don't get too close to the walls when I turn, or my wings will go numb. I learned that lesson my first week here.

My presence in the Iron Prison isn't helping my parents, either. Whatever moral support I had hoped to provide them has been impossible; I have not seen them once since we were brought here. The guards had to rip my mother's hands from my arm. Her mouselike tail lashed and went limp when they struck her. But even then, I thought they could not be too far. It's all one hallway, with cells on either side. But the Iron Prison is a much longer hallway than I had anticipated.

Five steps, turn, pick up another scraggly feather which has fallen off my wings, place it in the small pile in the corner. Anger and hunger cloud my thoughts, making it difficult to think of any plan of escape anymore. Those first few weeks, it was all I could think about. Now? Ha.

To think I had grand plans of sneaking myself and my parents out of this death trap.

Five steps, turn. Five steps, pick up a feather, place it on the pile. Now, I have set aside any plans of escape. I am focused on one thing, and one thing only: survival.

It's why, eventually, I bend down, my knees creaking, and pick up bites of the tasteless food and shove it in my mouth. Survival.

I go to pace my cell again, but stop. The whispers I have been listening to shudder to a halt and there is silence in the Iron Prison, not so much as a breath to break the smothering quiet. I pause, my ears straining to hear something, anything. A tiny part of me dares to hope. Is this it? Could this be a rescue attempt? Is it Eevee?

Every day since being imprisoned, I have imagined her face, the way it looked when I first saw her in Elfaeme, with a magical glow in her eyes and the orange flower markings on her temples. I loved tracing those marks with my fingers, watching her eyes close at my touch.

Footfalls echo down the hallway. I want to run to the bars and peer through, whisper to Eevee to remember what I showed her in the wyvern tunnels, to use her wings so she barely touches the ground, otherwise someone will hear her as she walks.

But when I stare out from my prison cell, it is not Eevee's face I see.

Nightglade himself stands before me holding a torch, dressed in black robes edged with white and silver fur. Across his face and the ruff of white fur around his neck are spatters of blood. Even the Unseelie King's crown on his head is dotted with ruby red droplets of blood, its intricate silver leaves and thorns tainted with death.

We stare at each other through the iron bars of my cell. I have no clue what could be on Nightglade's mind, why he has come to my cell after all this time, after ignoring me so completely I thought he forgot I even existed, but I am not going to ask him. I wait for him to talk.

He contemplates me, and under his steely gaze I'm hyper-aware of how thin I've become. How my hair is brittle and falls out at the slightest touch, how my once glossy wings are dull and have bare patches where feathers used to be. I don't break eye contact with him, though. I stare into the eyes of the Unseelie King and dare him to tell me what he wants of me. While I wait, I think of a haiku to calm my nerves.

I've become what you
made me. Bones and fire and a
desire to survive.

"You and I are going to chat," he says, his words clipped and to the point.

The words fracture in my mind. Nerves no longer calm.

A goblin with a snoutlike nose and forearms wider than my neck comes forward with a key and unlocks my cell, his hands covered with leather gloves to protect him from the iron. When the door swings open, I stay standing, immobile.

"Attempt escape, and your life is forfeit."

Nightglade turns without another word and the goblin grabs my too-thin arm and tugs me with him after the Unseelie King.

I crane my neck, peering through the gloom into the cells as I walk, but I can't see anyone who looks Gerald or Myska shaped. My heart, which has been beating in a dull, numb rhythm these many days, gives a painful thump. Where could they be? If it wasn't their voices I have been hearing, if I have started hearing things…The goblin grows impatient with my slow pace and growls, his grip so tight I know I'll have a goblin hand-shaped bruise on my bicep later.

We reach the end of the hall, the door

separating the Iron Prison from the Unseelie castle, and step through it. Out of the Iron Prison we go, yet I am just as imprisoned as back in that cell.

Casting my gaze at a window, my eyes drink in the night sky. It has been so long since I've seen anything other than iron bars, mold-covered, iron-flecked stone, and dirt floors in the weak light of a single torch. Stars glitter in the tiny window of the sky I can see, and I wonder if any of my friends are looking at the same sky as me. Where are Sean and Shannon, my cousins? Where are Eevee and Aspen? Or Eevee's friends, Cam and Maggie? Are any of them looking up at the sky tonight, empty without its moon, and worrying about how I am or if I am still alive?

A horrifying thought strikes me. What if they are here, too, somewhere in the Iron Prison, and we are all at the mercy of the Unseelie King?

Well, that is alarming to think about. My brain is split in two. I both want to believe they are not imprisoned, and also convinced it could be true.

"In here," the goblin grunts, tossing me through a doorway and slamming it behind me.

Nightglade stands by a fireplace at the opposite end of the room. Its warmth fills the small area and I shiver, suddenly aware of how cold and clammy I've been. I had gotten used to it to the point where I hadn't noticed it anymore.

"You may prove useful to me."

He walks forward and I flinch at his approach. Why can't I be brave when it really matters? But this is

the King who forbade my parents from living at the
Unseelie Court, simply because my mother is Seelie, the
King who forced them back to his Court when he
wanted to keep an eye on them, and me, just to get to
Eevee, the King who presided over numerous courtly
gatherings where the Unseelie fae loyal to him snubbed
me and bullied me and he said nothing, the King who
betrothed his own daughter to me to pretend he was
accepting of my parentage but really to bait Eevee and
break my heart, the King who tortured my parents
because I left. The King who imprisoned me, ignored
me, and is now intimidating me.

And I can do nothing but cower. I would cry if
I weren't so dehydrated. All my life, my parents
cautioned me to play it safe in Elfaeme, to not draw
attention to our family. It's why I grew up among
humans, learning how much they were like us, and yet
unlike. Learning to respect them for their courage
facing death after so short of lives, and for their
determination and perseverance. My parents
encouraged me to go to parties, set up play dates, join
clubs. When Jim Mortenson started coming around,
they were delighted. The more humans around us with
their human smell and human loudness, the less likely
we'd be tracked if the Seelie or Unseelie royalty ever
decided to search for us. Helping Eevee, unfortunately,
drew much more attention from the Unseelie King than
I had anticipated when I first met her. I wouldn't
change anything, though, and that knowledge fortifies
me. I straighten and square my shoulders, facing

Nightglade.

"H-how…" My voice rasps out, stuttering and raw. When was the last time I spoke aloud to anyone, aside from my circuitous whispers? "How can I be useful…" I take a breath; Nightglade's impassive face unnerving to me, "…from prison?"

A small, amused smile turns up the corners of his thin, lifeless lips ever so slightly.

"Precisely by being in prison, in fact."

The confusion must show on my face because he laughs, a low, cruel laugh utterly devoid of happiness. An empty laugh. The skin on my face and arms prickles painfully and my father's warning about the Unseelie King comes back to me.

"Beware his laugh. He can torture and kill without a sword."

Nightglade's laugh fades, as does the prickling sensation on my skin, leaving it feeling sensitive, like it had been scrubbed by the world's most abrasive loofah.

"You know we are seeking another Unseelie to take the crown of the Unseelie Queen."

He states it as if I do, in fact, know. I want to remind him I have been imprisoned since the Winter Solstice and the news here has been lacking, but I stay silent.

"Every new moon is another chance for someone else to take the crown."

A puzzle piece clunks into place. This explains the whispers from the cells. I'm young, I have not been alive for other coronations, so I didn't know the new moon was when the Unseelie crown chose another ruler, but there were obviously some in the Iron Prison who have been alive long enough to know.

Something is wrong, though. I furrow my brow as Nightglade perches in a high-backed wooden chair, steepling his fingers in front of his mouth.

My brain moves sluggishly, but a detail eventually rises to the surface.

It's been weeks. No, more than weeks, almost a couple months since the Winter Solstice.

The whispers about the new moon have happened twice.

"N…no one wants to…rule with you?"

I regret my cheeky question as soon as I ask it.

"You dare speak so to your King?" The look on his face is murderous, his gray eyes almost black like mine, though I doubt mine could ever look so terrifying and empty. He stands swiftly and strides to me until we're nearly nose-to-nose.

He lifts an arm and I flinch, anticipating the blow to come.

Instead, he places his index finger on my temple.

Paint shoots through my head like he's taken a nail gun and fired it.

An image blooms in the pain: my parents in a hanging cage in the throne room, clothes hanging off their skeletal frames, skin gray and patchy where not covered by bruises.

He removes his finger and the image fades,

though the pain stays, worse than any headache. I feel feverish and weak and sick to my stomach, like his touch has given me the flu.

"They mean a lot to you?"

White-hot anger fires in my heart. "They are m-my parents."

"That's not an answer. My parents were skilled and cunning and had high hopes for their child. They raised me to achieve my ambitions at all costs. They taught me how to garner loyalty, how to seek every opportunity for advancement. And when the time came, they knew their fate was sealed, their usefulness used up, except for one final task."

Horror fills me. "Y-you killed…"

He laughs, as though delighted I thought him capable of killing his parents with his own hands. "No. They died in a tragic accident, a fire at their home. Unfortunately, it meant that right after their funeral I needed to take their positions at court to carry on the family name. Maeve, our newly crowned Queen, was quite sympathetic to me, the poor soul who had lost both his parents and had so much to live up to."

I stand in shocked silence. He didn't kill them himself, but I have no doubt he had planned it, timed it so he could win the sympathy, and eventual love, of the new Unseelie Queen.

"So, you see, you puzzle me. You chose to stay with your parents out of…what? Loyalty?" Again, he laughs, but not the same skin-prickling laugh as before. "I assure you, they are unhappier knowing you are imprisoned than they ever were after you left them to go help your mate last year."

He stands, begins pacing, drawing ever closer. I don't dare to speak. Is he going to show me another image, this time of Eevee? I don't know if I could handle it, not while the afterburn of my parents looking so emaciated is still imprinted in my mind.

"Tonight's ceremony did not go as planned," he finally admits. "Banethistle was more than willing to take the crown, but I regret that he tried, because I have lost a loyal member of my Court."

Oh. Something is definitely wrong, then. I open my mouth to ask a question. "So, Banethistle, he–"

"Is dead," Nightglade finishes, his tone clipped and harsh. "The crown rejected him and killed him."

The crown of the Unseelie Queen has killed Banethistle? Nightglade might regret Banethistle's death, but I definitely do not. Not after what he had done to my family, not after he went undercover as Duluth High's substitute librarian last year, under the name of Abscons, to spy on Eevee. But it means Nightglade still needs to find another Unseelie Queen.

An awful thought occurs to me. Who died during the last new moon ceremony? Who was his first choice of Queen?

"Invoking the curse of the revoked crown succeeded." Nightglade has moved in front of the fireplace and is staring into its flames as though they might tell him why this hasn't made his life easier. "It deprived Maeve of her Queenly power."

And turned her to stone, I think, recalling how, from the back of the crowded room I had watched Maeve turn into a statue, Eevee's hopeful expression crumbling.

"But it has had an unexpected consequence," he continues, clasping his hands behind his back. "I need to learn more about the ceremony, about the crowns themselves. I have eight new moons left. 'Ten tries for ten queens,'" he says, sounding like he's reciting something he's memorized from a book. "'Ten tries for ten kings. And at the end, if none prove worthy, the crowns return to dust.'" He turns to me, an agitated light in his eyes, like twin flames had leapt up from the fire and into them. "To dust. My reign will be over if I can't find someone the Unseelie Queen's crown will accept as a worthy ruler, and I don't know what else to try. You will find that information for me."

"From prison?" I ask, raising an eyebrow.

"Not from prison. You're not an idiot, stop acting like one," he snaps. "No, you will seek out the Eldest and learn from them how I can rule the Unseelie Court by myself, after Maeve's upstart daughter rescues you."

"Why can't you–"

"Why can't I find out this information myself? I've tried. Unfortunately, the Eldest is a slippery one, and they have eluded my spies. They are sensitive to intention, you see. But if you were to search for the Eldest with the intention to find out the information I need in order to save your parents, that is a more noble intention than seeking information for power's sake. It should be enough to get past the Eldest's magic. Even better, if you go in the presence of your mate, who will want to learn the information for altruistic purposes," he bares his teeth, like Eevee's kindness and desire to help others physically causes him pain, "then the Eldest will most certainly allow you an audience with them."

"No," I whisper.

The Eldest. I have only heard a few stories about them. Like their name suggests, they are the oldest known fae alive. But they keep to themselves, only allowing a few fae to speak with them every few decades or so. Their knowledge spans more than centuries, it spans millennia. Nightglade is right about one thing. If anyone were to know more about the Seelie and Unseelie crowns and the coronation ceremonies, it would be the Eldest.

I shake my head, clearing it. "I won't do that for you. I don't even know where to look for them. And if you haven't noticed," I gesture around the room and toward where the goblin guard is posted at the door, "No one's rescuing me."

"Ah," he says, almost gently. "Not yet." I shiver. It's both a promise and a warning. "But if you refuse to help me, I am afraid your parents' lives are forfeit. If that is your final decision…" He steps toward the door and gestures to the guard to bind me.

"No, it isn't, I–just–let me think," I plead quickly. The goblin, who had been taking out his scratchy-looking rope with a look of excitement on his snouty face, puts it away in disappointment at a look from Nightglade.

My mind races, as much as it is able to race these days.

If I agree to seek out the Eldest with Eevee for Nightglade, my parents live.

If I say no, my parents die.

If I agree, I will be passing on information to Nightglade and betraying my friends.

If I say no, my parents die.

Their emaciated bodies are fresh in my mind.

They *are* dying.

And there's no guarantee Eevee will ever try and rescue me anyway.

I may never have to go search for the Eldest.

"Treat them better from now on," I say with a bravado I do not feel. "Feed them, house them in a more comfortable place, allow them some freedoms."

Nightglade shrugs. "Fine. Consider it done." His eyes narrow. "If you promise to uphold your end of the bargain when the time comes, that is. If you don't, they will die. Slowly and painfully."

I swallow, a large stone lodging in my throat. "I promise."

"Oh." He leans forward until I'm staring into his merciless gray eyes. "I'd like to think this goes without saying, but part of your duty is to keep your mission secret. From everyone. Do you understand?"

I shudder. Our little secret. I already feel like I am making a humongous mistake.

The look in my eyes must have been all the answer he needed. He nods, then opens the door. "We're returning the prisoner to his cell," he informs the goblin.

We march back down the hall to the door that takes us into the Iron Prison.

The guard throws me back into my cell and Nightglade's gray eyes gleam as he stares at me through the bars. He crooks a finger, then speaks in a low tone so the goblin, now marching back to his position by the door, doesn't overhear.

What he says to me makes my blood run cold.

Later, I curl up on the floor and listen to the whispers of the new moon. *Two deaths*, I think. *How many more will there be?*

I drift to sleep, my mind forming another haiku in response to the whispers, imagining what those who witnessed the ceremonies so far must be thinking.

How do I know when
a month has passed? I hear them
shout, "Another death!"

The Sign I've Been Waiting for Comes From a Strange Source

I should be at the first high school graduation meeting with my best friends, Maggie and Cam, today. Duluth High likes to start these meetings in early March to make sure all seniors are "set up for success" when it comes to graduation. For some reason, missing out on this meeting is getting to me more than my life on the run, more than restricted communication with my friends and family through text and email.

Both Maggie and Cam messaged me last night to say they'd let me know how the meeting goes today, and it took all my self-control not to text them some snarky response. Maybe because the meeting's a reminder of everything I could be doing with my friends right now if it weren't for the fact that I'm an eighteen-year-old fae on the run from the Unseelie King.

So instead of sitting in a threadbare auditorium seat and exchanging jokes with Cam and Maggie, I'm sitting on a squeaky hotel bed while Aspen shops for a dinner we can make in our hotel room's kitchenette. A cheap laptop balances on my crossed legs, and I jiggle my foot impatiently, growing grumpier with each passing second.

I pinch at my nose, which does nothing for my irritation whatsoever. "It shouldn't take this long to upload a four-page essay on 'The Tell-Tale Heart,'" I mutter, standing up and hitting every single squeak of the bedframe in the process.

In the middle of pacing the small hotel room, I freeze. What was that? It sounded like a cough. Near me.

"Paper-thin walls, Eevee, that's what." Probably someone in one of the adjoining rooms.

I can tell myself that all I like, even if I don't believe it for a second.

It's okay. I can ignore mysterious sounds. Only a little longer until Aspen returns.

Plopping back down on the bed, I pull the laptop back toward me. Upload almost complete.

The one benefit of online school is I can work on it wherever, whenever, so long as I have internet. Considering Aspen and I stay no longer than a week in any one location, online school is the best option for finishing up my high school career. And really, I'm not minding it so far. I started in the second semester of the school year with a handful of other new students, and my online teachers seem nice, from the few times I've attended live sessions.

As I wait for my essay to upload (seriously, this hotel's wifi leaves much to be desired, I hope we go somewhere else soon), I open a new tab and pull up my email. At the top of the mostly empty inbox is the latest message from my little sister, Amelia.

To: puckeverlasting@email.com
From: cheese4life@email.com

Subject: Hiiiiiiii

Hi Eevee! I miss you so much. Jess asks where you are and what you're doing and when you'll be home like every day still. The dweebs even miss you I think. I caught them playing in your room yesterday.

You asked about mom and dad in your last email. They're the same. They act like you're doing a foreign exchange program or something. It's easier to let them think that. Jess finally stopped bringing you up in front of them, thank god. All it does is make them confused and then Jess gets angry and cries.

I know you can't tell us where you are or what you're doing. But wherever you are today, I hope you can come home soon. It's been over ten weeks you know. I know you know.

Love love love times a million,
Amelia

P.S. I'm going to the school's one act this weekend to cheer for Cam's awesome set designs they did. I hear Jim's lighting is awesome, too! Wish you could be there with me. I know you'll be there in spirit.

Ten, almost eleven, weeks. That's how long it's been since Amelia escaped from Elfaeme at the Winter Solstice Festival with Cam and Maggie. And it's been even longer since I've seen the rest of my family. But who's counting?

Finally, the essay uploads. I move to close the laptop, but freeze part way. Was that another small cough?

Maybe I'm imagining things. I finish closing the laptop and stand to a chorus of creaks, stretching out my back until it cracks.

That must be it. I'm imagining things. It's been weeks since I've seen any fae, more than a month since my meeting with Folsom, when he told me I'd know when the time was right to return to Elfaeme. Since then, I've had nothing I could count as a sign, though I've kept looking.

And yet…

Maybe the sound I'm hearing is a squirrel. Aspen had wanted to stay somewhere warmer, so we're further south and it feels strange not to see snow outside, but it does mean there are more animals around. Squirrels are notoriously loud. Not just when they move, but in my head, all full of jittery energy and thoughts of hunger pressing into my mind.

I close my eyes and take a slow, steady breath, searching for any squirrely sensations. I've found that if I center my attention on a certain animal I know (or suspect) is nearby, I can make my mind hone in on it, like bringing a fuzzy microscope into focus.

Most of the time, I've learned to keep that sense fuzzy rather than focused. It's hard to concentrate on writing out a mathematical proof with birds' chittering anxiety and the endless hunger and greediness of squirrels distracting me.

Oh, right, I still have math to do today…

Mentally reprimanding myself, I frown, forcing my brain to clear and focus. Immediately, the impression of squirrels, plus birds and a few mice nearby, sharpens in my mind. Whoops, guess I went a little too wide with my focus. But none of them are close enough to have made the sound I heard.

And there it is again. I blink and the sensations of the animals go fuzzy. This time, the sound is almost like a sigh, a short exhale of breath.

If I were human, I wouldn't have heard it.

"'True!—Nervous—Very, very dreadfully nervous I had been and am…'" I whisper.

You've analyzed too much Poe lately, Eevee.

I unlock my phone and send Aspen a quick text. He's got to be on his way back already, right?

His response comes almost immediately.

A: *in the checkout line*
A: *but it'll be a bit*

He sends a picture of the line in front of him, which snakes across the aisle. In the picture, there's someone with a cart and a baffled look on their face who is apparently trying to figure out a way around the checkout line to continue their shopping. The woman ahead of Aspen in line has a cart so full it's taller than her, towering precariously like a miniature mountain of food topped with a bag of apples that looks as if all it'd take was a single breath to send them tumbling.

My brain does that annoying thing where it gets stuck in an anxiety loop. I replay the sounds I've heard in the last hour–small coughs, a soft sigh, both of which could easily be someone in another room, if it weren't for the fact that I have this creeping sensation that they were closer than the next room over.

I curl up on the bed, shoving the laptop to the side. Forget math. Like I'm going to do any more homework tonight.

But I can lull whoever's spying on me into a false sense of security.

Come and get me.

My ears take in all the sounds around me and my brain dutifully analyzes them to pieces, but I keep my eyes closed as if I were sleeping.

A minute passes. I listen and run through a variety of scenarios in my head. Grab them and realm-hop? Another minute. Practice some of the karate moves Sean taught me last fall on the intruder, maybe?

The bed dips and squeaks.

"You're really easy to sneak up on for a fae, you know that?"

I freeze in the fetal position, all potential scenarios draining from my head faster than sand through open fingers.

"I mean," the voice continues, "to be fair, you were nearly impossible to track. If I hadn't had that tip-off from Sir Cornelius, I don't think I'd have found you. And we're running out of time, so," the mattress creaks again as the intruder shifts position, "I'm glad I found you. I'll have to thank Sir Cornelius when I see him next."

I know that voice. Anger loosens my body from its paralysis and I sit up.

"How dare you–" I lose my train of thought and feel my jaw go slack.

Her left cheek twitches, like she'd smile under different circumstances, but the rest of her face is so solemn I'm surprised my reaction even elicited so much as a twitch.

"I thought–your voice–" I stammer.

Her face darkens. "I know. It's like my sister's."

She turns away, tucking behind her ear a strand of silvery blonde hair which has escaped her braid.

With only a few feet separating us, I can see now it's Jaila who's found me, not her older sister.

Honestly, it's better for Ilinor's health that her sister is the one to find me instead. I'm not sure I'd be able to keep myself from sinking a flaming fist into Ilinor's smug face. Even thinking about her makes the knuckles on my hands crackle and spark.

It's not just that she's Nightglade's daughter. I'd forgive her that offense if that's all she had going against her. After all, Jaila is also Nightglade's daughter and I'm not currently engaging in any flaming fist-throwing.

No, it's the fact that Ilinor enjoys going along with her father's twisted mind games, like becoming Quince's betrothed and befriending my sister to gain more intel on me.

"Why would Scamp–Sir Cornelius–tell you where I was?" I shake my hands, extinguishing the flames before they get, well, out of hand. The cat treats I bought for him the last time I was at the store with Aspen peek out the top of my suitcase in the corner. In a spur of the moment decision, which is entirely charitable in nature and not at all based on recently acquired information, I conclude it's best to donate them to an animal shelter rather than give that traitorous cat even a nibble.

"He told me where I could find you because he knows we're running out of time." Her face is turned away, her voice distant and overly casual for such a vague and dire statement.

"You said that already," I point out shortly, impatience frothing like carbonated bubbles in my chest. And maybe it's that impatience leaking out of me which makes my tone drip with sour vinegar. "If we're running out of time, we can't afford to repeat ourselves, can we?"

"Wow. You're kind of a jerk, you know that?" she says, matching my sour tones with venom of her own. "I have to admit, I don't know what the others see in you."

I pretend not to be offended by that, but it stings. "And I don't see why I should be nice to my stalker."

"I'm hardly your only stalker. And I'm definitely not the one you should be worried about."

"Thank you for that super clear, not-at-all ominous information. It'll really help my growing anxiety ulcer."

She huffs and turns to me, her pale green eyes, so like her sister's, flashing. "Do you want to hear what I have to say or not?"

I open my mouth, intending to point out that she obviously wants to share her information with me much more than I care to have it shared, but the door clunks against the deadbolt.

"Eevee, let me in, will you?" Aspen's voice is muffled. "We talked about this. I'd rather save the…" He drops his voice. "…phasing for emergencies. I don't think it's practical to phase in and out of our room when we can simply unlock the door."

In the space of time it takes me to look at the door and back to Jaila, she's vanished. I glance around the tiny room suspiciously. Did she realm-hop her way out of here?

But–no. Beneath me, the bed squeaks, and I'm not moving a muscle.

I launch myself forward, but catch only air. "Where are you?" I mutter out of the corner of my mouth, squinting around the room with just a little jealousy. I can make myself unobtrusive enough to be effectively invisible to humans if I really want to be, but my power doesn't extend to other fae.

Remembering Aspen waiting at the door, I unlock the deadbolt and let him in. He staggers into the room beneath armloads of food.

"I thought you were just getting dinner for tonight," I comment as he unloads the bags onto his bed with a sigh of relief.

"The berries were buy one get one! You can't pass up that kind of deal, Eevee!"

I squint at him. "You're sure you weren't raised in the Midwest? You're not going to start doing the Midwestern goodbye, are you?"

"The what?" he asks, pulling out a bag of chocolate covered caramels and ripping it open.

"Ah, the fruit sale definitely explains the bag of candy," I comment.

"These were on sale, too," he says defensively. "If you don't want them…"

"No, no, I didn't say that." I plunge a hand in the open bag of chocolates and grab a few.

This kind of back and forth banter is the routine Aspen and I have found ourselves in after a few months of living together. It's comfortable. I give him a hard time, he returns my barbs with some of his own, and we don't talk about anything serious like the fact his love/my birth mother is a stone statue.

Nor do we discuss Quince and his parents' imprisonment, or that we're living in hotels not because we're on some kind of bonding trip but because if we stay anywhere too long we'll be found by one of Nightglade's minions.

All good here.

I pop one of the chocolates in my mouth and watch him whisper some words of cleansing over a pint of raspberries. We have a sweet tooth in common, I've realized. I've spent my whole life not really seeing myself in any of my family, so to have this person suddenly appear in my life with similarities to me, like looking in a distorted mirror, is unnerving, even now, after living together for a few months.

He moves the rest of the groceries to the floor between our beds and sits, raspberries in one hand and chocolates in another. Looking temporarily flummoxed, he sets them on the comforter in front of his crossed legs after a few moments of indecision and reaches for the TV remote. The TV turns on, already set to the home improvement channel he loves so much.

"Aren't you going to sit down?" Aspen asks through a mouthful of raspberries and chocolate, looking over to where I stand, chocolates slowly melting in their aluminum foil wrappers in my hand. "I'm back now, we don't need to guard the door."

In surprise, I look to see I've moved to situate myself in front of the door to the hall. I don't even remember walking over here.

"Uh, yeah, right." I lock the door and make my way to my bed. As if the lock would really keep any fae out or in, but it makes me feel a little better when the door is locked and deadbolted.

I rummage through the grocery bags, extracting a package of pretzels and swiping the other pint of raspberries.

The pretzels are specially seasoned with honey mustard. I lick my fingers after munching on a couple, then hold the pint of raspberries out to Aspen. "Can you…?"

Without taking his eyes off the TV, he murmurs the cleansing words and flicks his fingers in my general direction. The magic flows over the berries, but also hits me in the face. It's a strange sensation, getting blasted with magical cleaning, like in the space of a second someone's scrubbed my face with a rough washcloth and lots of soap.

I touch my cheek gingerly. "Thanks."

A small huff of laughter from near the window catches my attention. So, Jaila hasn't realm-hopped out of here? I leap across my bed, pretzels and raspberries flying.

Aspen is so absorbed in the kitchen remodel on the screen, he doesn't even flinch at the airborne pretzels raining down around him.

I'm not exactly graceful, so my lunge probably looks akin to what I imagine a hippo jumping out of the water looks like, but it's effective. My hands close around an arm through the curtain, and I'm aware of the shape of her body now, even though up until this instant the curtains had looked perfectly ordinary and unassuming and not at all like a teenage fae was hiding in them.

We spend an intense couple of seconds scuffling for control over each other, impeded greatly by the heavy beige curtains.

"If it's a mouse, remember to release it outside," Aspen says absently.

How he thinks my frantic wrestling with a curtain (and Jaila behind it) is equivalent to spotting and hunting down a mouse is beyond me.

Jaila's arm twists in my grip and I feel her other hand grab the front of my shirt to pull me behind the curtain with her.

On this side of the curtain, the late evening sun glows like blood in the sky. My body squashes against the cool glass of the window, Jaila's grip on my shirt unrelenting.

"I don't want anyone else to know I'm here," she hisses, eyes narrowed at me, like she doesn't know whether to trust me or not. Which is fair.

I'm immediately suspicious, of course. I open my mouth to shout to Aspen that there's a fae intruder, not a mouse, behind the curtain with me.

All that escapes my lips is "Asp—"

But then her hand, the one not clutching my shirt, is lifting toward my face. I recoil, pressing myself as flat as I can go against the window. The look in her eyes is wild as her fingertips make contact with my temple.

Blinding flashes of rainbow mosaics dance dizzyingly in front of my eyes and the spots where her fingertips touch my temple feel like thousands of ants are burrowing into my skin.

Everything goes black for a second that lasts a thousand years.

In the black, through the painful buzzing in my temples, I hear chanting. Voices raised in harmony, like there's a ceremony taking place. My vision comes back, blurry at first, but when I rub my eyes, it's not Jaila or the beige hotel curtains I see. I stand on a platform of some kind, looking out into a crowd of fae. Snow glistens like red confetti in the light of the dying sun. The chanting comes from a group of fae clad in robes of midnight, their faces covered by wide hoods.

"When day turns to night
and the new moon's time will end,
place the crowns on the heads
of the new Unseelie sovereign.

Thus the Unseelie will be protected,
thus their new leaders will be filled
with power to use for the good of their folk
as the crowns' purpose is willed…"

Someone shifts to my right, and as I see the grim jaw, the steely gray eyes, it takes all my willpower not to scream and run away.

Nightglade. Jaila's sent me straight to Nightglade's side.

Even though I didn't trust her, I still feel betrayed; fear and anguish fill me until I might burst. Why did I let her touch me? How come I didn't realm-hop when I had the chance?

The chanting has stopped, I realize through my tangled, dazed thoughts. Somehow, Nightglade hasn't noticed I'm here, and hasn't acknowledged my presence at all. He turns to someone on his right.

"Bring forth the crown."

The crowd parts to let through a fae who looks like winter embodied. His hair, green and spiky like evergreen leaves, rustles in the cold wind as he walks toward Nightglade, reverently holding a pillow topped with the crown of the Unseelie Queen. It looks to be made of the purest silver, like its partner, the Unseelie King's crown. Though it's unadorned by any jewels, the way it gleams exudes a sense of luxury. Anyone wearing this crown would have to be considered beautiful. Anyone worthy of wearing this crown has to be worthy of following. My breath stops when it catches the light of the dying sun. Now it's a crown of fire.

Maeve's crown. Or at least it was. I bet she looked magnificent wearing it, a true Unseelie Queen.

And look how her Court has devolved without her.

In the clearing, all the fae fall to their knees and chant. "The time has come. The crown will choose. The time has come. The crown will choose."

The attendant carrying the crown lifts it high on its satin pillow, and my eyes follow the lines of his arms as his sleeves swish toward his shoulders. His skin is a twilit sky, a deep hue of blue dotted with white spots and constellations. He offers the crown to someone on Nightglade's right. I catch a glimpse of a sheet of silvery blonde hair, a hand with spidery fingers, and anger pulses at my temples. So. She finally shows herself (partly).

"What is all this?" I hiss to Jaila, not caring if Nightglade hears me. "Where have you brought me?"

Neither Nightglade nor Jaila respond.

Jaila's hands reach toward the crown with no hesitation.

On my left, I hear a sneeze.

"Gesundheit," I say without thinking, turning to face the fae with a cold.

Shoot. All those years of practicing my manners with my mom and dad are going to end by calling attention to myself and getting captured and–

And I'm facing Jaila.

Which means the hands reaching for the crown...

Wait.

"Gesundheit," I say again as Jaila sneezes a second time.

She wipes her reddened nose, her eyes focused on the figure to Nightglade's left, totally ignoring me. Also, when did she have time to curl her hair and change into a dress of the most gorgeous teal?

It hits me. I'm not actually at the Unseelie Court, this isn't happening in real time.

I think about Jaila's fingers on my temple, the pain like thousands of fire ants biting. Am I somehow in a memory? One of Jaila's?

With features so similar to Jaila, the fae to Nightglade's right can only be Ilinor. Which means she's about to become the Unseelie Queen.

Is that why Jaila brought me here? To witness

Ilinor's rise to power?

Nightglade shifts to allow Ilinor to take center stage. She stands rigidly, like she's trying too hard to look regal and imposing, as she holds the crown aloft, and the crowd in the clearing fall to their knees before her.

"The Unseelie's time is now!" Nightglade calls, and the crowd falls silent. His voice rings with power. "What good has it done to balance our power with the Seelie? How has it benefited us?"

I see a few of the fae lift their heads as if in thought, but no one answers their King's question.

After what feels like a minute of silence, Nightglade laughs. But Nightglade's laughter is not a sound of joy. It's a short, bitter huff, all happiness sucked out of it, dry, and sharp.

"In short," he continues, his voice edged like a knife, "it has not. Maeve believed in that balance, and see how that ended for her." He gestures to a shrouded figure next to the raised platform we're standing on. I had assumed it was part of the ceremony. Nightglade nods at the winter fae who had brought Ilinor the crown, and he walks over, pulling the shroud down so it pools at the statue's feet.

It's like getting punched in the gut when I see my birth mother's stony form. A reminder of how I failed to save her, failed to save Quince and his parents, failed…

"…as a unified Court, we will aim to strengthen the Unseelie claim to Elfaeme. Long have we kept to the shadows. But no more. Night shall reign!"

"Night shall reign!" echoes the crowd. My stomach tightens.

This is not good at all. An Unseelie Court ruled by Nightglade (bad enough) *and* his daughter (the one I really can't stand, not the one who stalked me)?

I've heard from Quince what Nightglade allows some of the crueler Unseelie to do to humans while he looks the other way. The wild fae tend toward mischievous pranks, and the Seelie have extremely misguided ideas of what caring for humans entails, but neither the wild fae nor the Seelie are intentionally cruel or harmful to humans.

With the exception of FREEDOM, I recall. A fringe group of fae made up of both Courts and wild fae, FREEDOM's whole goal is in their name: Fae Reclaiming the Earth, End Dominion of Men. If they've somehow teamed up with Nightglade…my blood runs cold at the thought.

Ilinor steps forward once more. Her arms are trembling slightly as she keeps the silver crown aloft.

"Behold," Nightglade declares. "Your new Queen."

The part of the platform Ilinor stands on rises up a couple of feet, so she is higher than the whole gathering. Her green, predatory gaze slowly rakes across the faces of all the Court members below her. Then, her face gleaming with pride, she lowers the crown until it's an inch from her head.

For a moment, nothing happens. I'm holding

my breath, even though this is a memory and not happening in real time.

Curious what Ilinor is waiting for, I find my attention wandering from Ilinor down to where Nightglade stands, the Unseelie King's crown adorning his dark head.

As I watch, his lips curve downward and he narrows his eyes at his daughter above him.

There's a metallic *shink*-ing sound I can't place. It almost sounds like someone drawing a knife, and I wonder if there's an assassination attempt about to unfold.

"Oh no," I hear Jaila whisper beside me. "No, no, no…"

My head snaps back to Ilinor. The crown is on her head, but something is off, something–

Did the crown have rubies when I first saw it? All along the crown are dots of crimson, catching the last rays of the sun.

"No," I say, echoing Jaila.

Ilinor's face is the color of a white lily. Her arms reach back up to the crown and grip it. She tugs, but it doesn't move. When her hands let go, they come away from the crown glistening red with blood.

"Father," she cries, her voice panicky. "Help me!"

She stumbles, falling off the platform, and no one moves to help her as she thrashes on the snow covered ground, struggling futilely with the crown on her head, which refuses to budge. Her wails fill the clearing, like a wild fox caught in a trap.

The snow around her turns pink and red with her blood. She gives up fighting the crown and stands, turning toward the platform. One unsteady step at a time, she moves forward until she is at eye level with Nightglade's knees. "Am I the Queen now?" she asks, her voice slurred. As she tilts her chin up to look at Nightglade, rivulets of blood run down both sides of her face. "Is this part of the ritual? Father?"

Nightglade's upper lip curls with disgust. If he had any other emotion upon seeing his eldest daughter bleeding to death in front of him, he doesn't show it.

"You disappoint me," he says, taking a step backward.

I don't even like Ilinor, but I would never have wished this on her.

Desperately, I wish Jaila would stop the memory, would bring me out of it and back to the hotel room, but I'm stuck here.

Ilinor's face cracks and falls at Nightglade's words, her pride broken, her life running out of her in streams of blood.

"Father?" she asks again, her voice weaker than before. "This is…" She leans, reaching out to him, and he takes another step back. "Part of…" Her head falls.

With another metallic *shink* the crown detaches from Ilinor's head. Ilinor lays lifeless, her upper body on the platform with her arms splayed out toward Nightglade. The Unseelie Queen's crown rests in a growing pool of her blood.

It's unblemished now, as if the blood can't touch it.

Nightglade stands with his eldest daughter's lifeless body at his feet, his face stiffening into a terrifying mask of calmness.

He picks up the crown and gently places it on its pillow, then hands it back to the winter fae for safe keeping.

"Next new moon," Nightglade calls, his voice an angry growl, betraying his true emotions. "We will try again. I had thought my eldest daughter would be a perfect candidate for Queen, but the crown disagrees." He pauses, his gaze shifting to his dead daughter, and I think how his eyes appear just as lifeless.

Is Nightglade admitting he made a mistake in letting Ilinor go through with this ritual? Is he going to admit it was a mistake to take the crown from Maeve?

"She must have been unloyal to me or to the Unseelie Court for the crown to judge her as unworthy."

I suppose it was too much to expect Nightglade to suddenly show a little character growth.

"From this moment on, at each new moon, anyone who is loyal enough to apply to rule as Unseelie Queen will have a chance to earn that right." His face is as hard as stone, like the statue of his ex-partner and ex-ruler.

"Nice," I mutter. "Your daughter just bled to death because the Unseelie Queen's crown rejected her, and now you're telling everyone that the only way to show their true loyalty is to apply for the same fate."

My commentary was, of course, lost on Nightglade, since this is a memory.

Jaila–the memory Jaila, not the current one who sent me here–lets out a whimper. When I turn to see how she's doing (or how she was doing? Being in a memory is more confusing than I thought it would be), I can't see her.

She's pulled a disappearing act.

Not that I can blame her. I would disappear, too, if I saw my father who I barely knew stand by and watch his daughter, my older sister, bleed to death.

Then my vision blurs and bursts of color dance before my eyes. The painful feeling of ants digging into my temples returns, and the first thing I sense is the smell of the musty curtains.

"I'll be back," Jaila whispers. Her face is close to mine, yet I'm already struggling to see her as she fades from my admittedly spotty vision.

"Jaila, wait." I reach toward her, and she flinches away from my hands. "I'm so sorry that happened. I didn't like Ilinor, but I know she was your sister, and that was awful. Do you want a hug?"

She hesitates, her appearance solidifying.

"It's okay if you don't," I say quietly. "Is there anything else I can do that you'd find helpful at this time?"

"There is, but we can talk later, once he's gone." She nods toward Aspen. "For now…" Her green eyes look at me hesitantly, and I don't see any of the pride or cruelty that glittered in Ilinor's eyes. I see longing, and pain. "I suppose a hug would be okay. Even if it's from you."

"Okay." I wrap my arms around her, my heart aching. I can't imagine how scared and confused she must be. For how independent she is, I have to remind myself she's only about the same age as my little sister, Amelia. We hug until I feel the tension in her shoulders relax.

"I still don't like you, you know," she says, her voice muffled.

"That's fine." I try not to laugh. "We don't know each other too well yet. You might change your mind."

"Maybe," she says as she pulls away.

I look her in the eyes. "I'm so sorry, again, about all of that."

"Yes. I am, too."

"I still don't understand why you shared it with me, though? Or why–"

"Eevee?" calls Aspen, with a fuzzy edge to his voice like he's speaking through a mouthful of food. "You get that mouse yet?"

The tiniest of smiles, which had appeared on Jaila's face after our hug, melts away at the sound of Aspen's voice. "Thanks for the hug, E. I'll be back later."

As she disappears, my thoughts jumble together. Ilinor is dead. Nightglade's on the hunt for a co-ruler of the Unseelie Court, bent on tipping the scales so the Unseelie have the most power in Elfaeme. And poor Jaila is caught in the middle of it all. If I had to guess, I'd bet she's on the run so she doesn't suffer the same fate as her sister.

Not only that, but what Jaila called me just now? E?

She's connected to Folsom somehow, which makes me wonder what that old, froggy fae has been up to since I last saw him in Duluth.

Aspen's Nightly Excursions

Even though it's only eight-thirty and I usually go to bed around ten o'clock, I yawn and make my way toward the bathroom, hoping Aspen doesn't catch on to my charade.

"Long day, you know, lots of homework," I say with a sigh, closing the bathroom door behind me.

"Um-hmm…" Aspen says.

My last glimpse before the door closes is of him surrounded by empty raspberry containers, his eyes glued to the screen, where a sweatpants-wearing couple is talking to a realtor about their dream vacation home. The woman is dead set on having a place with turrets.

"Do you think he'll leave soon?"

I stumble and crash into the bathroom counter, my toothbrush clattering into the sink. "Do you enjoy sneaking up on people?" I whisper to Jaila.

She points to me. "You're not a person."

"Ugh. Whatever."

I run the water as hot as it will go and hold my toothbrush underneath it, masking my emotions as best I can from Jaila. My fae identity is still new to me, and having grown up as a Minnesotan with the Ackers, it's still hard to get used to the idea that, unlike the rest of my adoptive family, I'm not human. It's like taking the "black sheep of the family" feeling and multiplying it by a hundred. Besides, the last person to remind me that I'm not human was my best friend, Cam, who is the most supportive friend, but was having a tough time with the idea that their friend (me) isn't human and is also entangled in political plots of another realm entirely.

Truthfully, I get why it was so hard for Cam. I'm also grateful they've come around to the idea and are using their creative mind to come up with ways to make sure they can stay in my life safely, along with Maggie.

Fudge, I miss them both.

"Acorn for your thoughts?"

I turn off the hot water and tap my toothbrush forcefully against the edge of the sink. "Acorn?"

"Fae money," she says, waggling her fingers at me dramatically. "Or so some humans pretend, anyway. Isn't the human phrase 'penny for your thoughts?'

So…what was that look you had on your face?"

I can't say it's nothing, so I don't answer.

"Fine," she says, lifting her eyebrows. "I was only curious. Your hug helped me earlier, so I thought I'd return the favor. You know, a kindness for a kindness."

I lower the toilet lid and sit down. "I miss my friends, that's all. I haven't seen them in over two months, ever since–"

"The winter solstice," she finishes. She flips her braid over her shoulder as she alights on the edge of the bathtub next to me. Her whole face is solemn as she studies me. "We're both on the run. It's one reason I thought I'd seek you out."

"What, to start a Faes on the Run Club?"

She crosses her arms. "Sean and Shannon didn't tell me about your awful sense of humor. It may have changed my mind, had I known."

The mischievous sparkle in her eyes indicates she wouldn't have changed her mind about seeking me out.

"I have a fabulous sense of humor," I say with dignity, not allowing her to see the momentary shock I felt when she name-dropped Sean and Shannon.

"Debatable," she replies, and now I definitely see her lips press together as though holding in a smile.

We're interrupted by a knocking at the door before I can ask her what her connection is to Quince's twin cousins.

"Eevee? Who are you talking to in there?"

"Do your invisible, 'can't see me' thing!" I whisper to Jaila, but the spot where she had been sitting on the edge of the tub is seemingly empty. "Er, yeah. Like that. Good job."

Opening the door, I see Aspen dressed in his fae clothing. Unlike his 'human costumes,' his fae clothing is simpler. Brown capris made out of cotton, paired with a mottled green shirt and a yellow vest. Forest-inspired colors. He's barefoot, and I'm already anticipating the dirt he'll track into our hotel room when he returns from his nightly jaunt to the Sweetbriar Wood.

"Hi. You heard me talking?"

He frowns. "I thought I did." His eyes scan the part of the bathroom he can see. "But no one's in there with you?"

"Does it look like there's anyone else in here?" I ask, opening the door wider and hoping Aspen doesn't have some kind of fae ability to see things that are invisible.

"No, it doesn't," he admits. "So what were you doing, then?"

I shrug, which he luckily accepts as an answer.

"Since you're getting ready for bed, I thought, if you didn't mind, I'd head to Elfaeme early," he explains, gesturing to his clothing. "There are some folk I need to see, and I'd have a better chance at meeting them before it got too late."

"Who?" I ask, raising an eyebrow at him. "Who are you seeing every night?"

"Oh, various folks," he answers quickly. "Nothing you need to be concerned about. And you promise—"

"I promise not to follow you to Elfaeme tonight, yes," I respond, suddenly as tired as I've been pretending to be.

"Good." He shifts his weight from toe to heel in the silence that follows. "Well, yes. Right. See you in the morning, Eevee."

Patting my shoulder, he turns, steps, and disappears from sight. One step in the hotel room, the other somewhere in Elfaeme, on his way to meet someone in Elfaeme. Again.

"That was sketchy," Jaila says, materializing to my left. "He gives me the creeps."

"Aspen?" I ask. "Creepy?" Though Aspen and I don't get along, I don't think I'd go as far as to call him creepy. Kind of a negligent, emotionally distant father figure who doesn't know what to do with his life now he's lost his lover and gained his long lost daughter, sure. But not creepy. "Why would you say that?"

"You don't get that vibe from him?" She shivers. "I don't know. Something seems off about his face. I can't focus on it."

I shrug. "I can see it just fine. You're not missing much."

"What's he doing in Elfaeme?" she asks innocently.

I give her a hard look. "Like I'd tell you."

"You don't trust me. I don't trust you. I get it."

Holding her hands up in a gesture of truce, she grins. "But come on. You're not curious what he gets up to every night?"

Every night?

"How long have you been spying on us?" I ask her, frowning. The thought of Jaila hanging out in our room, invisible, while I did homework or joked with Aspen while he watched his home improvement shows makes my skin feel like it's crawling with beetles.

"Long enough," she replies. "Long enough to know you're not as at peace with living in hiding as you let on. Long enough to know it's weird that Aspen goes to the fae realm every night and makes you promise not to follow him. Long enough to know you want to. So, where does he go?"

My frown is a full on scowl now. "Why are you really here, Jaila? To find out information for daddy dearest?"

Jaila pushes me into the door until it slams open, the doorknob digging into my back. The air whooshes out of my lungs.

"He may be my father," she says in a tone so cold it freezes me in place. "But he is not, nor will ever be, my 'daddy dearest.'"

We stare at each other, her face so close to mine I can see the purple smudges underneath her eyes.

"Okay," I say after a long moment. "He isn't your daddy dearest. I shouldn't have said that." The arm she's pressing into my chest loosens its hold. "But why else would you want to know where Aspen's going?"

Her eyebrows raise. "What shocks me is why you wouldn't want to know. If he were my father, I'd want to know exactly where he's going and why."

"With a father like Nightglade, I don't blame you."

She drops her arm completely and steps away. "I don't want your pity. I want—"

"What? What do you want?"

"Currently?" she asks, a mischievous grin on her face. "To know where Aspen's gone."

I groan. "I've promised not to follow him."

"Right," she presses. "Which is strange, don't you think?"

I hate that she's right. Of course I've wondered what he gets up to. "Sure, it's strange," I admit aloud. "But I assume he's meeting with old friends or whatever. Making up for the time he'd spent away with Maeve."

The green in her eyes grows brighter, more intense. "Every night? Even though he has a daughter to care for? He puts you at risk every time he leaves, Eevee. What kind of father does that?"

"I don't know, I…"

"Let's go see what he's up to," she presses. "Just for a little bit. Then I'll tell you why I'm here. But I've been watching him leave you every night and it makes me mad just thinking about it. I want to see if where he's going is worth it." She pauses. "It probably isn't."

"I've promised not to follow him, though," I reply, my response sounding weak even to me.

She taps her nose. "But you haven't promised not to follow me."

I throw my hands in the air. "What good are fae promises if all you do is find the loophole?"

"Isn't that the fun part?" she asks, tilting her head. "The challenge? The chance to test your wit against someone else's?"

"I—"

"Besides," she concludes, "we don't have to stay long. Just long enough to see what he's up to. Then we can come back to this room and I can share some information about Quince with you."

This gets my attention. "Quince? Have you seen him? How is he? What do you know?"

"I promise to tell you everything I can when we return," she says.

"Even I can see the loophole in that promise," I protest.

"I should hope so," she replies. "After all, you're fae, too. But the question is not whether you trust the promise. It's whether you trust me to follow through with it."

"You know I don't."

She laughs for the first time. "You're a strange fae, you know that?"

"I didn't grow up in the Courts. Which I know you know."

I exit the bathroom and pick up the remote to

turn off the TV, which Aspen always forgets to do.

"I do know that," she says, following me into the main part of the hotel room. "Which is why I'm surprised you're not in Elfaeme every chance you can get. It's your home."

"It isn't safe for me there," I reply shortly, sitting on my bed and tugging on a pair of tennis shoes.

Her face looks puzzled. "It isn't safe for anyone in Elfaeme. But that shouldn't prevent you from being there. And Aspen shouldn't be preventing you from returning, either. It's in your blood, Eevee. Don't tell me you can't feel the difference. Here on Earth, our fae magic is harder to do. We're not as light or free."

I stand and tug on a purple hoodie, then dig in my suitcase for my backup jacket and toss it to Jaila. "If we die tonight, I'm blaming you."

Looking down at the flannel jacket, she's quiet. "I appreciate this," she says quietly.

"Right, well…" I take a deep breath. In for a penny, in for a pound, as the saying goes. And I've had a feeling this whole day that something was about to change, that I wasn't going to be living on the run with Aspen much longer. When Jaila showed up, that feeling intensified. "Aspen always comes back with dirt and dead leaves on his clothes and feet. He hasn't told me where he goes, but I am relatively certain it's back to his home in the Sweetbriar Wood."

She nods thoughtfully. "I suppose that would make sense. It's as good a place as any to start."

The flannel jacket I've given her is much too big on her. It was one of my dad's–Todd Acker, not Aspen–that I'd stolen from him after Aspen and I escaped from the Winter Solstice Festival. It's warm, though, and still has a faint cedarwood smell on it from my dad's cologne.

She folds the sleeves three times, then looks me in the eyes. "Follow me."

"Ow, that's my foot you're stomping on like an elephant," Jaila complains in a whisper.

"Well, I wouldn't be stomping on your foot if you'd move over," I grumble. "I can't see anything from here, and I don't want to fly and risk anyone seeing me."

The bush we're hiding behind wouldn't provide much cover in the daylight, but the stars are out and the decorative lanterns around the clearing where I'd danced with the wild fae do little more than look pretty, if you like rustic, woodsy lanterns with colored glass.

Being back here is like sliding into an old, comfortable pair of shoes. It feels more like returning home than it did when I snuck back to Duluth, and I'm not sure how to feel about that. There's a sensation in my heart, like a peaceful sighing, that happens when I come back to Elfaeme, especially to the forested areas.

Back on Earth, it's like holding my breath. When I return to Elfaeme, that breath releases.

"Guess you're stuck on the ground with me, then." Jaila turns her attention back to the jostling, dancing fae in the clearing. "Are they always dancing? Don't they do anything else?"

"They're not constant partiers like your Seelie friends, if that's what you mean," I say, even though I'm not one hundred percent sure that's accurate. I've had very little contact with the wild fae since Olearia had Scamp track me down and bring me here to warn me about Maeve's power waning. Much good that warning did, since she still turned to stone.

Jaila sniffs huffily but doesn't respond. "I'm going in. It's impossible to see anyone clearly from out here."

The branches next to me rustle, which is the only clue I have that Jaila's moved at all. I watch the grasses carefully and note a footstep without a body, then another. Jaila seems to be heading right to the middle of the dancing mob. I cross my fingers and keep an eye on the situation, hoping she avoids arousing suspicion by bumping into anyone accidentally. Her ability to go invisible may keep her from being seen, but it doesn't make her impossible to touch.

While she's scouting the sea of dancers, my thoughts return to what she'd said to me. *It isn't safe for anyone in Elfaeme. But that shouldn't prevent you from being there.* If it weren't for my mom and dad, for my sisters and brothers, for Cam and Maggie, would I even want to keep living on Earth? Returning home to Duluth, even briefly, didn't feel so much like returning home as paying someone a visit. And in all my recent travels with Aspen, we've never been to a location that gave me the same sense of peace and belonging that returning to Elfaeme, to the magical woods, does. Though, that's maybe because none of the hotels and motels we stay in are near any forests.

I don't know what to make of that. Until Jaila appeared, I had been resigned to my life on the run, thought I had accepted I'd lost and my life was going to be a lonely one, living from hotel to hotel in different places on Earth, until Nightglade died or was overthrown.

But am I being too cautious? Overthinking the situation?

Should I really let someone like Nightglade have so much influence over how I live my life?

My immediate answer: no. But if not…what is it I really want from my life anymore? Is it possible to have a mid-life crisis at age eighteen?

The leaves next to me rustle again. "I didn't see him," Jaila says, appearing at my side in the same spot as if she'd never left. "Is there anywhere else he could be?" Her cheeks are flushed and her green eyes gleam in the starlight. She's loving this kind of covert activity.

"I don't think so," I whisper back. A thought occurs to me. "Did you see a really old fae with goat legs and curly ram horns?"

She shakes her head. "The only one with

distinct head features I saw had antlers.”

“Which aren’t horns,” I muse. It’s late, but maybe visiting Olearia is worth a shot? “I’ve thought of someone who might know where Aspen is,” I say aloud.

We creep away from the clearing and I hope my memory doesn’t fail me now. Once I’ve visited a place, I’m pretty good at retracing my steps. Olearia was the wild fae who’d sent Scamp after me, and seemed invested in Aspen’s wellbeing when Maeve’s powers were waning. Olearia didn’t care for Maeve, so if it weren’t for the fact that Maeve’s powers were also protecting Aspen from the Unseelie King, I doubt she would have bothered helping me. It stands to reason Olearia would keep up to date on Aspen’s comings and goings now that he’s returned to the wild fae.

“She might be asleep,” I warn Jaila once we’re out of earshot of the clearing. The path we walk on is well-worn, a winding dirt path that reminds me of deer paths in the woods in northern Minnesota.

“If she is, we’ll just go back to the human realm,” she says brightly.

“We could go back now,” I mention, slowing my pace. “I don’t know if you realize how old she is. She was probably asleep before eight this evening.”

Jaila laughs. “I don’t know if you realize that us fae are different from humans. Or have you always needed the eight hours of sleep every night that are recommended for mortals?”

“I–” I’d always had a hard time falling asleep at

night, especially when the moon was full or any kind of storm or rain was going on outside, pattering on the roof like a friend knocking on the door. My pediatrician had told my parents it was probably my ADHD.

Something must show in my face as Jaila turns to look back at me, because she nods. "Yeah. I thought so. My point, E? Olearia may not be as much like your typical old mortal as you may think."

E again. "When we get back," I say, lowering my voice as we approach Olearia's log cabin, "you're going to tell me what your connection is to Folsom."

A wide smile grows on Jaila's face. "You're not as slow as I thought."

"Thanks?"

We fall silent and tiptoe forward. Jaila doesn't have wings to help her footsteps fall silently on the leaf-covered, mossy ground, but even though she's right behind me, I can barely hear her. I don't trust my own feet to step that quietly, so I use my wings like Quince taught me to do when we were sneaking around the frozen wyvern tunnels beneath Crystal Lake with Sean and Shannon, looking for another of Maeve's clues she'd left for me. If I had known then that in a few short months Quince would let himself be captured by Nightglade to stay with his parents, who were also prisoners, would I have allowed him to keep hanging out with me? Nightglade wouldn't have considered him or his parents as much of a target if it hadn't been for me. My heart twists painfully. I don't think it's felt whole for a long time, if ever, but the last few months have left it bruised beyond recognition.

My resolve hardens. Quince and his parents deserve to live their lives outside of Nightglade's influence. And so do I. I'll learn what I can from Jaila about Quince's situation, and then I'll track down Sean and Shannon and we'll figure out a way to help him, which I should have done long before now.

I'm done surviving on the run. It's time to live, whatever that life might be.

Ahead of us, I can see a warm yellow glow of light through the trees. Maybe Olearia's awake, after all. We slow our pace even more, and if I squint, I can see the beginnings of Olearia's overgrown flower garden that spills out from the front walls of her cottage. Pointing at a tree near the window on the far side of the cabin, I give Jaila a significant look. She moves her chin in a gesture of understanding and we make our way to it, keeping to the outside of the tangled underbrush that surrounds Olearia's place.

As we inch closer to the tree, I can hear the low murmur of voices coming from inside. So, Olearia isn't alone?

We situate ourselves behind the tree, each of us taking turns poking our heads out to peek at the windows, then I crouch down, careful to keep my wings from poking out on either side of the tree. How do fae with wings even sneak up on anyone anyway?

"I don't know if we should go and knock, not if she has company," I say under my breath to Jaila.

"Let's wait and see if her company leaves

soon," she suggests, her eyes still gleaming with the thrill. "It's a stakeout!"

"That could take all night."

"Ooh, you think it's *that* kind of visitor?" Her hands cover the giggle threatening to burst out of her.

"Wha–ew, no, that's not what I meant at all!" I say vehemently as soon as I realize what Jaila is insinuating. "I just–you know what, you take first watch."

"On it." She turns her face to the cottage and studies it intently. Around us are the sounds of the nocturnal forest creatures waking up. Frog calls compete with the chirp of crickets, and somewhere off to our left is a rustling in the underbrush, probably a mouse, though I don't really care to focus on the animal emotions around me at the moment.

The side of her face tightens, her mouth turning down in a grim line.

"What is it?" I whisper. "Do you see who else is with her?"

Instead of answering, she gestures for me to look, her eyes still focused on the cottage.

Slowly, I peek around the tree trunk and look toward the side window. I can see the green hues of the spring wall from here. Olearia's cottage walls have been painted in murals that depict each season, and the wall dedicated to spring is full of green, dotted with white wildflowers. Silhouetted against the green background is a short figure with curly rams horns–Olearia. There are two other fae in the room with her. One, winged, is pacing, and the other stands erect, nodding at whatever the other two are saying.

Then, the one who's standing turns toward the window and the light of the fire catches his hair, which is a glossy mane of red, tied neatly at the nape of his neck.

I duck back behind the tree. "Oakspirit?" I hiss to Jaila. "What's the Seelie King doing here?"

She shrugs as if to say, "Beats me."

"You're all buddy-buddy with the Seelie Court," I say, and though I can hear the accusation in my voice, I don't do anything to hide it. "You really don't have any idea what he's doing here?"

Immediately, she gets defensive, her whole body vibrating so that her silvery blonde hair trembles. "For your information," she says, her voice frosty, "the Seelie have only ever tolerated me at their Court. I was treated as the Unseelie outsider that I was and am, and only kept around because I was something different, something that could be used against my father someday if they wanted. I've never been more than a pawn to them." Her eyes shimmer with angry tears. "So, no, I don't know what Oakspirit is doing here any more than you."

I don't know how to respond, how to comfort her. There's another rustle in the underbrush, closer than before. Whatever animal is moving around out there is bold or stupid for getting so close to us.

Studying the hard lines of Jaila's too-thin face, my feelings are a jumble of distrust and pity. Though I don't particularly like Jaila, I can understand why she acts the way she does. If I'd always been tolerated, treated like a pawn in a political game even as a child, how would I have turned out by the time I turned fourteen, like Jaila? Instead, I had camping trips, potlucks, family board game nights, and adoptive parents who treated me as one of their own.

Jaila breaks eye contact first, looking back to the cottage. She covers her mouth and I peer around the tree trunk curiously to see what's surprised her.

My stomach does an uncomfortable swoop, as if I were on a roller coaster and had just plunged a hundred feet. The pacing fae with the wings?

It's Aspen.

I duck behind the tree again before he can see me. "Fudge nuggets," I whisper.

"Meow," answers the cat at my feet.

I look down and groan internally. It's not just any cat. It's a skinny, dusty-colored cat with a missing right ear and green eyes, not unlike Jaila's.

"Scamp?" I ask at the same time that Jaila whispers, "Sir Cornelius?"

Right, she's probably only seen him at the Seelie Court, where, for some reason, he's able to speak and goes by the name of Sir Cornelius instead of Scamp. I had named him that when I had thought he was a stray cat that stopped by for scraps behind Gramp's Diner where I worked, back when I had a place I could call home.

I don't need my ability to sense animal

emotions. Scamp conveys his reproach for me clearly enough in his eyes and the irritated twitching of his bushy tail.

Bending down, I reach toward him. "You didn't see us here, okay, Scamp? Please don't tell anyone."

He throws a significant glance at Jaila, then stares at me again, and I feel the curiosity emanating from him, with a healthy dash of disappointment and anger.

"Please, Scamp," I whisper again, urgency making my voice louder than I intend. "The one thing Aspen's ever asked of me is not to follow him. And, technically, I was following Jaila, not him…" I trail off feebly, the excuse sounding lame even to me underneath the disapproving gaze of the cat.

With the air of mischievous chaotic abandon that comes on cats right before they knock a vase off the counter, Scamp trots off in the direction of the cottage.

"We need to get out of here, now," I say to Jaila.

"Don't need to tell me twice," she responds. "Meet me back at the hotel room. I'll tell you what I can about Quince."

She disappears.

I glance back once at the cottage. The silhouettes of Olearia, Aspen, and Oakspirit have gone still. The shortest one, Olearia, heads toward the window, her expression hidden in shadow.

Keeping the hotel room firmly in my mind, I

step backward, just as I see someone open the front door of the cottage.

Then it all melts away, the dark trees with their even darker shadows, the frog song, the cozy cottage, replaced by the musty hotel room and police sirens in the distance.

Jaila's tapping her foot on the ground, looking like a rabbit ready to bolt at any sign of trouble.

"I'm not staying long," she starts before I can say anything. "So if you want to know about anything other than Quince, that'll have to wait."

"What about Quince?" I ask, dread making my skin prickle. "Is he okay? What about his parents?"

Her head tilts. "I don't know about his parents. But someone told me Nightglade's changed his mind about finding the most loyal fae to claim the Unseelie Queen crown."

An image of Ilinor's lifeless body at Nightglade's feet, blood pooling around her from the crown's puncture wounds, flashes in my head. "What does this have to do with Quince?" I ask, the words suddenly hard to form over the lump in my throat.

"It seems he wants to keep his loyal followers as loyal followers." She's talking quickly now, her eyes darting around for any sign of Aspen reappearing. "He…tried again at the new moon in February. This time with Banethistle. Same thing happened. So now," she gulps, "now he says the crown must want him to have full control over the Court."

"But the Queen's crown needs to be claimed," I

say.

"Yes," she agrees.

"So…"

"So he's going to start trying with Unseelie fae he doesn't care about," she finishes. "Like his prisoners. Like–"

Like Quince. Or his parents.

"When's the next new moon?" I ask.

"March sixth."

Now I know why she began her visit earlier today by telling me we were running out of time.

March 6th is two days from now.

I'm Done Surviving on the Run

"Meet me in the hotel lobby in half an hour if you decide to come with me."

Like that, Jaila disappears, and I feel the clock ticking in my head.

If I leave, I'll possibly be destroying any trust Aspen has in me.

If I stay, Quince may not survive the next few days.

Besides, Jaila had referred to me as "E." That has to be the sign from Folsom, which means he thinks it's time I return to Elfaeme.

I pull a small overnight bag out of my suitcase and start packing.

"What were you doing in the Sweetbriar Wood, Eevee?"

I freeze, a pair of leggings in my hands. "I could ask you the same question," I say as calmly as possible, folding the leggings and placing them in the bag. I avoid looking at Aspen, skirting around him to get to the bathroom for my shampoo and face wash, but he steps in front of me, his arms folded. His blond hair is disheveled, and panic tightens the lines around his eyes.

"You risked a lot with that stunt. How did you follow me without breaking your promise?"

"I didn't follow you. I followed–someone else."

Glancing up at his face, I swear I see a hint of some emotion, pride maybe, but then it's replaced by fear. "You could have been followed."

"What, like you? We both know you messed up a while ago, Aspen. Why else would fae have been hot on our trail?"

"I am your father," he yells. "I'm doing my best to look after you!"

Rage like cold ice covers my body. "Don't you dare. My father is Todd Acker, and he's currently dealing with the effects of some kind of fae magic or another, or he'd have looked after me much better than you."

Aspen's mouth works furiously. Finally he spits out, "That's unfair. I'm trying. I've never–"

"No, you never had to be a father," I agree. "So stop pretending to be mine just because we share DNA.

I didn't come looking for you and Maeve because I wanted to replace Todd and Penny. I wanted answers, I wanted to expand my family, ideally. I did not want another adult giving me input and advice when it's not needed."

His face flushes. "Now listen here–"

"I'm going. Something's come up and…I need to help."

His eyes widen, the skin on his forehead crinkling. "What could you do to help the situation in the Unseelie Court that isn't already being done by other fae in Elfaeme?" he asks. "No, Eevee, I want you to seriously consider my question."

"I don't know," I force out. "I only found out I wasn't human about six months ago. There's a lot I don't know about myself or the world I was supposed to grow up in. But things have changed. I've learned…new information. I need to go back."

Aspen's whole body grows still, and the look he gives me is grave. "What did you hear?"

I turn from him and walk back to my bed.

"Eevee," he says warningly. "What did you hear? I'm your father, I–"

"Stop," I say, suddenly weary. I look at him, turning partway to face him. "It's clear from how you've acted the last couple months that you don't really want to be a father."

The look on his face is shocked, as if he'd been slapped.

"Or maybe you do," I amend. I'm already

regretting some of what I said. I take a breath. "Maybe you want to be a father to me." I study him. "I'm not sure you're ready, though."

He's quiet for a moment, his eyes on the floor, then he lets out a huff of air and meets my gaze, his bright green eyes awash with unshed tears. "Maeve and I had to live with our choices every day." Aspen raises a shaky hand to cover his eyes. "Every. Day. It weighed on us. Both of us. We wondered how you were doing, if any powers had started affecting you early, if you were ever confused or felt like you didn't belong. But you know what we didn't have to worry about?" He's deadly quiet now, and he lowers his hand, so I'm pierced by the look of anguish on his face. "We never worried about your safety while you grew up with Todd and Penny, thinking you were a human child. We never had the gut wrenching fear we experienced while Maeve was pregnant that each day might be your last if we were caught by Nightglade. Among the humans, you were safe for a time. You should be grateful they were willing to adopt you."

Grateful.

My gut seethes.

"Grateful?" I ask, the word foreign in my mouth. I laugh. "Grateful? Not neutral, or fine, or okay, or making the best of the situation. But grateful because Todd and Penny were willing to adopt me? Do you know how messed up that sounds? No matter how good your reasons were, and–" I hold a finger up to stop him from speaking, because these are words that have been on my chest for so long, locked away where I didn't have to acknowledge them, but now they're all pouring out, like a break in a dam, "–and I acknowledge you had valid reasons. I do. Those reasons don't change the fact that placing me with a new family, even as a baby, was a traumatic experience for me to live through. I know you've been living in hiding for almost two decades, so you may not be totally current with the times, but what other people who experience trauma are told to be grateful for it?"

He closes his mouth, his thumb rubbing against his index finger.

I shoulder my bag, feeling like a rag wrung out to dry. "I'm not a baby anymore, or even a child. I'm an adult. I'll be turning nineteen later this year, if I live that long. I think I'm old enough to decide if I want to return to Elfaeme to help a friend." I pause, then add, "I'm sorry you and Maeve had to make so many tough decisions. I'm sorry after everything that you lost her to the curse of the revoked crown anyway. But please stop letting your past decisions dictate our relationship now. We have a chance to start fresh. When you're ready."

He doesn't move from the bathroom door, but his thumb rubs against his index finger and a line appears between his eyes as he regards me. I decide to get toiletries somewhere else, and exit the room. When I glance back, he's gone, presumably back to the Sweetbriar Wood.

Some of the sympathy I had felt for him evaporates. It's unfair to make the comparison, but I know Todd wouldn't have run away from a difficult discussion with me.

A dark stormcloud settles over me as I make my way to meet Jaila in the hotel lobby.

Quince

Each day the next new moon draws nearer, the third one since the Winter Solstice Festival, I grow more and more hopeful, yet depression lingers.

Maybe Eevee's seen the sense in not rescuing me. Maybe she's said her goodbyes, given me up as a lost cause.

As I count down the days, waking up each morning in the same cell with no visitors and no rescuers, I hope it's true.

It's strange, though, that the same thing I hope for also makes me feel like I might as well die.

I hate Nightglade for the deal he offered me, but I hate myself more for accepting it.

If Eevee never rescues me, though, then I'll be okay. I'll never have to go through with the deal.

I watch a droplet of condensation slide down the moldy stone wall across from where I sit.

Am I worth rescue?
I don't think so. Why don't you
forget about me?

"Breakfast!" calls one of the guards. She's not as awful as some of the others. At least she doesn't sneer at me while I eat, like the goblin who works a couple nights a week.

I force myself to stand and move toward the iron bars of my cell. Half the time lately, my food hasn't wanted to stay down. Being in such close proximity to the iron does that to the stomach.

She slides the tray of food through the small opening in the bars at the bottom and I push my half-empty tray from last night out to her.

I'm a few bites into the lumpy, tasteless oatmeal, when I notice she's still hovering in front of my cell. I let my spoon drop. "What?" I ask.

She glances left and right, her tusks gleaming in the flickering light of the torches. "I'm taking a shift tonight, too," she says quietly.

"What?" I ask again, this time because I have no idea why she'd share her shift schedule with me.

"I have it on good authority that tonight is a worthy time to work," she whispers, fast. "For fae who are loyal to the crowns."

"O…kay…?"

"Stay awake," she whispers, then hurries off to the next cell, loudly chatting with the cell's occupant, who doesn't answer her cheerful questions.

My mind moves sluggishly through the conversation I just had. Then, when most of my oatmeal is gone, it dawns on me.

Someone is going to rescue me tonight.

I silently pray it won't be Eevee. Let it be Sean, or Shannon. Anyone else.

If it's Eevee, then the deal I struck with Nightglade will begin, and I'll have to somehow guide us to the Eldest without making it obvious.

I've spent months in this prison, but I have a feeling my nightmare is about to begin.

Old Friends in New Places

Jaila's silence and lack of questions is appreciated. After I stormed out of the hotel and agreed to return to Elfaeme with her, I worried my declaration would be followed by a peppering of questions. But she had simply nodded and said, "I know where we can phase to that's relatively safe. All the moonstones that lead directly to the Unseelie Court are being guarded. Tomorrow, though. No offense, but you look like a zombie."

Which is how, after we found another hotel to stay at, got some fitful sleep, and revived ourselves with two cups each of the hotel's bitter coffee in the morning, I find myself back in Elfaeme for the second time since my run-in with Folsom in January. This time, instead of traveling to the In Between, where right now it would be a cool spring morning, we arrive in the cold, majestic lands of the Unseelie. I step away from Jaila and immediately slip on the glittering ice of a frozen pond.

Jaila walks silently to the pond's edge, while I opt to fly (a safer option for me if I want to avoid bruises). On the horizon ahead of us, lit from behind by the morning sun, is an enormous castle. Where the Seelie castle had been covered in all things lush and green, the Unseelie castle is stark, its bare stone walls with their swirling patterns of gray and white their own declaration of simple beauty.

She beckons me forward and I fly to join her, touching down at the edge of the pond. "How close is the Iron Prison to the castle?"

"It's in the castle," she answers, her hand up to shield her eyes from the sun as she scans the barren, snow-covered landscape around us. "There's a direct entrance to it from one of the hallways near the throne room."

I'd been nodding as I listened, but my chin slows to a stop and I swallow when her words sink in. "You…we have to sneak into Nightglade's castle without being seen?"

She hadn't mentioned this detail before.

"It's not like he spends his whole day there." She rolls her eyes.

"Okay, but I still feel like that's something you

should have mentioned earlier," I protest.

The green eyes she turns to me are so much like her sister's, but with an undercurrent of uncertainty Ilinor never possessed. "Would you have come with me if I told you?"

I want to say "Of course!" but I can't. "I would have considered it a little more carefully," I answer instead.

By the way her shoulders droop, I guess that wasn't the answer she'd hoped to hear.

"It makes accessing the Iron Prison more complicated is all," I add, keeping my tone soft.

Jaila turns, her expression guarded. "You know why I came to you."

As if I could forget the memory she'd shared, Nightglade standing over the bloodied body of his eldest daughter, her eyes empty and her limbs lifeless. Or the information she shared. How, after two coronation attempts with fae he considered worthy, Nightglade has decided to look elsewhere, to stop risking the lives of those closest to him. And since he's bound by the magic of the crowns, he has to find someone the Queen's crown will accept. Someone he can overpower.

My resolve hardens, thinking of Quince in prison, waiting for what will most likely be an execution rather than a successful coronation. There's no guarantee Nightglade would choose Quince at the new moon on March 6th, but I'd rather not take a chance.

"I know. And I appreciate how you worked so

hard to find me."

Snowflakes dance swirling pirouettes through the crisp air, obscuring our view. I follow their dance to its conclusion, in a glittering array on the ground, and chew on my lip.

"Problem?"

"Possibly," I answer. "I can fly, so I won't leave any footprints, but I'm not sure I can fly while carrying you around, at least not for long. Also, I kind of doubt how stealthy we'd be if we attempted it."

Jaila, like her father and sister, doesn't have wings. But even without wings, and even though she's young still, she handles what powers she has with expertise. From what I've seen, her powers lie in her ability to hide, to share images and memories with the touch of a finger, and in her razor-sharp claws she can protract and retract at will. That last trait she had in common with her sister, though I don't know what Ilinor's other powers were. And now…

My insides do a squeeze and a backflip simultaneously, thinking of the blood running down Ilinor's lifeless face, burned into Jaila's memory, and now mine. Ilinor's in no position to show off her fae powers any longer. And if we don't do something soon, Quince might be the next victim in Nightglade's quest for a co-ruler of the Unseelie court.

I wrench my thoughts away from the past and focus on the present only to find I can't focus on Jaila at all. Suppressing a grin, I whisper to where I think Jaila's standing, "So? Ideas?" As I wait for her to respond, a thought crosses my mind that when Jaila eventually grows into her full powers in a few years, she will be terrifying. Hopefully whatever happens between us here is enough to place me in her good graces.

She allows herself to be seen, reappearing in a spot about five feet further left than I'm looking and indicates the pond behind us. "Already got that covered."

No trace of footprints across its surface or leading from its edge to where we are now.

I look at her, my eyebrow rising. "But you can't fly. How…?"

"No. I can't." She grins, a small expression, her lips hardly tipping up, but her eyes sparkling.

Shaking my head, I say, "You're a mystery within a mystery, Jaila."

Her smile widens. "I like it that way."

The way she blooms under the tiniest bit of praise from me gives me pause and I feel my heart soften a little to her. It can't have been easy, growing up with minimal memories of your mother before she turned gwyllyon, estranged from your sister, depending on the goodwill of fae who have ulterior motives to get to her father who, until recently, she had only known by name.

"So, no risk of leaving footprints. Where do we go from here?"

"Onward!" She gestures overdramatically toward the setting sun and the castle in the distance.

The trees we venture around not only offer

occasional shade from the setting sun, but also occasional obstacles to me as I fly. I'm grateful, though, because they also obscure us from too many prying eyes.

"You know…" Jaila glances up at me, then away. "Quince was kind to me, when most other fae usually just ignore me."

I fly low, so I'm level with Jaila. "Was this before or after he wrestled you to the ground at the Seelie Court?"

"After. Before, he believed I was my sister." The slight tightening of her lips is the only clue Jaila gives me to what I've already suspected: she and her sister, almost strangers to each other, did not get along in their short time together at the Unseelie Court.

"Quince is kind, and thoughtful." I warm, thinking of him, though there's an ache in my chest, too. More than anything, I hunger to hear his laugh, to feel his arms around me, to feel that sense of peace I haven't found in anyone else. "He understands feeling out of place in Elfaeme, too."

She makes a noise of agreement. "His parents."

We're both quiet. Talking about Quince has made all of the emotions I'd pushed down–anxiety, fear, longing–rear their heads, snapping at my heart. It takes all my effort to stay aloft, to keep flying toward the castle, when a large part of me wants to collapse to the ground and huddle in a ball.

We're almost to the edge of the treeline when Jaila holds up a hand and catches my leg. "Piggyback," she hisses. "Now."

I hover, confused, and she yanks me out of the sky.

"What the–Jaila?"

"Piggyback," she hisses again, turning away from me.

I hesitate. "I don't want to crush you, plus I'm carrying my overnight bag, and…"

She looks over her shoulder at me, pulling a face. "You're barely bigger than me, and I'm stronger than I look. Just do it. Now!"

Without a chance to ask why, I hop onto Jaila's back, wrapping my legs around her torso. She stumbles forward under my weight, but catches herself and straightens her shoulders.

"This will take a lot of energy for me to hide us both, but it'll be easier to do with you close to me," she says in a low voice. With my arms around her, I can feel her rapid heartbeat in her neck.

"I don't know how you've been hiding your tracks up till now," I say. "And I really don't think I can lift us fully in the air, but I can maybe get us a couple inches off the ground, if that'll help."

Her head bobs next to mine. "That would help, yes."

My wings strain with the combined weight of the two of us, but not as much as I'd feared they would. I beat them furiously, letting Jaila guide us forward out of the treeline and across an expanse of empty, snow-covered hills.

The castle looms in front of us, a mile away, then half a mile. The minutes drag by, and my wings are like jelly on my back but I keep moving them, sweat pouring down my temples and into my eyes. Circling the castle is a wall, where lone figures prowl atop it with military precision.

One wingbeat. Another. Then something happens that I've never experienced before. My wings, which had held me aloft with relative ease ever since I figured out how to fly, fold in on themselves, the strain too much, and Jaila stumbles. One of the figures on the wall hesitates and, my heart thumping wildly in my throat, I force my wings to open and flap, open and flap, but we don't move. Beneath me, Jaila whimpers.

"I'm tired. But I'm not the one running while wielding magic and holding someone on my back. You must be exhausted," I say, acknowledging her efforts.

"Can't…think…about that," she pants.

With effort, she takes one step forward and then another. My wings lift us out of the snow, and we make a beeline for the wall as a team: me and my wings holding us aloft, Jaila steering us where we need to go.

Jaila slows to a stop at the edge of the wall and I lower us to the ground. We both sink to our knees, panting.

"Do you think any of them saw us? Will they notice that spot in the snow where we stopped?"

Her shoulders lift noncommittally. "Whether they did or not doesn't change what we have to do."

"No, but it might change how we do it."

Her eyes widen at the same time I hear the sound of leather on stone, a steady rhythm of footfalls. As one, we press against the wall and hold our breaths. I keep waiting for the steady rhythm to slow to a stop, but the footsteps continue without pause until the sound fades.

"I tracked the pattern of the guards' movements when Nightglade had me here for some forced family time. We have to be quick, before the next guard appears," she whispers. "The wall is mostly ornamental, a show of power and strength." She snorts. "Like most sneaky enough fae can't just fly or climb over it."

The amount of information she gleaned from her time at the Unseelie Court, a total of fifteen days from just after the Winter Solstice to the first new moon in January, astounds me. Her mind is like a steel trap, where mine is more like a steel sieve. Strong, but with lots of holes for forgetting key information.

I scan our surroundings, taking deep breaths and trying to let my heart rate settle. Over the wall, then into the castle to find the hall near the throne room (hopefully unoccupied). It's easier to concentrate on our current task, making our way to the Iron Prison to bust out Quince, than on how close we were to being discovered or on the complicated emotions I feel over my argument with Aspen.

Even thinking Aspen's name is enough to kindle my rage again. Why he thought he could pull the dad card, when he was in hiding for most of my eighteen years…

Breathe, Eevee.

"It's now or never!" Jaila whispers to me. "Another guard will be here in a minute." She clambers up the wall like a spider and hefts herself to the top.

"You gotta be kidding me," I grumble. My wings beat half-heartedly behind me, my muscles burning, so I end up doing a weird half-flying, half-spider climb after her up the wall. Jaila pulls me to the stone floor and we crawl to the other side.

"See the buildings around the castle?"

I peer over the edge. From a distance, the castle is the only part of the Unseelie Court that's visible. But up close, I can see there's an entire village sprawled around it. Fae folk wander to and fro, and I even smell cinnamon and the yeasty scent of fresh-baked bread coming from an open square filled with street vendors.

"Yes."

"We're heading to the building with the snake sign on it."

"So, not to the market?" I clarify, my stomach grumbling. It's a little early for lunch, but the stale granola bar I ate at the hotel this morning was not enough fuel for how much flying I've been doing.

Apparently my question is worthy of a withering stare.

"Fine, fine. To the snake place!"

We climb down the other side of the wall, Jaila much more gracefully than I, and she tugs me into an alleyway, leading me from one side street to another.

"What if someone recognizes me?" I hiss as we

casually blend into the crowd on a busier street, easing our way to another small alley. Jaila has the power to go undetected if she wants, but I have distinct orange flowers on my face that, after my stunt during the winter solstice, I'm sure many would recognize. Not to mention my uncanny resemblance to Maeve, their former Unseelie Queen.

"I gave you a cloak for a reason, dummy."

"Gave it to me would imply it was yours to give," I grumble under my breath, but tug the cloak's hood over my head. I hope she left the vendor some money before she took it. Maybe it's just a false sense of security, but having my temples and my face obscured in the cloak's shadow makes me feel calmer, less anxious about being recognized as Jaila leads me to the snake place.

We wind down first one street, then another, until we are in a part of town louder and dirtier than the outer rim. Every building here is in some level of disrepair: windows boarded up, dust coating the stone walls, roofs patched up. Then we turn left, and the street widens. Across from us is a building in immaculate condition compared to the squat stone buildings around it, though it still shows signs of age. I can tell that the owner, whoever it is, has put a lot of time and effort into making it look warm and inviting. Its exterior is dust-free, and the light shining out of the windows is warm. It's taller than the other buildings on the street, with two stories instead of one.

I glance up at the sign hanging above the door.

On it is a painting of a large green snake coiled around a black rock. Beneath this, in faded black letters, is the name "Snake & Stone Tavern."

Jaila darts through the crowded street, directly toward the two story building, and pushes open the wooden door. I scramble to catch up to her, sliding inside just as the door closes, and the smell of beer hits my nostrils.

The tavern is crowded, considering it's late morning on a Tuesday; nearly all the seats are filled with fae laughing and shouting over each other, beer mugs rising in toasts, and servers hoisting trays of food above the heads of the customers. We wind through the horde, and I keep my head down, hoping no one thinks anything of my orange wings, and seat ourselves at a table in the corner.

A prickling sensation, as of being watched, travels down my neck and I glance around. None of the patrons seem to be paying any attention to us. But then

I notice the barkeep staring in our direction, the mug in her hand forgotten. Beer dribbles down its side as it tips toward the floor.

I quickly duck my head. "Is there a reason you've brought us here?"

"It'll be easiest to do what we need to do under the cover of dark. Plus, I thought you wanted to eat?"

"The barkeep is staring at us," I mutter, tugging my hood lower.

Jaila turns on the bench.

"Don't look!" I say quickly, and Jaila shifts back to me. "Otherwise she'll know we know she's looking at us."

"Eevee. Relax. She can't see me unless I want her to. My invisibility isn't all or nothing. I can choose who sees me and who doesn't."

Jaila turns around again, then looks back at me with a grin. "Ah. That's what I'd hoped."

"You hoped a fae with hair that I'm pretty sure is partly made of fire would pay attention to me?"

"I hoped Kenna would be here today, even though it's a Tuesday. She's a fire nymph who really likes beer. She took over this establishment after its previous owners got bored of running a tavern."

I raise my face so Jaila can get the full blast of my skepticism. "Listen. This place reminds me of Cam's parents' brewery back in Duluth, but just because someone likes beer doesn't make them instantly trustworthy to me."

"We can trust Kenna," Jaila replies with calm

confidence. "She knew my mom before my mom turned gwyllyon. Hold on."

Jaila darts over to the barkeep, who sets down the mug of beer to talk to her. I gnaw on my lip as I watch. From their body language, the way Kenna's face showed no surprise at seeing Jaila, the casual manner in which Jaila leans on the counter toward Kenna, reassures me only marginally. After a few minutes, Kenna hails two of the servers. They both set down their trays and bustle to the kitchen. One returns almost immediately with two plates of food. Jaila smiles happily at Kenna as she takes the plates, then rushes back over to our table.

"Here, you wanted food, right?" She plunks down a plate of beans and buttered bread. "Eat up. Kenna says the previous owners asked her to keep a lookout for you." She eyes me curiously. "How do you know them?"

I shake my head, bewildered. "I don't. I know you trust Kenna, but I have a bad feeling about this. What if she sent that other server to go get the previous owners? Then our cover would be blown." I stand, pushing my plate away. "We should go, find somewhere else to hide until nightfall."

Jaila's cheeks are stuffed full of bread. "Ca we'eet urst?"

My stomach growls again. I sit and pull the plate back toward me. "Fine. We eat, then we hide."

While we eat, I keep an eye on the kitchens. The second server still hasn't returned, not that I can see. Unless he slipped back into the tavern without me noticing? I scan the crowded tavern, looking for his dark hair or the silver hoop earring in his right ear. The tavern's front door swings open and four fae enter. I turn my attention back to the food. Where had that server gone? And how much time do we have before he returns and we're caught?

"Hope you don't mind, the place is quite busy," says a polite-voiced fae, one of the four I saw entering just now. Without waiting for a reply, he sits next to me on the bench and waves his companions over.

I shovel food into my mouth, panic rising in my throat making it difficult to swallow. Crap crap crap.

"Wonderful, even Eevee doesn't realize it's you when you use that voice!" exclaims one of his companions with a frivolous glee that I recognize immediately.

My panic subsides, replaced by confusion. "What the fudge, Shannon?" I ask angrily, pulling back my hood and glaring at where he sits next to Jaila, a satisfied smile plastered on his face.

Jaila looks from Shannon to me, a line between her eyebrows.

He chuckles, nudging her in the shoulder with familiarity, then waves to me. "Hello, Eevee. Miss me?"

Sean touches my elbow. "We're glad to see you. After hearing you'd returned to Elfaeme, we have been keeping a lookout."

After hearing I'd returned to Elfaeme. Anger seethes in my gut. I have one guess as to who tipped them off, and his name starts with A.

"Who are your friends?" I ask, indicating the two fae at Sean and Shannon's sides. In the dim light of the tavern I can't see much. They're both cloaked, like me, but the hands they have resting on the table are green. Or is it a mottled blue?

"You see!" Shannon crows delightedly. "A perfect disguise." To me, he winks and lowers his voice. "A little bit of fae glamour goes a long way, you know. Look more closely at 'our' friends."

I frown, focusing more closely on the other two fae. What did he mean, by emphasizing *our* friends?

The two fae with Sean and Shannon are close in height, though the one sitting next to Sean on our side of the table is broader. If I had to guess, I'd say they were both some kind of tree or water sprites. Neither has wings, but they each have pointed ears and their eyes are like the reflection of leaves in a clear pond. Then the one sitting next to Sean shifts and I *know* that shoulder hunch, like they're trying to be smaller than they are.

"Cam," I breathe. I look over to the other, who's grinning impishly at me. "Maggie. What? Why? …How?"

The last time Cam and Maggie were in Elfaeme in disguise was at the Winter Solstice Festival, and their disguises then were nowhere near this level.

I turn to look at Sean and Shannon and jab a finger at them. "You two are a bad influence! How could you let them come here?" I eye my friends with growing alarm. "And what did you do to them? They look…"

Maggie's grin widens. "Fae-bulous is the word you're looking for, E. We look fae-bulous." She winks, and my brain sees two images superimposed, one in front of the other, both the human Maggie and the fae-Maggie, the green…or is it mottled blue? skin over her brown skin, twiglike hair over her Afro.

"It's a fae glamour," Cam explains quietly, and even though I'm in a corner of a tavern surrounded by fae, I immediately feel at ease. I've wanted to hear their voice for so long. After years of friendship, going months without being able to talk to them except through text or email has been torture.

Tears well in my eyes and the room grows blurry. "F-fae glamour?" I stammer.

Jaila tosses a linen napkin at my face, glancing between me and my friends wistfully, like being apart from friends was something she wished she could experience, if only to have someone to reunite with someday.

I hastily swipe the napkin across my face and set it on my plate. "What do you mean, like a disguise?"

"We do love a good disguise," Shannon admits, flipping his long, blonde hair behind his shoulders with flair.

"Don't I know it," Jaila mumbles around a mouthful of bread.

"But this is a bit more than that." Sean gestures

to Cam and Maggie.

Never one to like being on display, Cam crosses their arms and one of their legs bounces, the bench jiggling with the movement.

"A perfect illusion." Shannon raises a finger to poke Maggie in the face.

She does an odd flick of her wrist and then swats his hand away. "Oh no you don't."

Shannon shakes his hand a little, as if Maggie's light swat had stung.

"Nearly perfect." Sean's words are calm but they have an undercurrent of warning as he watches the boisterous crowd at the Snake & Stone.

"Is that why their skin keeps changing color?" Jaila asks, curiosity lighting up her features.

Cam flushes, yanking their hands out of sight, and Maggie, after a questioning look at Sean, tucks her hands into the purple cloak she's wearing.

"I can't do fae glamour myself," Jaila continues with the air of a scientist chatting about a favorite subject. "At least, not yet. I hear it's tricky to get right. Maybe in a few years I'll see if I can do it as well as—" She cuts herself off, the pointed tips of her ears red.

When it's obvious she isn't going to finish her thought, I ask, "If the illusion isn't perfect, should they even be here?" Warring emotions ricochet around my heart. Happiness to see them, even disguised as fae. Worried they're putting themselves in unnecessary danger. Elation. Anxiety. Fear.

Maggie scoffs, raising her color-shifting fists.

"I'd like to see anyone try to get us." In her right hand is her phone, which she waggles in the air with a significant look at Cam, who coughs.

"We haven't tested that yet," they say.

"Yeah, well, we have other things up our sleeves, too, don't we?" Maggie pockets her phone.

Sean and Shannon's silence is a loud response to my question about whether my friends should be here with a less-than-perfect illusion as cover. My irritation with them can wait, though. "Why are you in Elfaeme, Cam?" I ask.

They tilt their head toward me. Sean opens his mouth to answer and I hold a finger up to him. His eyes narrow, and I get the distinct feeling he's thinking of at least seven different ways to murder me, but I focus on Cam.

"We…" Cam looks to Shannon, who shakes his head. "We can't say."

"We can say why we're here, in this tavern, though, right?" Maggie asks, looking from one twin to the other.

"Of course," Shannon replies smoothly.

Maggie looks across the table at me, and I can't believe I didn't notice before how pinched and tired her face is. Maybe the illusion covered it.

"The barkeep–Kenna?" She looks to Sean and Shannon for confirmation, and they both make sounds of agreement. "Kenna. She knows Sean and Shannon, and she's one of the fae who've been keeping an eye out for your reappearance. When she saw you today–"

"Hold up." A thought hits me like a flying tackle from a wyvern. What had Jaila said? *She took over this establishment after its previous owners got bored of running a tavern.* Snake & Stone. S & S. I resist the urge to roll my eyes, but only just. "You guys were the previous owners of this place."

"Guilty!" Shannon winks. "Sean can still brew the best pear cider. He'd chill the glasses with his magic, too, so the drinks were always ice cold. And I'm a little out of practice, but I used to do this trick where I'd pour the drink and flip it in the air–"

"As fascinating as our lives as tavern-owners were," Sean interrupts with a stern look at his brother, "Eevee had asked why we were here."

Shannon waves for Maggie to continue.

"Wait, I want to hear more about that drink trick."

I kick Jaila under the table.

"Ow!"

"Well, we figured you came back for a reason, E," Maggie says, leaning in toward me. "We're a little busy with our own thing, so we don't have long, but we wanted to see how you were doing, and if we could help with anything."

Warmth fills me from head to toe. All those months of intermittent communication, of my only companion being my birth father who was in mourning for his partner, and all that time worrying we'd grow apart. And yet here they are, Maggie and Cam, illusion-ed up and risking their lives to come help me when I really needed it.

"You guys are seriously the best." My voice is thick. I get up and move to hug Cam, but find myself bumping into someone at the table behind us instead. "Sorry," I mumble, keeping my face down.

"Sorry," Cam says at the same time, taking their hands out of their cloak and adjusting something I should have noticed earlier–one of their daisy chains. Unlike the prototypes, which were simply daisies twisted around thin iron wire, these are longer-lasting, encased in resin. They see me looking at the charm and nod, before slipping it back up their sleeve.

Jaila, who I've never heard giggle before, is giggling. "What just happened?"

I sit back in my spot on the bench. "They're smart, that's what."

Maggie leans on the table in front of Shannon until she's within a foot of Jaila and whispers, "Fae protection charms. Especially effective when they're against our skin."

She adjusts hers so it slides down the long-sleeved shirt she's wearing under her cloak and rests on the skin on her wrist.

"Yeah, I get that now." Jaila presses up against the wall and Shannon, who was even closer to Maggie than Jaila, somehow manages to slither away from Maggie and her protection charm by going under the table and popping up at the end of it in front of a server who's passing by.

"So." Maggie relaxes back into her spot with an

air of satisfaction. She readjusts the charm so it no longer touches her skin and pulls out her phone, holding it up next to where the charm is hidden. "We're as prepped as we can be for–"

"Helping you," Sean interrupts with a cutting glance at Maggie. She clamps her mouth shut and I feel my curiosity rising. What is it they're up to?

"Yeah. Sure. Helping me," I echo with skepticism.

"He couldn't say it if it weren't true," Shannon quips. He swipes a drink from the tray of a server walking by and sits down. As he passes me, I feel him press something into my hand. When I glance at him, he shakes his head and mouths, "Read it later."

"What are we helping you with, is the question." The look Sean gives me is sharp, like he's trying to cut through to my inner thoughts.

I slip the small, somewhat bulky envelope from Shannon into my sweatshirt pocket, and Jaila and I catch them up on Nightglade's failed coronations and our goal for the evening.

When we're done, Sean is tapping his chin with a faraway look on his face and Shannon's eyes are sparkling with glee.

"Sounds like you'll need a distraction while you two break into the prison tonight."

"I agree with Sean. Does this mean we get to ride Fearghas again?" Maggie asks. She has a reckless, happy smile on her face I recognize, because it's the same look I have on my face when I fly.

"Fearghas?" I raise an eyebrow at Shannon. "You named the wyvern?"

"I did! And he's been a delight to train!" Shannon declares, his whole body radiating with pride. "He's flying above right now, but he'll come when I need him."

"And you're okay with this?" I cross my arms, spearing Sean with an icy gaze of my own.

"Fearghas has been worthwhile to train," Sean admits reluctantly. "He's helped with some of our recent missions."

He gives Shannon a significant look, probably telepathically yelling at his brother not to say anything else.

This explains what they've been up to since I last saw them depart from the Winter Solstice Festival riding the wyvern–Fearghas. Leave it to Shannon to devote his time training a horse-sized, two-legged, flying beast.

Maggie pulls her phone out, swipes to unlock it, then laughs. "No service, I keep forgetting. Man, E, what do you do when you need to look something up on the fly here?"

"Books, mostly?"

Cam leans forward and clears their throat.

We all turn to them and I think their cheeks are flushed but it's hard to tell with the fae glamour.

"I have an idea for a distraction. Maybe."

Cam's Subterfuge

"Do you think Cam's idea will work?" Jaila whispers to me as soon as we've split off into our three groups.

A large part of me wishes it could have been Cam or Maggie coming with me tonight to break Quince out of prison. But not only would that be too dangerous for them, neither of them have any lockpicking skills, and Cam has another part to play. I think back on how Jaila vigorously swung her lockpicking kit in front of Sean and Shannon, how her stance widened and she *insisted* she be the one to come into the Iron Prison with me.

It's probably some kind of personal desire for

revenge, I tell myself. I'd want to get back at
Nightglade, too, if he were my biological father.

One thing's for sure. She didn't insist on
coming with me so we could bond over small talk.
We're both silent as we make our way to the main
doors of the Unseelie castle. There are two guards
posted outside it on either side of the doorway, both
dutifully standing at attention, their eyes scanning the
stairs leading up the doors for any who'd dare try and
enter the castle without permission. It's a stark contrast
from the Seelie castle, which was much more open and
inviting to visitors.

"We wait here for the signal," Jaila says. "Then
we make our move." Misgivings about the plan must
show on my face because she adds, "No hesitation. We
get the signal, we move, that's it. Got it?"

"Got it," I grumble. My stomach tightens.
There are so many things that could go wrong with our
plan before we ever get the signal.

Night has fallen, and the sky above us is
clouded, obscuring the stars. I know if it were cloudless
we'd see a nearly new moon. If this doesn't work, if we
can't get Quince out tonight, he might be the one
Nightglade chooses to participate in the coronation
ceremony tomorrow.

Somewhere up there, Sean and Maggie are
circling on the wyvern, Fearghas, ready to provide
backup if needed.

Please let this work, I plead silently as I watch the
guards with Jaila. The Unseelie nightlife is coming alive

as we wait. Sounds of music and singing drift down the streets of the town surrounding the castle. Each alley and roadway lights up with balls of light in various hues, purple, blue, green, white, and yellow, which move lazily above the streets.

"Will-o'-the-wisps," Jaila answers when she sees my puzzled expression. "Some of them like to spend time on Earth waylaying travelers, of course, but the biggest concentration of them live here in the Unseelie realm."

The stall we're hiding behind, situated near the base of the castle steps, must sell leather products, because the warm, kind of smoky, musky smell permeates the fabric and the wood of the stall. It reminds me of the smell of a horse saddle, the one time I went horseback riding at a summer day camp.

In front of us, coming up the street, I see two fae. One carries a notepad, and my heart quickens.

"It's them," I mouth to Jaila, and her eyes narrow as she watches their approach.

It's still strange seeing Cam disguised as a fae. In the dreamy light of the will-o'-the-wisps, their disguise is infallible. Even as they near us, I can't pick out any defining feature which would hint at the fact they're actually human.

Next to them, Shannon has opted for a simpler disguise, dressed in a hooded crimson robe. His batlike wings have been painted so instead of black, they're a shimmery hue of orange, like lava. His hood obscures his face too much for me to make out any features clearly, but knowing him, he's smiling. Deception is his favorite game.

Cam fiddles with the pencil in their hand as they both approach the guards, who are now observing the two with watchful, yet bored, expressions.

With a sweeping motion, Shannon produces an easel from underneath his robe and sets it up at the base of the steps. I have no idea where he even found an easel in the town at this hour.

Placing the notepad on the easel with care, Cam takes their pencil and puts it to page while Shannon makes a show of watching what Cam is drawing. He waves a few will-o'-the-wisps over so they crowd above Cam's head, a jostling mix of colors.

"Don't be so obvious, Shannon," I mutter.

But the guards are now watching the scene with more interest.

"Isn't it a little late for drawing?" one asks, the one nearest to us. Her voice is high, yet resonant.

Now I know Shannon is grinning. I hear it in his voice when he replies, "Not for my friend. They're an apprentice, you know. Still trying to make a name for themselves. And they thought, what better way to practice shadows than at night?"

"But why here?" asks the other guard, the tip of his javelin dipping a little as he watches Cam draw.

Shannon laughs delightedly. "Because of you, of course!"

"Me?" the male guard asks in surprise.

"Him?" the female guard, the one nearest us,

asks incredulously.

"And you," Shannon adds with a small bow to the female guard.

She shifts her javelin from one shoulder to the other. "You don't say?"

Cam clears their throat and lifts their eyes from the drawing they're working on. "I've been working on drawing portraits in twenty minutes or less." Their voice is shaky and hesitant, and I can see the tension in their shoulders, but with an encouraging nod from Shannon, they continue. "It's a little more challenging with how dark it is and with two subjects to draw instead of one, but if you let me draw you, you could keep the finished drawing."

"Only twenty minutes, you say?" the male guard asks. He exchanges a look with the female guard.

"And you get to keep the drawing," Cam reminds them.

"Well…" The female guard surveys the empty marketplace, the stalls all covered and vacant.

"It's only twenty minutes?" asks the male guard.

"It may take a little longer with drawing two of you," Cam hedges.

"Hmm." The female one taps her chin.

Turning to his guardmate, the male one wheedles, "Oh, c'mon, Nena. No one's here except these two. I'll let you keep the original, and we can pop over to Earth to make a copy for me."

She grins. "Oh, fine."

"Wonderful!" Shannon claps his hands. "You

two will be the perfect subjects for my friend to practice. Your wings, Nena, are the most beautiful white. They will simply pop in the drawing!"

She preens the feathers on her wings. As her face turns toward me more, I see her face has feathers on it, too, with two round, yellow eyes like an owl's trained on Shannon.

Cam whispers something to Shannon.

"What's that?" the male guard calls. "What'd he say?"

"They," Shannon corrects.

He scratches at his chin beneath his tusks. "My apologies. What'd they say?"

"Oh," Shannon sighs. "It's nothing."

Cam's brow crinkles as if in frustration. "Nothing? The staging is all wrong. It'll be okay, but not the best."

"What's wrong with the staging?" asks Nena.

"Well…" Shannon hedges. "It's just that, you're so far apart from each other, you know. On either side of the doorway. Which, I know is where you're supposed to stand when you're on duty. That's why I said it's nothing. You can't move, you must do your duty and stay at your posts." He turns and proceeds to peer over Cam's shoulder, then makes a disappointed clucking sound. "Though I see what you mean," he says in a stage whisper to Cam.

"Is it going to be an issue?"

"I'm not sure, Nena," Shannon replies with a hefty sigh. "I do see what my friend means, though.

The angle from here. It's…not flattering. We'll do our best, of course."

In the silence, all we hear is the scratching of Cam's pencil against the paper. "We don't have to stay right here in these spots, do we, Ash?" asks Nena, facing her guardmate.

Ash grunts in agreement. "So long's we're keeping an eye on the doors for any intruders, should be fine."

"Only if you're sure," Shannon says. "I wouldn't dare ask you to do something against your orders."

"It's only twenty minutes, and it's not like there's anyone else around," Nena says, flapping her wings and flying silently down the fifteen steps until she lands in front of Cam's easel.

"This would be much better for lighting as well," Cam admits. "Then I can sketch in a few details of the castle behind you."

Ash marches his way down the steps to join Nena, and Shannon busies himself with posing them until Nena is standing, aiming her javelin point at an invisible attacker, and Ash stands stiffly at attention, both of their faces directed toward Cam, whose pencil is now flying across the page.

"Now, hold that pose," Shannon says loudly.

Jaila jabs me in the ribs.

"Ow! What?"

"That's our signal!"

Fear snakes around my chest and squeezes.

"Right. Are you sure you can keep me invisible again? We haven't had a lot of time to rest."

"It's only for a short distance." Her jaw is set in an obstinate line, and I know there's no arguing with her on this.

At the base of the steps I can hear Shannon chatting with Nena. "–and you've been working as a guard for almost seven decades? My! Don't you ever want to try another career, just for fun?"

"It's now or never," Jaila says, gesturing for me to get on her back.

I tamp down my jitters and hop on, flapping my wings as she runs toward the doors to keep her feet from making sound on the steps.

The doors loom before us, its dark wood shining dimly in the light of the will-o'-the-wisps. With practiced ease, Jaila turns the handle, and we both hold our breath as it click-thunks open. I look back at Cam and Shannon. Cam's eyes, glamoured to look like a fae's with the appearance of a leaf-covered pond, glance up at the doors and quickly back to their page. Not missing a beat, Shannon moves in front of Nena and Ash, near Cam, keeping the guards' eyes trained on him. We slip inside and close the door behind us.

"We have twenty minutes, at most," Jaila says, lowering me to the ground once it's clear the hallway is deserted. "That's not a lot of time."

"We knew that going into this," I reply.

The halls around us are dim, lit only by the occasional torch in wall sconces. Even though we're above ground, the dimness and the stone remind me of the cave where the Unseelie hold their big gatherings, like the Winter Solstice Festival, and I shiver.

"The Iron Prison is down this way." Jaila walks confidently, but her voice is thin, like she's holding her breath.

"Did you go there often when you were here?" I ask curiously, because I just realized I don't know much about Jaila's time at the Unseelie Court.

"My f–Nightglade had his favorite noble, Banethistle, show me around. The prison was part of that tour. Along with some remarks from Banethistle about how no one was safe from the prison, not even those related to the King."

Banethistle. The name puts me even more on edge. His ratlike face swims before my eyes, taunting me with all I don't know about him. He had been one of Nightglade's most loyal nobles, willing to take on the job of substitute librarian at a human high school to spy on me, willing to be the second fae to die in pursuit of the Unseelie Queen's crown, but his past is a mystery. The only things I know for sure are that he did something to Quince's family, something Quince hasn't told me, and that he was terrified of Sean and Shannon when he saw them at Duluth High's library.

She glances at me over her shoulder, a wry grin on her face. "They didn't trust me even then, since I grew up around the Seelie. My mother made Oakspirit and Hibiscus promise to let me grow up at the Seelie Court. It was one of the last things she did before she turned into a gwyllyon. And no," she adds, wrapping her arms around herself and picking up the pace, "I don't want to talk about it."

Fair, I think. *I'm not sure I'd be able to talk about it, either, even if I didn't have a time limit like we do now.*

Jaila hesitates at one juncture, pressing against the wall and holding a finger up to her lips at my raised eyebrows.

"–simply unsettling, you know? Do you think it was one of his glamours?" asks someone in a breathy voice.

"Hard to say," another voice says in a haughty, icy tone. "His illusions are fairly convincing. I was a guest at that dinner–"

"No! How did you get an invitation?"

"He rewards those who are loyal, Trina, you know that. And the fae they brought out, well, let me tell you, when the glamour was stripped away, she was no more than skin and bones. His glamour can fool even the most eagle-eyed. I think he likes to remind us of that…"

The voices fade away. To be on the safe side, Jaila and I wait another minute before continuing on.

The next few corridors are empty, but that doesn't stop us from peeking around every corner and moving as cautiously as we dare with a time limit to keep in mind.

I don't have to ask Jaila if she's leading us in the correct direction. The closer we get to the Iron Prison, the more I want to turn around and go back the other way. This feeling is more than nerves, it's like with each step that creepy-crawly sensation gets exponentially stronger, until we're in front of a nondescript wooden door at the end of a hall.

"Is this it?" I whisper, eyeing it.

We've made it to the entrance to the Iron Prison easily. Too easily, if you ask me.

Behind this door is where Nightglade keeps his prisoners close at hand, including Quince and his parents.

So why isn't anyone guarding it?

Doubt seizes me for the first time. Will Quince even want to leave if his parents are here? He refused to come with me at the Winter Solstice Festival, choosing instead to remain with his parents and be imprisoned with them. What makes me think he's changed his mind in a couple of months?

"There'll probably be someone on the other side," Jaila mutters to me. She reaches down and pulls out a small dagger. "If we're lucky, it's someone who's loyal to the Unseelie Queen."

My heart sputters at the mention of my birth mother. "But she's–"

"Stone, yeah," Jaila agrees in a hushed tone. "But she has followers, E."

At the mention of the nickname I'd given Folsom, I grow quiet, an image starting to form in my mind.

Of a loyal follower to the Unseelie Queen.

So loyal, he'd allow himself to lose his place at

Court and follow her into exile.

So loyal that, after her powers had been revoked and she'd turned to stone, he still worked to gather together those who would oppose the Unseelie King, the one responsible for her final fate.

"I see," is all I say.

"We need to hurry," she says. "I'll go invisible and open the door. If it's someone I recognize as being loyal to the Queen, we'll be able to go in with no trouble."

"If it isn't…"

Her face is grim. "We fight, and fast."

I ignite my fists so they both crackle with flames. "Right. Let's do this."

She cracks the door open, pulling it toward us on silent hinges, and looks through to the dark hall behind. At least, I assume she's looking. As soon as the door opened she disappeared.

"You won't need those fists," she whispers in my ear.

"I'm keeping them anyway," I decide as she opens the door further. The guard posted at the door sits on a stool, leaning against the cold stone wall, her eyes shut as if sleeping. "If not for fighting, at least for a little light."

At each cell, I hold up my fists, illuminating the inhabitants.

Most are asleep, or so tired they don't do anything more than blink at the sight of my flames.

"My Queen," one says in a croaky voice. "You

wear the face of my Queen, youngling." He weeps into his grimy hands.

The further we go down the prison halls, the more my heart sinks into my feet. Many of the stalls are empty, but the ones with occupants feel emptier somehow. Like the fae who are imprisoned are husks, nothing more.

One, a female with large, scabbed patches on her otherwise periwinkle skin, hisses at the light of my fisted flames when we walk by. My stomach squirms to see her gripping the iron bars of her cell. Even being this close to the iron makes me want to turn tail and run. To grab it and hold on? I don't know how she isn't puking with the nausea that comes with touching iron for so long.

"Over here," Jaila says, tugging on my elbow, and it's like getting a static electric shock all over when I follow her to the cell she's indicating.

Suddenly, I don't care about the iron or caution. I run the last few feet, holding my hands out until they're close to, but not touching, the iron bars of his cell. The flames crackle as I gaze into the tiny space.

Quince's cell.

"Oh, Quince," I whisper, tears filling my eyes.

The eyes looking out at me from underneath his greasy hair are dark, glittering, and wary. A flash of some emotion–disappointment?–flashes in them and is quickly replaced by fear.

"You shouldn't be here." His voice is sandpaper scratching on gravel.

"Well, we are, so shut up and let us save you."

His face is unreadable, but he stands and shuffles forward.

"Eevee, I need more light," Jaila mumbles out of the corner of her mouth.

My eyes stay fixed on Quince, but I move my hands closer to where Jaila works on the lock.

"Your parents," I say in a low voice. "Where are they? We can try to get them out, too, if you need us to."

I don't know how successful we'd be, I can feel the clock ticking as Cam draws the two guards outside, but I wouldn't be able to consider myself Quince's friend, let alone girlfriend, if I didn't try and help him save his family, too.

"They're…" He swallows, as if each word is painful. "They're safe. For now."

I study him. If they're safe, why doesn't he look happier, or more relieved? And why are they safe but he's still imprisoned? Something doesn't add up, but I can't spend time worrying about that right now.

"Then let's get you to safety, too."

He stares at his feet while Jaila struggles with the lock. Finally, we hear a soft click. None of us move.

"Someone's going to have to touch the door to get him out," Jaila says, pocketing her lockpicking kit. "And since I had to touch it while picking that lock, I vote not me. I've had enough of touching iron for the day." She shudders, then her eyes dart back the way we came. "And…I have something else to check out quick."

"Wait, what?" I ask.

Quince grits his teeth and pushes his cell door open.

"That wasn't part of the plan," I accuse Jaila.

"We still have a little time left. I promise to be by the castle doors before the twenty minutes are up."

Before I can offer any other protests, Jaila disappears from view.

I swear. I guess Quince and I are on our own.

"Are you okay to move fast?" I ask him. Seeing him closer to the light of my flames, he's skinny, barely more than skeletal. His face and arms, which had a healthy glow before, are dull and covered in spots of red, flaky skin.

"I'll manage," he says, not meeting my eyes.

I want nothing more than to hug him, to spend time together doing something not dangerous. Tears threaten to spill down my cheeks. Like the date we'd had right before the Winter Solstice Festival. We had pretended to be normal human teenagers for a few hours. Shopping, lunch at a food court, and ending with a movie. Suddenly, I want that more than anything, to just be regular—fae, human, that part doesn't matter. But someone other than the daughter of the former Unseelie Queen. Someone other than the fae whose actions had essentially led to Nightglade invoking the curse of the revoked crown. If I hadn't been so determined to find my birth parents, or if I had at least been quieter about it, maybe Nightglade wouldn't have renewed his interest in doing away with his ex-wife. Maybe…

Ugh, cut out the thought spiral, Eevee, I think firmly to myself. You've got your kind-of-boyfriend to save, and you're not out of the castle yet. Save the self-blaming thoughts for later, like when you're trying to sleep after all of this.

"We don't have a lot of time," I tell Quince, who's struggling to keep up with me as we fly back the way Jaila and I came in.

His arms are wrapped around himself, and his wings, I realize, have bare patches where glossy, black feathers used to be. The feathers that remain are trembling with the effort of flying.

"I'll manage," he repeats.

"But—"

"How do you plan to deal with the guard at the Iron Prison entrance?"

Worry and frustration burn like acid in my throat. I clear it, then say, "Just follow my lead."

We fly past the guard, who still appears to be sleeping, though I'm unsure if she's actually sleeping or if she's connected to Folsom in some way.

Again, I'm struck by how easy it has been to break Quince out of prison. The halls in the castle are still eerily absent of any fae. I guess Nightglade doesn't approve of late night wanderers of his castle halls?

Still, should it be this easy?

We make it to the front doors and I touch down. Shaking my hands to release the flames still flickering across my knuckles, I press my ear to the cool wood.

"–really coming along, now. They should be done any minute! You're doing wonderfully at holding your poses. I'm impressed!" Shannon's voice is muffled, but as cheery as ever. If he's worried about us making it out, none of the strain shows in his tone.

Here's where it might go south. If I can't open this door quietly enough, our whole ruse will be exposed.

"What are you waiting for?" Quince asks. His hand nervously tugs at one of the small horns on his head.

"Jaila," I say, my jaw tight.

I continue listening to Shannon gab away, my impatience growing with each second. What could Jaila be doing?

A horrible thought occurs to me. What if she's betrayed us? What if she slipped off to go tell her father that she's succeeded at bringing me here, and in a plot to help one of his prisoners escape, no less?

He'd have all the evidence he needs to execute me.

I glance at Quince, suddenly more nervous than I have been in the past half hour. What if I've just led us both to our deaths?

"You've got an ugly nervous face, you know that?" Jaila asks from my left. When I turn, there she is. She catches me looking at her, and the worry lining her face smooths away.

"Where'd you go?"

"We need to get out of here," she replies, refusing to answer me. "Why haven't you opened the door yet?"

And without any more preamble, Jaila takes the circular, silver handle, and pulls.

In the air, a wyvern cry pierces the air at the same moment, masking the sound of the door. Relief floods through me. Of course Sean and Maggie would be keeping an eye on the door, ready to cover for us when we opened it.

Cam glances up from their drawing, panic in their eyes.

"My arms hurt," I can hear Nena complaining.

"Yeah, let's see the picture already," Ash says restlessly, breaking pose.

Jaila, Quince, and I sprint toward the edge of the marketplace, ducking behind stalls, until we make it to the side alley where I stored my bag. Luckily it's still here.

Did we leave the door cracked open? I wonder as I lift it and sling it across my shoulders. I can't remember. I guess it doesn't matter at this point, but I hate thinking we might have created a problem for Shannon and Cam.

"No time to catch our breath." Jaila scans the alley, then turns to where Quince and I have slowed. No will-o'-the-wisps light up this alley, and the darkness is like wearing a cloak of invisibility. I feel safer already. "We need to get to where we can phase out of here."

"Where are we realm-hopping to?" Quince leans against the alley wall.

"Anywhere on Earth, to start," I say.

"But then back here, right?" he asks, his voice sharp.

I exchange a look with Jaila, who's tapping her fingers on her forearm. Now that Quince is no longer imprisoned, that means he won't be the one Nightglade chooses to place in the coronation ceremony tomorrow. But can we live with ourselves if we leave anyone to that fate?

"Yes, of course," I say finally. "I just need to stay on Earth long enough to connect to WiFi and send a text to Maggie and Cam to let them know we made it out safely. Once I hear they're safe, too, we can come back.

"Maggie and Cam?" Quince comes toward me, panic on his face. "Why do you need to hear if they're safe?"

"They've kind of partnered up with your cousins," I explain.

"Oh, that isn't good," he mutters.

"Earth first," I say. "Then we can catch up."

As I follow him out of the alley, skirting through the Unseelie town to a spot where Jaila knows we can realm-hop from, I study his back. It's like looking at a stranger's, and I wonder if I came too late to save Quince.

A Pit Stop for Clothes and Coffee

The alleyway Jaila has us appear in on Earth is a comfortable temperature, warm enough to wear a t-shirt, but cool enough that I'm okay in my sweatshirt for now. Even better, it's deserted.

"I love coming here," Jaila says, happier than I've seen her in the last few days.

"Where is here?" Quince asks, his voice gravelly. In the light of the cloud-covered sky, his face is gray, the line of his cheekbones sharp.

"I couldn't stay in Elfaeme after what happened to Ilinor," Jaila explains, leading us out of the alley. "Not for long stretches of time, anyway. So most of my time was spent touring different countries on Earth. To answer your question," she calls, taking a left onto a sidewalk, "we're in New Zealand. And it's daytime." She gestures to the cloudy sky above.

"New Zealand. But it was night when we left Elfaeme?" I ask, tugging my sleeves up above my elbows.

"Oh, and I suppose time has always lined up for you when you went back and forth between Elfaeme and Earth?" Jaila retorts.

"Well…yes?"

"But you never traveled to New Zealand, or this part of the world at all, from Elfaeme?"

"No," I admit.

She shrugs. "I don't know how the time works between the realms. All I know is sometimes it lines up and sometimes it doesn't."

I try to exchange a look with Quince to see if he has any more insight, maybe from his accidental realm-hopping to Sweden that one time, but his brows are furrowed, his gaze on his feet, which I just realized are bare. The excitement I had initially felt at being here diminishes. "We need to get you some shoes while we're here, Quince. Maybe some new clothes, too. And a shower."

He lifts his shoulders. "I guess. But then we'll head back?"

"You can head back whenever you want, for all I care. For the record, though, I helped get you out of prison once, I won't do it a second time." Jaila studies a sign posted in a shop window. "Ranch hands wanted for sheep farming. Huh." She stares at Quince with her green eyes. "Why are you so eager to get back after you just escaped?"

"I…" He runs his hands through his greasy black hair, which is matted in a few places. "Part of me is concerned about who Nightglade will choose to be in the new moon ceremony tomorrow. Don't get me wrong, I am…" As he pauses to think of a word, I mentally fill in a few for him. Glad? Grateful? Ecstatic to be free? But instead he finishes by heaving a sigh. "I'm mentally trying to wrap my head around the fact I'm no longer imprisoned. And I don't want to go back to the Iron Prison. But I don't want anyone to die tomorrow."

The questions circle through my head like whirlpools. One that I don't have an answer to yet is why the coronation ceremony hasn't worked for Nightglade so far.

"He's going to keep trying until he finds a fae both he and the Unseelie Queen's crown can agree on," I say aloud.

Quince shakes his head. Jaila motions at us to stay put. "Wait out here. I'll get some shoes and clothes in here quick." She disappears into the thrift store, named the One Stop Op Shop, according to the brightly printed rainbow letters above the door.

"What do you mean, shaking your head no?" I ask Quince quietly once Jaila's dashed inside the shop.

"'Ten tries for ten queens. Ten tries for ten kings. And at the end, if none prove worthy, the crowns return to dust.'"

"What is that from?" I take Quince's shoulders and inwardly wince. They're so bony now. But I look at his face, the face which I've missed so much these last few months. "What is that from?" I ask again.

"I truthfully don't know what it's from," he answers, biting his lip. After a moment, he adds, "It's something I heard during my time in prison."

Lowering my hands from his shoulders, which he has held stiffly ever since I placed my hands on them, I ask, "And do you think it's true? Do you trust the source?"

He runs his fingers through his hair again, where his horns would be if we were in Elfaeme. "I don't trust the source, but I trust that the information is accurate."

We lapse into an uncomfortable silence. Quince doesn't look directly at me, but stands as though all his joints hurt. I'm about to ask him what happened to him in the Iron Prison, but Jaila bursts out of the shop door with an armful of clothes. Sitting on top of the clothes is a pair of shoes so yellow they're almost neon.

"These are the only ones which looked about your size," Jaila says with an apologetic shrug to Quince. "I don't understand how humans figure out their shoe size at all. It's different everywhere I go. Here." She unloads the clothes and shoes into Quince's arms. "Let's find a coffee shop somewhere. Eevee looks like she needs at least three cups to appear like she's actually alive, and I'm starving."

"As long as the shop has WiFi," I say, choosing to ignore the insult. I pull out my phone and nervously check the battery percentage. It's at 14%. Spending time in Elfaeme always drains it, unless I remember to turn it off, which apparently I didn't. "And somewhere I can plug in my phone."

"Do you have an adaptor?" Quince asks. "We're not in the Midwest anymore. We're not even in the United States anymore."

I grimace. "Shoot. No, I don't. We better find someplace with WiFi, food, and coffee fast. I promised Maggie and Cam I'd check in with them, and I want to make sure they're okay before we do anything else."

"Hopefully the shop has a bathroom you can change in, too," Jaila comments to Quince. "Your clothes really smell. Like a moldy basement."

"Thanks," he mutters.

We happen upon a café with a cute sign out front made out of repurposed wood in a downtown district filled with quaint stores. The whole district is bustling with people going about their shopping.

"Corner Coffee," Jaila reads, then peers inside. "Looks cozy. Food and beverages are on me!"

Quince shoves his feet in the yellow shoes, which are a few sizes too big for him, and follows Jaila inside.

"Do you want a coffee?" I ask, placing a hand on Quince's arm to stop him from making a beeline for the bathroom.

He scans the menu. "Iced mocha. Large, since

Jaila's buying." He frowns, adorably confused. "Wait. How is Jaila buying?"

"I have no idea," I admit. "Money doesn't seem to be an issue for her here."

"You know what, I'm not even going to question it at this point," Quince says wearily. "Can you have her order me a muffin, too?"

A wave of homesickness hits me at the mention of muffins, and it's like I'm back at Gramp's Diner just outside Duluth, waiting until the end of my dishwashing shift to buy muffins to bring home to my family.

"Yeah." I clear my throat. "Yeah, I can have her get you a muffin. Any particular flavor?"

"Something chocolatey if they have it." He leans in, as if to give me a kiss on the cheek, but then stops himself, looking self-conscious, and hurries toward the bathroom.

I relay Quince's order to Jaila and include mine–a large coffee, black, with a blueberry muffin–and we find a booth in the back corner of the café.

Each of the tables has a potted plant on it, and the walls are lined with shelves bursting with leaves and flowers, giving the café greenhouse vibes.

Jaila and I take turns bringing the food and drinks to the table. When we're all settled, I take out my phone and use the WiFi password listed on the menu to connect to the internet.

No messages come pouring in, which worries me, but I send a message to Maggie and Cam.

E: *back safe. u 2 ok?*

I set the phone to vibrate, then place it on the table. Quince slides into the booth next to me, his hair dripping wet. "I used the bathroom sink and the hand soap," he admits.

"Well, you smell better than before," Jaila declares around her egg sandwich.

My phone is disappointingly not vibrating with Cam or Maggie's immediate responses. I fiddle with the items in my pocket.

"What's in my pocket?" I murmur.

"Wha'd oo say?"

"You really should eat with your mouth closed."

She swallows and pulls a face at me, crossing her eyes and sticking out her tongue. "That's not what you said."

But my eyes are on the small envelope I've pulled out of my pocket. What had Shannon given to me at the Snake & Stone?

Underneath the table, I open the envelope and dump the lumpy object into my palm. A gold ring, plain, with some kind of runes engraved on the outside, and a single inlaid diamond barely larger than the period at the end of a sentence gleams against my skin.

The metal is warm from being in my pocket so long. I close my fingers over it. Why in the world–this one or Elfaeme–would Shannon give me jewelry?

From the envelope, I pull out a small slip of paper. On it is a short note.

Use this to call "Scamp" from great distances if needed. It only works once. Then it's worthless, unless you like gold.
~S

I hastily put the ring and note in the envelope and stuff it back into my sweatshirt pocket.

Quince swallows his bite of chocolate chip muffin and raises an eyebrow at me. His hair is still plastered to his head, giving him the appearance of a wet, confused dog.

"I was just checking something."

He doesn't press it, which is a relief.

Unfortunately, Jaila finishes eating within five minutes and begins tapping her foot on the ground. "When will your friends message you back?" she complains.

"I don't know." I stare at my phone, willing it to vibrate, but it doesn't.

"They're fine, I'm sure." Quince crumples the paper wrapper from his muffin and drops it on his plate. "We should leave soon. Head back," he lowers his voice, "to Elfaeme."

"And do what?" I demand, crossing my arms. "We just got you out of there. Are you ready to tell me why you're so eager to return?"

Beneath the table, his knee bounces. "I think we should learn more about the crowns, and the coronation ceremony." He fiddles with his napkin, ripping it to shreds above his plate. "The more we know, the better chance we have at stopping more botched ceremonies from happening."

"Yes…" I say slowly. "But who do you propose we go ask about it? We can't exactly go up to Nightglade and be like, 'Hi, yes, we think you're going about this ceremony all wrong and causing unnecessary death. Let us help you. Also, would you consider stepping down as Unseelie King, you're not doing the greatest job.'"

Jaila snorts. "That's an understatement."

Quince looks troubled as he smooshes the napkin bits into a pile. "I don't know. Maybe one of the older fae know more about what's going on?"

"What, do either of you have any grandparents still alive?" Then a thought occurs to me. "Do I?"

"I don't know about you, but I don't." Jaila scoots out from the booth. "I'm hungry still. I think I'll get a scone."

"We'd need a true fae elder," Quince says thoughtfully. "Not just any fae grandparent. Someone who's especially old."

We listen to the sounds of the coffee machines grinding, and if I close my eyes, I can imagine myself back in the Java Jive, working on homework with Cam while Maggie works behind the counter and joins us on her breaks.

"What about that one fae you met last winter?"

I blink up at Quince. "Olearia?" The wild fae

had been the one to send Scamp to look after me. With a chest built like a barrel, rams horns, and wrinkles on her wrinkles, she looked like a goat melded with a grandmother. An ancient grandmother. "Do you think she's old enough?"

"We have to start somewhere."

Jaila returns with her lemon scone already half-eaten. As she moves to sit back down, the screen on my phone lights up and my phone buzzes.

I snatch at it and unlock it, scanning the message with relief.

C: *we're back safe.*

Good, I type. *Keep it that way, please? Promise not to return to Elfaeme any time soon.*

I shut my phone off before I can get a response.

"They're okay," I say to Quince, whose face brightens with relief.

"So we can go now?"

"Go where?" Jaila asks, wiping the crumbs from her mouth.

I tell her Quince's idea, and she taps her chin. "We might run into Aspen there, if we're going to the Sweetbriar Wood." She shudders. "There's something about him…"

"I'm not exactly jumping for joy at the idea of running into him, either," I say grimly, "but Olearia may have insight into what's going on."

Jaila mumbles something about sheep I can't

quite hear, but stands. "Since you're both so eager to return to Elfaeme, might as well not waste time."

"To be clear, I'm not eager," I point out. "I happen to agree with Quince, though, that if we can find out anything about the coronation ceremony to help us thwart Nightglade, it's worth looking into. Before there are too many more deaths."

I smile at Quince, whose shoulders slump in exhaustion.

My smile falters. "And maybe we can rest there, too. For a little while."

Old, But Not Old Enough

As amazing as it was to be in New Zealand (New Zealand! Jess would be so jealous. She loves animals of any kind, and would be tickled to know I was in the land of the kiwis, if only briefly for a cup of coffee and the WiFi), returning to the Sweetbriar Woods feels like a breath of fresh air. Literally. The air here is fresher than any I've experienced, even when compared to all my camping trips with the Ackers.

If only it weren't for the sense of trepidation that I might run into my birth father at any moment.

Or the growing sense of guilt at the thought I may not feel like this when I am finally able to return to Duluth.

We've appeared in a section of the woods I recognize, not far from Olearia's cottage. Based on the confident way Jaila's walking through the trees, she recognizes where we are, too, from our sojourn here to spy on Aspen only a few days ago.

It's funny how time works, because it feels like ages ago to me.

In the dim light below the canopy, I see details I had missed during our hasty escape from the Iron Prison. Quince's wings are missing patches of feathers, and the ones which remain look like they're not holding on by much. As I watch, one falls off the bottom and lands on a rotting log.

"Time works weird between Elfaeme and Earth, doesn't it?" I muse aloud, partly because it's what's on my mind, partly to distract myself and Quince from needing to talk about his imprisonment. I can see it enough in his eyes, the way they shift and won't meet mine.

"There's not always a direct correlation." Quince wheezes as he catches up to me, clutching his side. I hadn't realized I had been moving fast, but I'm a notoriously fast walker on a usual day, and especially fast when I'm worried I may run into my angry birth father at any moment. "I'm sure there are some fae here who could explain the way time works between Earth and Elfaeme, but I couldn't explain the science behind it."

"Not to mention," Jaila says from ahead of us. "There are some places in Elfaeme more unmoored from time than others.”

“What does she mean by that?” I whisper to Quince, but he’s holding a hand out in front of him.

“Rain.” He lifts his face to the canopy. “Can you hear it, Eevee? It’s starting.” A tear trickles out of the corner of his eye. “I missed the sound of rain.”

I turn my face up and close my eyes. A soft pattering of rain on leaves reaches my ears. “I hear it.”

“And if we want to make it to Olearia’s cottage before it comes down any harder, we should pick up the pace!” Jaila shouts to us, her words full of laughter.

I take Quince’s hand, which is still held palm up, cupping a raindrop, and touch my palm to his, pressing the raindrop until the water connects us. He looks at our hands, then at me, and his hand tightens.

“Are you okay to fly, or would you rather jog? We don’t have to go fast if you’re not up for it.”

“I’m up for it.” His gaze is steady as he looks into my eyes, like he’s searching for something. “But I don’t want to go fast. I want to walk through the rain with you, Eevee.”

Heat rises to my cheeks as I lace my fingers through his. “Go on ahead of us, Jaila!” I call, still looking at Quince. “We’ll be there as soon as we can!”

I listen to the sound of the rain. Most of it

doesn't fall to the forest floor where we walk, the leaves in the canopy providing an effective umbrella above us.

This moment is nearly perfect. I have Quince back with me, and we're strolling through a forest in Elfaeme. I sense animals like squirrels nearby, but also know more wondrous creatures lurk in the shadows, waiting to do mischief. Creatures only found in Elfaeme. There's magic around every corner on Earth, if you know where to look, but in Elfaeme, magic will often jump out and surprise you.

But it isn't completely perfect. Quince's "Quince-ness," what makes him who he is, has been overshadowed by this survivor of the Iron Prison. He's not the same. He has a hardness to him, a distance that hadn't been there before. All I want to do is reach across the chasm between us and hug him to me.

Instead, I squeeze his hand and slow to a stop. Olearia's cottage is visible through the trees, her overflowing flower garden a shock of color in the middle of the forest.

Quince looks quizzically at me, an expression so familiar it makes my heart break and sing simultaneously. He's back, he's safe. He may have been irrevocably changed by what happened in the Iron Prison, but with time, hopefully he'll be able to heal.

"We haven't had a chance to rest since your rescue." I reach a hand to his face, but his eyes pull downward and he turns his face away.

"I'm fine. I didn't have a lot of space to move in the Iron Prison. It's nice, getting to stretch my legs, eat muffins."

"I don't care about muffins, I'm just so glad you're with me." My voice cracks. The months of guilt and surviving from hotel to hotel in the human realm, cut off from any news from Elfaeme, not knowing if Quince was even alive or not, feel like a bad nightmare I'm finally waking up from.

From the direction of Olearia's cottage, I hear Jaila knocking on the door.

Quince tenses. "We should catch up with Jaila."

"Wait." I dig in my heels and keep Quince's hand in mine, pulling him to a stop.

"Wait for what, Eevee?" he snaps, his eyes flashing.

I drop his hand, his words like a hornet's nest of stings. "Nothing, apparently."

He lifts a hand to his mouth. "Eevee, I'm sorry, I'm exhausted and beyond stressed, and there's this thing–" His face spasms. "I can't, I–"

I'm reminded of Jess, the younger of my sisters. She has trauma she's still dealing with from her young life with her birth parents, and being adopted. Because of the trauma, she has separation anxiety, and sometimes fixates on things which make her seem younger than she is. She also has a hard time handling her emotions when she's stressed, often going from zero to a hundred, throwing her pencils and screaming when she can't figure out the answer on a worksheet she's doing with dad. Just as quickly, she calms down, and is all apologies and hugs. So I say what dad says to

Jess when she apologizes after losing control.

"Thanks for apologizing, Quince. I'm sorry you're having a tough time right now. I'm here for you. If you want a hug, I would love to hug you. If you would like some space, that's okay, too."

He exhales, and some of the wild, defensive energy I had seen in his face dissolves. "I need some space right now, I think." Ducking his head, he adds, "Partly, it's…I couldn't wash everything in the café bathroom. I can smell myself, and it's a weird combination of floral hand soap and months of sweat, which, let me tell you, is not a great pairing."

I snort, and a slow smile spreads across his face. "Okay, fair. We'll save the hug for when you're no longer vying for the award of smelliest fae."

We join Jaila at Olearia's front door.

"She hasn't answered yet. Do you think she's out? Or taking a nap?" Jaila asks, stalking to one of the windows. She cups her hands above her eyes and peers through the glass.

I chew the inside of my cheek. If Olearia isn't home, I don't know how long I want to hang around. "Maybe we try again later? Head back to New Zealand or somewhere else on Earth to rest and recoup?"

"I don't think I have another realm-hop in me," Quince admits.

"Well, that settles it." Jaila plops down on the path leading from Olearia's door into the woods and crosses her arms behind her head.

I sit next to Jaila and the butt of my leggings are

immediately soaked from the recent rain. The events of the last day all catch up to me at once.

Realm-hopping to the Unseelie lands with Jaila and sneaking into the town surrounding the castle.

Finding Sean and Shannon (or rather, Sean and Shannon finding us) in the Snake & Stone, with Maggie and Cam disguised as fae.

More sneaking, this time into the castle itself to get to the Iron Prison.

Leaving the Iron Prison with Quince.

Regrouping in New Zealand to confirm with Maggie and Cam they both made it out safely.

Returning to Elfaeme to see if Olearia knows anything about the coronation ceremony to help us stop what has become a monthly slaughter.

Quince sits on the other side of me. When I lean over and place my head on his shoulder, he doesn't move away. I feel my eyes closing, and I breathe deep, taking in the heady smell of Olearia's flowers. They smell sweet, with a hint of citrus and mint. It's soothing. And even though my butt is wet, my exhaustion wins.

How do I know my exhaustion wins?

Because the next time I open my eyes, it's to the sound of crickets and the smell of some kind of herbed stew cooking.

My stomach growls and I stretch. The whole outer side of my left leg is wet from having tilted even further onto Quince, who is curled on the ground, snoring softly. Rubbing the grainy sleep from my eyes, I stand. Jaila isn't laying next to me anymore, but I hear voices from inside the cottage, so I push the door open.

"Shoes off," Olearia barks as soon as I'm about to take a step inside. She's exactly as I remember her. Short, with a torso shaped like a barrel, a head of gray hair covered with curly rams horns, and furry legs ending in cloven feet.

I kick my shoes off on a woven mat outside her front door and glance at Quince.

"Let him sleep, no one will disturb him here." Olearia beckons me inside, then turns to the wood stove where a pot of stew is burbling and steaming.

From the overgrown flower garden, I hear a swishing and some of the stalks bend and sway, though no wind moves through the trees. In my head, I'm hit by the sensation of prideful duty. Squinting, I think I'm able to pick out two pinpricks of light in the garden, near where Quince sleeps.

"Keep an eye on him, Scamp," I whisper.

If an eye roll were an emotion, that's what I feel from Scamp right now.

"Well, of course you're going to do your job, I wasn't trying to imply–"

"The longer you argue with my cat, the less stew there will be left for you to eat," Olearia says. "This young one is set to eat my whole pantry."

Shutting the door behind me, I sit down at the table next to Jaila and Olearia scoops a ladleful of stew into a wooden bowl.

Jaila loudly scrapes the last of the stew from her

bowl. "This was delicious."

"A recipe passed down from my ancestors. Special to the Sweetbriar Wood, as it includes herbs and mushrooms found here and nowhere else." Olearia smiles in a kindly, grandmotherly way at Jaila. "You must be going through a growth spurt."

"Maybe." Jaila collects her bowl and spoon and walks over to the wash tub on the counter next to the wood stove.

"Did Jaila tell you why we've come to see you?" I ask around mouthfuls of stew. It's too hot to eat and burns my tongue and the roof of my mouth, but Jaila's assessment of it is spot on. It's delicious. Swimming with flavors similar to basil and rosemary, with a hint of earthiness and something I can't quite place.

Olearia regards me with her coal-dark eyes. "Not yet. Even if she had, I'm curious to hear it in your words, Aspen-daughter."

At my birth father's name, I stiffen. Olearia clucks, tipping a cup to her mouth and taking a sip. "He's worried about you, you know. He came to me as soon as you left."

"I don't want to see him."

She sets the cup down and sighs. "He would like to know you are safe. He means well. But Aspen has always flitted around, much like a bird."

An apt description, I think. Before spying on him with Jaila, I had only seen Aspen in the fae realm once, at the Winter Solstice Festival, and the events of that evening had zipped by so fast I hadn't much of a chance to reflect on his fae appearance. Spending so much time on Earth with him, I had gotten used to his more humanlike appearance. On Earth, as much as it pains me to admit this, he looks like a hot dad, with his wavy blonde hair and dimpled smile.

Side note: why couldn't I have inherited those dimples?

When I rescued him from the fae realm, I had been more focused on how close to death he looked to really take in his fae form. Both of my birth parents were winged, though not all fae are. Quince's mom, Myska, has a mouse-like fae aspect when she's in Elfaeme, for example. And neither of Quince's friends I had met at the Fall Equinox Celebration, Carl and Mindy, were winged. Aspen's wings are feathered, like Quince's, though I don't think I'd describe Quince as one who flits around. If anything, he has a Labrador-like energy to him. Or, he did. Before he willingly went into the Iron Prison with his parents.

"The only time I saw him settle in one place for long," Olearia continues to muse, blowing some of the steam off her cup, "is with *her*."

Right. Olearia has no love for my birth mother, Maeve. She considers Maeve to have been a mistake in judgment on Aspen's part. I let my spoon clatter to the table.

"Nightglade got his revenge on her in the end," I say, my jaw stiff. "He turned her to stone."

Olearia shakes her head. "The curse of the revoked crown is what got her in the end."

"Same difference."

Olearia purses her wrinkled lips. "Maeve knew the consequences of taking the crown, Aspen-daughter. There's always a sacrifice. You can't allow so much magic to course through you without giving up something in return."

"Eevee?" Quince's voice floats through the window, full of panic. "Where are you?"

"Inside," I call, glad to end this conversation with Olearia. With Quince awake, we can learn what Olearia knows about the coronation ceremonies and get out of here before Aspen makes an appearance.

Quince opens the door and shambles inside, looking half asleep still.

"Shoes!" Olearia barks, though her gaze softens when she sees how disheveled Quince looks.

He starts, looks around and finds the mat with shoes on it. Slipping off his oversized yellow sneakers, he pads inside, barefoot once more.

Soon Olearia has him sitting at the table with a full-to-the-brim bowl of stew. "Eat up," she says, her eyes crinkling.

Quince doesn't need telling twice. He digs in, and Olearia's gaze moves from him to me. "Olearia, we're hoping you might know some more about the coronation ceremonies," I admit under her questioning stare.

"Because you're so old," Jaila quips.

Olearia scowls fiercely at Jaila. "Old, am I?" she asks, then she wheezes out a laugh like the sound of book pages flipping in a dusty room. "I suppose it's true, I have a few years under my belt. What do you need to know about the coronation?"

I tell Olearia all we know. How the ceremony has failed twice so far for Nightglade (which she already knew), and what Quince had heard during his time in the Iron Prison.

"Where did you hear that quote, hmm?" she asks, and Quince sinks into his seat.

"When I was in prison, like Eevee said," he mumbles into his stew bowl.

"I see…" Olearia leans back in her chair until it's balancing on the back two legs. "What is it you wanted to know, then?"

"Well." My mind goes blank, an unfortunate side effect of being asked a direct question I already know the answer to. "Um."

"Has this happened before?" Jaila cuts in. "Is there a way to stop it? And what does it mean, the crowns will return to dust?"

"You ask many good questions." Olearia leans forward again, her chair legs thunking to the floor. She rests her chin on her age-spotted, knobbly hands.

"If you don't know, do you know who would?" Quince asks. His whole body is turned toward Olearia, his eyes lit up with focused intent.

"Hmm." Olearia closes her eyes. "Let me think. It isn't as easy as you may think, living as long as I have. The memories are harder to recall with each year I live."

Quince has abandoned his bowl of stew and instead watches Olearia as she thinks.

"Yes," she says after a few minutes. She opens her eyes. "Astute question from your mate, Eevee."

"Oh, he's...I mean–"

She waves a hand, like the status of our relationship is of no concern for her, she's already made up her mind. "I may be old, but I'm not old enough to have been around for the making of the crowns. And even if I were, the wild fae always preferred to stay out of the politics of the Seelie and Unseelie Courts. The only time we've swayed one way or another is when the rulers of one or both of the Courts sought more than what the crowns could give."

I frown. "More what? Power? Magic?"

Her smile is wry. "Both, usually. When that happens, things get thrown all out of whack, even for us wild fae."

"So–"

"Things have been changing for a while now," Olearia answers my question before I can ask it. "Decades." She pushes her chair back and stands, though she isn't much taller standing than sitting. "The question is," she collects the remaining bowls, cups, and spoons from the table and carries them to the wash tub, "what are we going to do about it this time?"

"What have you done in the past, when the Seelie or Unseelie rulers have overstepped their bounds?" Quince asks, his head tilting.

"Me personally? I look after my own here in

Sweetbriar. But I think you mean to ask, what have the wild fae done?"

She looks over her shoulder, a sly, amused expression on her face.

"Yes, what have the wild fae done?" Quince clarifies.

A clattering of wooden dishes is the only answer we receive at first.

When Olearia turns to face us again, the front of her simple white shift has splotches of water across the chest and arms.

"They've helped balance the power." Her raspy voice is intense. "They've gone where they were needed."

"If the power imbalance is being caused by Nightglade, we need to go to the Seelie, then?" Jaila wrinkles her nose as if smelling something rancid, like someone's smelly gym socks. "Get them to fight against whatever Nightglade is doing?"

Olearia shakes her head. "You're all so young and ready to go to battle. That's not the way we handle things in Elfaeme. We don't have direct wars between the Unseelie and Seelie. What a waste of life! Covert missions, assassinations, are one thing. But outright battle? No, this problem requires a more subtle solution." She taps her chin. "There is one who is older even than me, if you can believe it." She winks at Jaila. "According to legend, they are thought to be the oldest fae in Elfaeme."

Next to me, Quince clutches at the edge of the

table with white knuckles.

"And this old fae might have some ideas of how we can deal with Nightglade?" Jaila's whole body tenses like she's ready to throw a punch.

"They might. I can't recall where they live. But everyone calls them the Eldest."

To the Gnomes We Go

Though she insists we stay the night, at the look on my face, Quince quickly interrupts Olearia to say how much we appreciated the offer, but we should get going.

Warmth blooms in my chest and I shoot a grateful glance at Quince.

"If you are so bent on leaving, at least let me send some food with you." Olearia opens a cupboard and rummages through it, returning to us with some bread and apples, which I slip into my suitcase.

"Do any of you know where the gnomes or dwarves live?" Olearia asks once the food is safely stowed.

"I do," Quince says, while Jaila and I shake our heads. "Or at least, some of the gnomes, anyway. One of my best friends is a gnome."

"Might be a place to start." Olearia wipes her hands on the front of her shift, then folds her arms over her chest. "Gnomes and dwarves have special relationships with the Eldest."

We bid farewell to Olearia. As I'm slipping on my shoes, her shadow falls over me.

"Are you sure you don't want to see him?"

No need to ask who she's referring to. I straighten.

"I'm not sure I'm ready to see him yet."

Who I really want to see right now are my adoptive parents, Todd and Penny Acker. To be enveloped in one of mom's bear hugs, her messy bun tickling my nose, and chat with dad while he bakes some kind of new hot dish. But their condition, if Amelia's emails are any indication, has only gotten worse. If any of my siblings so much as mention me, mom and dad go misty-eyed and foggy-brained for minutes. Until I can figure out what kind of fae magic is causing that and how to reverse it, it would be too painful to see them.

It's also too dangerous to go see them. So long as I'm nowhere near them, the fae following me won't be either. And any fae who may be near the Duluth house on the off chance I return would find it difficult to get close to any of my family, thanks to the fae protection charms Maggie and Cam have made.

"Can I tell him where you are heading at least?"
she asks softly.

"I don't want him coming after me, just to tell
me to play it safe and live with him in some hotel on
Earth."

She nods, looking thoughtfully at me. "You
worry for your freedom. But, Aspen-daughter, don't
you think he worries about it, too?"

"His freedom or mine?" I ask, bitterness
stinging my tongue. "Because the time we spent
together it seemed he was always trying to escape from
me and return here whenever he could."

"Does it seem that way?" she ponders. "He
never told you what he was doing?"

"No, want to clue me in?" I shoot back.

She raises her shoulders. "Your guess is as good
as mine. I was happy to see him handling his grief over
Maeve's–"

"Turning to stone?"

"–by engaging rather than hiding. By rekindling
his friendships with fae from his home."

"Like you?" I ask. She doesn't look surprised,
so I'm relatively certain Scamp had told both her and
Aspen I had been spying on Olearia's cottage a few
nights ago.

"He would see me occasionally, yes. And you
know what he'd talk about every time?"

I turn to follow Jaila and Quince.

"He'd talk about all the experiences he was
having with his daughter," she calls as we retreat into

the woods. "He's so proud to be your father."

Tears sting my eyes as I walk away. "Then he can tell me that himself whenever I see him next. Because he didn't say any of that to me when we were together," I mutter.

Olearia whistles for Scamp, who bounds out of the garden. I pause and watch as he jumps into Olearia's arms, then I take a shuddering breath.

"Let's get out of here," I say, when Jaila and Quince turn to look at me.

We walk in silence, Jaila and I striding side by side behind Quince, who pauses every few miles, looks around, and sets off in another direction.

I have never spent prolonged time outside during the night in Elfaeme. The times I've been here past sundown have usually involved some kind of fae creature or monster attacking us. The shadows in the underbrush are inky, so completely black they could be hiding anything.

My skin crawls. I wish my ability to sense animals could extend to other creatures. Out of curiosity, I try to tap into my animal magic, broadening the signal in a way to try and sense something else. But all I get is a massive headache by the time we stop to rest.

Jaila heaves a sigh and stretches out on the edge of a river we've been following. The air around us is like the first spring morning after a long winter, still cold but with a hint of something warmer on the horizon.

"How long has it been since you visited the gnomes?" I ask Quince, who's studying his hands. Is he actually thinking of which way to go? Or is he thinking of his parents, who, as far as I know, are still imprisoned?

His chuckle is self-deprecating. "Funny story."

Jaila sits up on her elbows. "You've never visited them before, have you?"

My eyes widen and I search Quince's face. "Is that true?"

"No. I've visited them. It's just…" He runs his hand through his hair and tugs on one of his short, black horns. "You know when you go along for a ride in a car–"

"No," Jaila interrupts. We both ignore her.

"–and you either draw, or read, or sleep, and you don't really pay attention to which roads the car has gone down until suddenly you've arrived at your destination?"

I lower my head into my hands. "Your parents were the ones to take you to the gnomes?"

"Well…yes."

Jaila groans. "Why didn't we stay with Olearia tonight then? I've used all my energy to keep a shadow over the three of us as we've walked."

"A shadow?"

"It's not as powerful of a camouflage as my usual," she explains to me. "But I figured it'd be better than nothing. And now I'm exhausted, it's almost dawn, and we won't have anywhere safe to rest unless either of you know of anyone who lives here," she gestures at the river, "aside from the usual naiads."

"I'm not leading us on a wild goose chase," Quince retorts. "I have a vague idea of where to go. Gnomes are earth-dwellers, and they prefer mountainous settings. There's a small concentration of gnomes in the northern mountain range, but most of those mountains are home to dwarves. However, I recall the weather being warmer when we'd visit Carl and his family, so I think we need to head to the southern mountain range, the one in Seelie territory. I've been keeping an eye out for a moonstone, because..." He bites his lip and looks down at his knees, which are tucked up to his chest where he sits. "I don't think I'm up to full strength yet. Going from the Unseelie Court, to New Zealand, to the Sweetbriar Wood, all in the span of a few hours? I...I don't think...even with the nap I had on Olearia's front doorstep..."

"Hey," I say, placing a hand on his arm. "It's okay, you don't have to explain yourself."

"Why didn't you say you were looking for a moonstone that leads to the Seelie lands earlier?" Jaila asks, bounding to her feet.

I look up at her. "Do you know where one is?"

"Duh." She scoffs. "The Seelie tried their best to mold me to be their perfect Unseelie pet, no better than the humans they care for, but any chance I could get, I'd escape and find a way out. I always came back," she admits, reddening, "but I liked knowing the ways I could leave, if I ever decided to leave permanently."

I'm left with more questions about Jaila's past than answers. Like, who was caring for her, and how awful was it that she wanted to run away so often? What kept her coming back? Was it her fear of her father, Nightglade? If so, how did he eventually find her and convince her to come back to the Unseelie Court?

We're not close enough that I can ask her any of those questions, but she's getting to know my facial expressions well, because she says, "I like my freedom. I thought life at the Unseelie Court, with the King as my father, could give me more money and freedom than my life with the Seelie. Until…"

"Until Ilinor died," I finish.

"So Nightglade chose Ilinor for the first coronation ceremony," Quince says, a queasy expression on his face. "She was the first casualty."

"I didn't like my older sister," Jaila says. "I had met her a few times in my life before this last year. My caretakers thought my mother would've liked her daughters to know each other. Every time we met, Ilinor treated me like scum for being raised by the Seelie." She wraps her arms around herself, her eyes on the river. "I never wanted her dead, though."

The edges of the sky where it meets the land are tinged with pink and light blue, which means, if I'm keeping track of time correctly even with our confusing realm-hop to New Zealand, it's now the morning of March 6th.

There will be another ceremony tonight.

And, most likely, another death.

"You said you knew of a moonstone that'll get us to the Seelie territory?" I ask Jaila.

"I do! And, we're in luck. It'll bring us pretty close to the Greenwater Range. Those are the mountains you were referring to, right?" She directs this last question to Quince, who nods. "Great!"

The world comes alive around us as we follow Jaila. Birds call to each other, though some of the birdcalls are unfamiliar to me. When I reach out my senses to feel for the birds, I find a few awake and even sense a nest of babies still asleep. They'll wake up soon, though, I can feel their gnawing hunger. There aren't enough birds around for all the birdcalls I'm hearing, though, and the hairs on my arms raise. So much about Elfaeme is a mystery to me.

Jaila re-traces our steps on the path we had been following through the forest, backtracking for about ten minutes, then, at a split in the path, she heads left instead of right, the way we had come from previously.

"Not far now!" she calls in a whisper. I catch her turning her head to listen to the bird-and-fae-calls as she walks.

"How are you holding up?" I ask Quince. His face is covered in a sheen of sweat.

"About as good as I look," he jokes.

My brows draw together. "Hopefully we can rest with the gnomes for a little bit. But with the coronation ceremony coming up tonight..."

"Eevee." He pauses, wiping a hand across his forehead. "I know I'm not usually the one with the negative outlook, but I don't know if we'll be able to stop the coronation ceremony tonight."

Ahead of us, Jaila does a hop-skip and pats a birch tree lovingly. "I recognize this tree. We'll be to the moonstone in a minute."

I slow my pace. "I thought that's why you wanted to get back to Elfaeme so quickly after we broke you out of the Iron Prison. To stop Nightglade from going through with another coronation ceremony."

He stuffs his hands in the pockets of the sweatpants Jaila had picked out for him at the thrift store in New Zealand. "It's complicated," he says finally.

"Over here, you two, what's taking you so long?" Jaila pops her head up from behind an enormous bush.

Quince hurries over to Jaila without looking at me, and I frown after him. If he didn't want to come back to Elfaeme to stop the coronation ceremony tonight, then why did he insist on returning as soon as possible?

"Eevee, I'm going to leave you behind if you don't get your butt over here," Jaila calls in a singsong voice.

I grind my teeth, but launch myself into the air and fly over the bush, coming to a landing in front of the moonstone on the other side.

Like other moonstones I've seen in Elfaeme, this one has a shifting pattern of lights across its surface, a sign its magic is active. Most fae prefer using moonstones to travel large distances across Elfaeme. Realm-hopping to Earth and back takes a lot of energy, which could mean life or death when you return to Elfaeme. Moonstones don't always take you wherever you want to go in Elfaeme. Some only go to specific locations, and they only ever connect with other moonstones. Last year when Quince and I had been searching for the Seelie, we'd had to find a specific moonstone.

"Does this moonstone only lead to the Greenwater Range?" I ask. The Seelie are protective of their territory, it would make sense if most of the moonstones leading to their lands would have limited usage, versus the moonstone in Sean and Shannon's backyard, which can be used to travel to many different moonstones, so long as the user knows where they are going.

"I think so. Are you both ready?"

I mentally steel myself. Traveling by moonstone is my least favorite way to travel across Elfaeme. I'd much prefer to fly, or realm-hop. But Quince isn't up for doing either, and Jaila can't fly.

"Together?" Quince asks, with a concerned look in my direction.

"Yes, please," I say, smiling at him. We had traveled together during my first time using a moonstone, going from Sean and Shannon's backyard to Crystal Lake. Once there, we had angered a bunch of wyverns in our search for one of the clues left throughout Elfaeme by my birth mother Maeve.

In a way, I'm grateful for those clues. At the time, I had been upset, confused, even angry sometimes, that she had left me a glorified treasure hunt instead of a direct address where I could find her.

But through my search for my birth mother, I had found Quince. And his cousins, Sean and Shannon. I learned more about where I had come from, and I had seen more of Elfaeme than I might have otherwise.

My smile falters, then falls. I'll never be able to explore any of it with the birth mother who had written me those clues.

"You know it works the same if we go alone or together, right?" Jaila asks. "I'll meet you there."

She reaches down, touches the moonstone, and disappears.

"We should go," I say. "We don't have to go together. Jaila's right. It'll work the same either way."

Quince takes my hand in his as I reach an index finger to the moonstone. "Let's do it anyway."

I don't protest.

Curious Caverns

I'm never going to get used to moonstone travel.

Jaila laughs behind her hands as I gasp and dry heave. My heart feels like it's going to explode. "I—really—think…" I take a deep breath and try to shake off the awful squeezed like a tube of toothpaste sensation. "I think fae who travel by moonstone when they're young are less affected by it. That's my theory, and I'm sticking to it. Every time I travel, I feel like I'm going to die."

"Oh, it's not that bad," Jaila says, lowering her hands. "It's a few uncomfortable seconds, and then you're done."

Quince shields his eyes from the morning sun, his gaze on the small mountain range in front of us. It reminds me of pictures I've seen of the Appalachians, with tree-covered ridges. The sharp scent of pine is in the air, and some of the valleys between the peaks are blanketed with a wispy fog. It doesn't look like the gwyllyon's fog Quince and I had lost ourselves in last year, but it makes the hairs on the back of my neck stand on end regardless.

"Is this a bad time to also mention I've never actually been to Carl's home?" He lowers his hand and grimaces at us. "We'd always meet them outside for a picnic." He grins, his eyes misty with memory. "Carl and his family would always show up late, or early, but never on time."

Jaila makes a strangling motion in the air toward Quince. "I know you've been imprisoned for months, so you're used to keeping your thoughts to yourself, but…gah!"

"I had kind of hoped you'd know how to find their home, maybe?" Quince asks her.

She rolls her eyes. "I'm carrying the mission so far. I hope you both know that."

"Do you know how to find them?" I ask.

She taps her chin. "No."

"Shoot." I gnaw at my lip. "Now what?"

Quince narrows his eyes at the mountain range. "I can't imagine the picnic spot is far from where the gnomes live." He walks purposefully toward the mountains. Jaila and I exchange a look, then jog to catch up.

"Why?" I ask.

"Gnomes are wild fae, creatures of the earth. Their homes are in the mountains themselves," he explains. "The picnic spot is in that valley up ahead," he points to the valley directly in front of us, "underneath an enormous pine. Very little sunlight comes through."

"Ooh, perfect for gnomes," Jaila says.

"I thought you didn't know how to find them?" I tilt my head, my brows furrowing.

"Well, they're there somewhere." She indicates the mountains. "Underground. Unless they have the right charms, too much time in the sunlight can turn them to stone. It makes sense that an above ground picnic spot for them would be shaded, and close to an entrance to their home."

"Gnomes can manipulate the earth masterfully, it's where they're most comfortable. So the entrance to their underground home may not be easy to find," Quince warns. "Even if we're in the right area, there's a good chance we'll walk right by their front door and never know it."

"Here's hoping some of the gnomes feel like going picnicking today," I say.

The weather here is too warm for the sweatshirt I'm wearing. I breathe and relax my shoulders, then feel my wings go non-corporeal, like someone just lifted a weight from my back. I quickly remove the sweatshirt before my wings become solid again, and stuff it in my bag.

"Nice shirt," Jaila comments.

I look down at the shirt I'm wearing, then laugh. "Thanks. It's a great quote, huh?"

"'Lord, what fools these mortals be!'" Quince reads. "From *Midsummer*, right?"

"Yep! Cam got this for me a while ago. I found it in my drawer, after Aspen and I escaped from the Winter Solstice Festival, and decided I couldn't live life on the run without it."

"A solid choice." The corners of Quince's eyes crinkle.

"I know." I grin back at him. "Cam has good taste."

It's midmorning by the time we arrive at the gnome's picnic spot. Unfortunately, no gnomes are currently occupying it. Quince paces, an apple in hand from the small bushel Olearia had gifted us.

I offer an apple to Jaila, who shakes her head. "I'm still full from the stew last night. I may or may not have had a few bowls before you woke up," she confesses.

While we wait to see if any picnickers arrive for a midday meal (unlikely, as the sun is now beating down on us, but you never know), I practice trying to extend my animal sensing magic some more. It would be so much more useful if I could use it to sense nearby fae as well.

It takes a few minutes until I think I sense something. It's foreign to me. Not like the typical woodland creatures I'm used to.

But Jaila breaks my concentration with a yelp. "Someone's coming!"

She, Quince, and I huddle together, watching the fae approach. Whoever it is, they're short, bearded, and holding a parasol.

"Not Carl," Quince whispers. "But maybe they know him." Quince waves as the gnome approaches, faster than I'd think was possible for how short his legs are, a friendly smile on his face.

"Didn't know this spot was goin' ter be occupied today," the gnome says. His voice, while high-pitched like Carl's, is rockier, gruffer sounding. He comes to a halt beneath the large pine. "I'll tell m' lad and lassies to–"

"We're not staying long," I interrupt. "Or at least, we don't intend to. We're actually looking for our friend, Carl. Do you know him?"

The gnome's face splits into a smile, showing off his white, square teeth. "Know 'im? Carl's m'nephew. Wonderful lad."

Quince peers down at the gnome. "Are you Uncle Urlin?"

"How'd you guess?" The gnome beams at him.

"The flowers braided in your beard," Quince says, grinning now. "Carl used to tell me he couldn't wait until his beard grew in so he could braid flowers in it like you."

"Yeh should see 'is beard now!" Urlin exclaims. "Grew in all'a'sudden. Bushy like yeh wouldn't b'lieve."

"Can you bring us to see him?" Jaila asks, her mouth working like she's trying to keep from laughing.

"Can I?" Urlin muses. "I'm s'posed to wait here fer m'lad and lassies. They like playin' games on th' way to the picnic site, so I walk ahead and get it all set up for 'em." He strokes his beard. "I take 'em picnickin' once a week, keep 'em outta the home all day, so m'wife, Fulna, has some time t'herself," he confides. "So…er, no, I don't s'pose I can bring you m'self. But the entrance is down an' around, thatta way," he gestures behind him. "Behind a big rose bush. Yeh can't miss it."

We thank Urlin, who's already busy setting up a picnic blanket beneath the shade of the pine, and head off in the direction he indicated.

It turns out, "down and around" and "big rose bush" are not as helpful of tips as we thought. As the hours pass, we get sweatier, and more irritable.

Another fae is going to die tonight, I think, swatting at a bug. *And there's nothing we can do to stop it. Not this time.* A mosquito lands on my arm and I slap it away. Why do there have to be mosquitoes here and on Earth? I guess nowhere is perfect.

Urlin and his six children find us knocking on a cliff behind a rose bush.

"I wondered if yeh had found it," Urlin says,

twirling his parasol above his head.

His children all stare at us with wide brown eyes.

"This here's m'kids." He points his parasol at one who looks like a miniature version of himself, minus the beard. "This is m'eldest, Marpo, my only boy. These here," he pats each of the rest on their heads, "are m'girls. Julna, Gilvi, Lessi, Jolmi, and m'littlest, Molbi Pell." He smiles down at them, all fatherly pride and warmth, and I have a sudden desire to see my own dad, Todd.

Molbi Pell, who had been crouching to pick a purple flower, stands up when Urlin touches her head and flashes us a shy smile.

"C'mon, then." Urlin lifts Molbi Pell up and rests her on his hip, then shakes his head at us in amusement, his eyes twinkling and his flower-studded beard waggling. "Yer barkin' up the wrong rose bush."

I'm equal parts relieved he found us and exasperated that he needed to, but if it means we'll be with the gnomes soon, then at this point, I don't care.

We walk behind Urlin and his children, who all chatter in hushed tones, occasionally looking over their shoulders at the three of us, until we come to a rose bush we had somehow missed.

It's huge, like Urlin said. But it's partially hidden behind rows of lilac and other foliage.

He steps around the rose bush and I hear a grinding sound.

"Door's open!" he calls.

"Yay!" His children dash around the rose bush after him, nearly tripping over each other in the process.

When I round the bush myself, I gasp.

In the cliff wall is a perfect, stone door, complete with a handle made from a polished opal and a small window that had been carved to have a crosshatch. In each of the four sections of the window is a neatly inlaid stained glass design. My favorite is the design in the upper right-hand corner, a little scene of a blue-capped gnome holding a mushroom up, smiling gleefully. All three of us duck as we enter the cave.

"Welcome to Curious Caverns!" I hear a voice call. A female gnome, who I think must be Furla, as she is currently surrounded by all six of Urlin's children, waves to us. "I hear from Urlin yer lookin' for our nephew!"

I gape at my surroundings. It's the coziest cave I've ever been in, honestly. I can see four halls stretching out from the entrance, which seems to serve as a market square. It's a large, open space, filled with bearded gnomes as far as the eye can see, bustling up and down each of the adjoining halls. In the center of the market square is a fountain with a tree made of stone in the center. Water cascades from the branches into the fountain below. Around it sit a few couples holding hands. One young gnome is in the process of clambering up the edge of the fountain, while her parents laugh and lift her into their arms instead. Above us, the cavern is lit with crystals in a rainbow of hues.

"We are," Quince answers. His face looks as awestruck as mine feels right about now.

Furla smiles warmly at us. "His home is in the far left hall, three doors down on the right."

I'm immediately grateful that Furla's directions are more precise than Urlin's.

"Come see us soon!" Furla bends and picks up Molbi Pell, who wraps her arms around her mother's neck and babbles happily, showing Furla the purple flower she found. "We're in the second to left hall, eleven doors down on the left."

It's a short walk to Carl's home, but in that short stretch of time, I'm impressed by the attention to detail the gnomes have for their home. Curious Caverns is decorated with gold, silver, and jewels galore, all of them polished to a shine and gleaming in the light of the crystals from the ceiling. Everything seems to have been made with care, and positioned with love.

Carl's door, like the others, is adorned with artwork to distinguish who lives where. The words "Carl's Residence" are carved into the stone frame, followed by what looks like a more recent carving: "and Mindy's."

"I wondered when those two would make it official," Quince says as he raises a hand to knock.

The door opens with the sound of stone scraping across stone, and Carl's face pokes out. He looks almost exactly as I remember him. Short, with bulky shoulders, and a round, warm face with rosy cheeks. Only now, like Urlin said, his beard has fully grown in. When I had met him at the fall equinox, he was beardless. Now, a dark brown beard with glints of red in it reaches halfway down his waist. And, just like his Uncle Urlin, it's braided with flowers. Though, where Urlin's beard has a frazzled look to it, most likely from his children tugging on it, Carl's has the glossy appearance of having recently been oiled.

"Quince?" he squeals in his high-pitched voice. He takes off his pointed blue hat, revealing the rock horns on his head, and bows to me and Jaila. "And friends! What a surprise! Do come in!"

"You remember Eevee, from the fall equinox, right?" asks Quince, sitting down in a plush armchair. Behind the armchair, I think I see a fire burning merrily, until I get closer. There's no wood burning fireplace in Carl's house, but instead the gnome equivalent of an electric fireplace: a cluster of red, orange, yellow, and white crystals built to look like a fire in a hearth. There's a wood cook stove, though, with a pot of soup steaming on it. I follow the stove pipe, which disappears into the earthen roof, and wonder where the smoke goes.

"I remember Eevee, 'course," Carl answers. "Make yerselves at home. Mindy should be back soon. She likes ter soak in the sunlight when she can. It's the tree in her," he says in a confidential tone to Jaila. "Always needin' extra sunlight. And who're you?"

Quince completes the introductions, and Carl strokes his beard. "Right. Well, nice ter meet yeh. Soup should be ready in a few hours. Oh! Where're my manners. That's Clay." He gestures to a mud puddle in the corner of the room.

I give Quince a quizzical look, but he seems to be as puzzled as I am. "Uh…are you getting into pottery making?"

Carl throws his head back and guffaws. "Pottery makin'! No, that there's m'buddy, Clay."

We all regard the mud puddle, which burbles in hello.

"He's…he's not a gnome," Jaila says hesitantly. "Right?"

Carl finds this hilarious. "What're y'all sayin' about gnomes up der anyway? No, we dunno what Clay is. Sometimes he'll shape himself into a biped, kinda dwarf-lookin'. Though he can never get the beard right, can yeh, Clay?"

Clay's bubbles burble sullenly.

"Anyway," Carl continues, walking over to the wood stove to stir the soup. "He might not get the beard quite right, but he can karaoke all night long with the best of 'em. Maybe you'll get to see it. Yer stayin' a few, yeah?"

He turns hopeful eyes our way.

"Oh, I don't know," I answer. "We're kind of on a mission of sorts? Someone we know said the gnomes may be able to tell us about where to find the Eldest."

Carl sets the soup spoon down on a leaf-shaped, wooden spoon rest and strokes his beard again. "The Eldest, eh? My grandpa used to talk 'bout the

Eldest a bit. He might have a nugget or two of wisdom to share with yeh."

Jaila grins excitedly. "Awesome! Can you take us to him?"

"Now, hold on. Yeh just arrived, and I am due some time to catch up with m'friend." Carl crosses his arms, emphasizing the muscles in his bulky shoulders. "Eat, rest, chat a little, then I'd be happy ter help."

I understand the impatience Jaila is feeling, but at the carefree smile Quince turns my way, I know I'm not going to push Carl to introduce us to his grandfather any sooner than he wants. This is the happiest I've seen Quince since Jaila and I rescued him.

Mindy joins us with half an hour to spare before the soup is ready. Her hair, the pale color of a spring leaf, is tied back in a single braid down her back. She ducks through the door, her mouth turned down into a grimace.

"FREEDOM's not far from the picnic spot, Carl. I was talking with the trees, and they told me there's been more activity going to and from FREEDOM's main center of operations. They're up to something. You know, I think–" She catches sight of Quince squeals, practically jumping for joy as she dashes over to us.

"Now it's really going to be a party tonight!" She pops her bubblegum and beams at me and Quince, then heads over to help Carl with the soup.

As we sit down at the stone table, which Carl proudly states he carved himself, I dip my spoon in the soup, thinking how happy and peaceful this moment is, and wondering guiltily whose life Nightglade has chosen to risk at the coronation ceremony tonight.

Quince

It shouldn't feel this nice being back with my childhood friends, eating soup, laughing, and listening to Carl's friend Clay belt out "R-E-S-P-E-C-T!" while giving the thumbs up to Eevee.

Eevee laughs and claps along. "I can't believe this gnome-made karaoke machine," she says, her eyes sparkling in pure delight. "Isn't it amazing how it can play whatever song you want, in whatever style you want? How do they do that?"

I murmur something about gnome magic, but she's already back to clapping and chatting with Mindy.

The deal I made with Nightglade weighs heavily on me. It's too late now to back out of it. Though I am starting to doubt I ever had a choice to begin with.

Eevee suspects something, too. It is getting harder and harder to talk to her without revealing anything, and the promise I made to Nightglade, the deal we struck, is binding. I am physically incapable of saying anything to Eevee.

This is why I wish I hadn't been rescued. No rescue, no having to dodge Eevee's worried glances and probing questions.

I look down at my hands. There has to be a way out of this deal. Some way I can hint to Eevee that I've messed up, and...

Oh no. I blink. How long have I been sitting here, thinking and staring at my hands? She's giving me a probing look. Please don't follow it with a worried question. Please–

"Quince, are you okay? Carl asked if we'd like to stay the night, since his grandpa's usually asleep by now. You kind of zoned out there."

See? Worried question. I force a smile on my face. "Yeah. Sure. That sounds fine."

"Bathroom is down the hall," Carl says.

Behind him, Clay finishes yet another alternative rock cover, and melts into a mud puddle on the floor.

Carl's home is bigger than it seems from the open dining room/living room/kitchen area. The hall I walk down to get to the bathroom has open doorways on either side, all leading into bedrooms, guest rooms, and even a workout room with rocks he must use in place of weights.

The bathroom ends up being all the way down the hall. It is a spacious room, with a linen curtain that can be drawn for privacy when it's in use. I pull it closed and wash my face in the sink.

When I lift my face, water drips from it onto the oversized t-shirt Jaila had bought for me in New Zealand. At least, I'm fairly certain she bought it. Though she wasn't in the thrift store for too long.

I stare into my reflection in the burnished silver mirror. Like a lot of the decor I've seen so far in Curious Caverns, the mirror's frame is encrusted with jewels like how some kids make picture frames from seashells or macaroni, but it is made with much more skill than a child gluing macaroni to a wood picture frame.

"Who are you?" I ask.

I am a stranger
to myself. How can I live
with what I must do?

I bury my face in the fluffy pink hand towel.

Vague Directions Lead to Monsters

Leaving Carl and Mindy and the gnomes of Curious Caverns after staying with them for a few weeks proved to be harder than expected.

We had intended to stay only a few days, but Carl's grandpa proved an elusive gnome to find. The visit was hopefully worth the wait, but I'm not sure. He mostly rambled on with stories about the Eldest, and when we finally got him to share where he thought the Eldest was, his information was imprecise, to say the least.

One thing he said, as we were thanking him, has stuck with me, though. He crooked a twisted, arthritic finger to us to get us to lean in, and then, in a warbly whisper, he said, "If it were me, I would find the Fae of Many Faces. Only the Fae of Many Faces has seen Eldest in the last hundred years. If you can't find the Eldest with the verses, you could try and find the Fae of Many Faces instead."

We thanked him again, and he gave us a rheumy-eyed smile, then closed his eyes. Quince shut the door as quietly as he could, and we returned to Carl and Mindy's. Carl opened the door, an anxious look on his face, which immediately crumbled when we told him we planned to get going.

"We should try and find the Eldest with the couple of weeks we have left before the next new moon," Quince explained to a teary-eyed Carl.

None of us could resist Carl's tears. So when he suggested we stay for one more night, we accepted his offer immediately. I don't think any of us really wanted to leave the gnomes.

Well, it turned out the rest of the gnomes of Curious Caverns wanted to join Carl, Mindy, and Clay in wishing us farewell.

First, the gnomes insisted on throwing us a going away party, which they held in the large market square near the entrance. The best part of the party, in my opinion? At each of the tables were jewel-encrusted party favors in the shape of mushrooms and snails, not to mention lots of dancing. Even Clay materialized out of his usual mud puddle to bust a few moves on the dance floor and sing some David Bowie songs with the band before returning to his puddle after some particularly enthusiastic applause embarrassed him.

Then, Carl and Mindy insisted we join them for a small after-party at their home, which turned out to be only marginally smaller than the original party and involved a lot more food and toasts to our health and lots of gnomes gifting us with gold and jewels we had no way of feasibly bringing with us.

At that point, we needed to rest from all our partying, as Quince and I could barely string two words together and Jaila had passed out in Carl's cushioned armchair sometime after the eleventh toast.

Finally, though, we made our way out of the Curious Caverns to the sound of many farewells and "Come back soon"s.

Carl directed us to a moonstone, and luckily his direction-giving is more like his Aunt Furla's and less like his Uncle Urlin's, because we find it with no issue.

Quince yawns. "Remember what Carl said, this will take us to the Unseelie lands."

"Why did you yawn?" Jaila complains, her jaw cracking as she yawns in response. "Of course we remember, he just told us."

We'll appear in a part of the Unseelie territory I haven't been before, and I'm more than a little relieved to know it's far from the Court.

Like last time, Jaila uses the moonstone first. This one is only the size of a small dog, and its light is dimmer than some of the others I've seen. Maybe it'll go dormant soon, like the Mage Stone?

I grit my teeth. If this one is smaller and has less magic in it, I'll have to travel alone.

"It should take you there no problem," Quince reassures me. "But it'll help if you think of winter when you touch it. Do you want to go next?"

These last few weeks have been so good for Quince. He almost looks like his old self again. Even more importantly, he's been sounding more like himself. Every now and then I'll catch him looking off in the distance with an odd, pained expression on his face, but I've learned not to ask too many questions until he's ready to talk.

"You can go," I say, smiling up at him.

He traces the flower markings along my left temple. "Only if you're sure."

"I'm not. If I don't appear, please come looking for me."

"Always."

Touching the moonstone, he disappears.

I wait for a second, in case the moonstone needs time to recharge. I eye its shifting, murky light with trepidation.

"Here we go again."

An uncomfortable few seconds later, I'm gasping for breath somewhere where the air is sharp in my lungs. I shiver, glad for my sweatshirt. This winter wind is chilly after the breeze-free caverns we'd been staying in.

But at least now we have directions as to where we can find the Eldest, even if the directions are somewhat vague and based on a few lines from the famous poem by Lydia Marie Child, who may or may not have known about the fae. We have more food than we could possibly eat, but the gnomes seemed to think it was barely enough to survive on and tried to sneak more in our bags before we left, and in my pocket I have the envelope from Shannon, with the ring still safely stowed. Carl and Mindy agreed to hold onto all our party favors for us until we could return for them, as they eventually realized we didn't have the strength of gnomes to be able to carry our weight in gold and jewels across Elfaeme.

Ahead of me, Jaila hunches forward under the weight of her backpack. She trudges with the energy of someone who has gotten very little sleep after excessive partying—in other words, not a lot.

"Walk me through the directions to the Eldest one more time," I say to Quince, who is squinting somewhat angrily at the bright sky above us, which we haven't seen for a few weeks and, admittedly, is more bright than it needs to be right now. "How do we know we aren't being pranked by the gnomes somehow? The directions just happen to sound super similar to 'Over the River and Through the Woods?' I mean, how likely is that?"

"Again?" His voice is weary. "We've gone over it so much already. It's just as unclear as before. But I don't think Carl's grandfather would deceive us intentionally."

"You're right." My stomach churns. I don't like

vague, I never have. And I also don't like this new distance Quince has since Jaila and I rescued him from the Iron Prison. It's like a part of him is closed off to me, and he's usually an open book. I remind myself sternly how much he's improved over the last few weeks, and that he probably needs more time to heal from his awful ordeal.

Jaila mumbles, but it's hard to tell if she's talking to us or is mumbling to herself.

"What'd you say?" Quince asks her.

She turns. "I think we're going the wrong way."

Quince huffs in annoyance, his breath puffing out in a cloud in front of his face. "I mean, it's hard to tell, isn't it? 'Over the river and through the wood/to the Eldest's house we go/though wind stings the nose and bites the toes/as we make our way through the snow' isn't directions to the Eldest so much as a poorly written quatrain ripped off a human's poem."

My eyebrow raises. I'm no poet, but I hadn't exactly pegged Quince for being one, either. I suppose there's a lot I don't know yet about Quince "currently-freaking-out-about-our-lack-of-directions" Florentz.

"And he said no one except the Fae of Many Faces has seen the Eldest in the last hundred years," he continues almost-yelling at a Jaila who looks very much like she regrets saying anything, "which means our directions are nearly a century old and most likely incorrect."

I stare at Quince. I know we're all sleep-deprived, but it's not like him to snap at anyone. What's going on with him? I understand the importance of the deadline as much as he does. No one wants another fae to die (or be forced to be co-ruler of the Unseelie Court with Nightglade…now that I'm thinking about it, I really don't know which is worse), and you don't see me snapping at Jaila, no matter how much she mumbles about which river we should be going over or which part of the woods we're traveling through.

Jaila fiddles with the end of her braid, which Carl had plaited for her. Like his beard, he had braided a number of flowers in it. "It's just—well, we're supposed to go over the river and through the woods."

"And we did go over the river," I added helpfully. "Like ten minutes ago."

She nods. "And through the woods. But where are the trees now?"

My brow furrows. What does she mean? We're in a forest, there are trees all around…I scan our surroundings. Okay, so, yes, there are trees all around us, but we're currently in a bare patch of land.

And it isn't just that. I can see why Jaila feels we've veered off course (if we were even on course to begin with). There's a heaviness to the air despite us being out in the open, and a sensation prickling the back of my neck like someone or something is watching us. Not to mention a radio silence in my head, which seems loud compared to the buzz of animal feelings and images I'm used to tuning out. I focus on picking up any sensation of animals around me. There. Far off, so faint I can barely feel it, I pick up on the consciousness of a fox curled up beneath a tree. But there are usually many more animals in the middle of the woods, even in a snowy landscape like the one we're in.

"So we wandered into a glade or something." Quince shrugs.

"A big glade," I mutter, turning in a circle. Nothing.

So why can't I shake the feeling of being watched?

"There are trees up ahead. We'll head back into them and continue on this pointless quest." At the side eye I give him, he sighs. "Okay, not pointless. It very much has a point. It's a pointy quest."

"Partying with the gnomes last night really did a number on you, huh?" I comment lightly.

"I should've known better than to engage in a wrestling contest with Carl." Quince rubs the back of his head ruefully. "I'll be sore for weeks."

"He had to show off for Mindy." A smile breaks across my face, the first since we left the gnomes of Curious Caverns.

My smile quickly fades and I whirl to check a movement I saw in the corner of my left eye.

Jaila jumps and gasps. "Eevee, what?"

"Oh. It was you. Why are you sneaking around?"

"I'm not, I was…oh, whatever. We're almost to the edge of this 'small' grove." She uses air quotes around the word 'small,' and it makes me wonder if using air quotes was a human thing first or a fae thing?

I miss what she says next, but then she trudges away and I follow, eyes still roving the grove for…what? Nonexistent animals? We're alone, the gnomes were careful about where they brought us in the Unseelie territory.

And yet.

We're nearly to the treeline in front of us when I hear a snap. This time, Quince and Jaila spin around with me.

"Who's there?" I mean to shout, but it comes out as more of a garbled inhale.

"What was that?" Quince hisses at the same time.

Beside us, Jaila is silent. Her eyes are wide, so wide I can see the whites all around her pupils, and her face is as white as the snow at our feet.

Other voices, not our own, repeat our words. It's not an echo, though. Their voices are deep, and their tone mocking.

"Who's there? What was that?"

Their laughter is worse, like deep, braying donkeys in a discordant chorus.

Jaila's fingernails elongate into claws, but her whole body trembles.

"Are you okay?" I keep my voice low so the voices–whatever they belong to–don't repeat my words.

The tiniest shake of her head. Her breath is coming in short gasps. A whispered, "No," and then she sinks to her knees, her eyes shut tight and her hands, no longer clawed, clutch at her chest.

I wrap my arms around her, this fae who is the same age as my sister, Amelia. But where Amelia is curly hair and laughter and sweet petunia soap, Jaila is bony edges and frowns and snowy mountain air. Yet I hug her to me, wondering how often she's been hugged since her mother turned into a gwyllyon and she'd been raised among the Seelie, kept as far from her father in Elfaeme as her mother could manage.

"Don't look," she whispers, eyelids fluttering open so she can meet my gaze. "Don't look at them."

"I won't." I keep my voice calm, soothing, but inside my head multiple thoughts collide. *What's happened to Jaila? Who do those voices belong to? What can't I look at?*

I gently lower her to the ground. "Quince and I can take care of this. Then we'll find somewhere we can rest until you feel better."

As I stand, a hand claps over my eyes. "Don't look."

"Jaila told me that," I say, louder than I mean to.

"Jaila told me that, Jaila told me that!" Braying donkey laughter, closer this time.

My heart thuds in my chest. "What do you know that I don't, Quince?"

"Fachan," he whispers in my ear, his hand still covering my eyes. "I can take care of this. I know exactly what to say to them to make them go away."

"But—"

"Keep your eyes closed."

My face feels cold as his hand leaves it. I do as he and Jaila suggest and keep my eyes closed, but I hate feeling useless.

What can I do? I cast about for ideas. I could fly into the air and try to escape and get help, but I don't know if the fachan have any long-range weapons, and I don't like the idea of leaving Quince and Jaila with the fachan, whatever fachan are. The fox I had sensed earlier nudges at the edge of my brain. The noise the fachan are making has disturbed him; I can practically feel his little heart hammering. In fact, if I concentrate, I know I could pinpoint exactly where he is.

Which makes me think…what if I use my sensing powers to find out where the fachan are and how many we're dealing with? That would be helpful information to know. And before we found the gnomes, I thought I had sensed something other than animals. If that's true, I think I can do this.

I focus all my concentration on the glade we're in, not even a hundred percent sure if this will work. It's like going from one art medium to another. You could be great at drawing still lifes of flower-filled vases, for example, but creating a vase out of clay after only having drawn vases would most likely conclude with a moderately vase-shaped vessel at best. Unless you were an art savant.

Come on brain, focus. Stop thinking about vases!

At first, I don't sense anything at all, except the

fox. I can hear Quince murmuring something, but I can't make out any words. His voice is coming from about fifteen feet in front of me, so I use his voice as a way to orient myself as I concentrate.

It works.

Well, kind of.

I can sense…something. It isn't animals, those come easily to me. But it's fuzzy at first, like that prickling, crawling sensation you get all over your body after you've discovered a tick on you and are convinced there are more (horror upon horrors when there actually are more, as I unfortunately know firsthand after many Acker family camping trips). Ultimately, not a comfortable sensation to have in one's brain.

But useful. Because those prickly, crawly feelings begin to coalesce. I center all my attention on those uncomfortable sensations, and a blurry connection forms. I can feel them, and Quince.

My moment of elation at learning this new application of my old skill is short-lived, however. There are three entities around Quince, who is talking so softly I can't hear what he's saying to them. But they seem to be listening. Their presence in my mind feels slimy, but currently subdued.

It's the fourth entity, the one sneaking slowly forward off to Quince's right, I'm concerned about.

All I sense from that one is wicked malice.

"Quince, look out!" I shout, stupidly, because of course we're both averting our eyes and not looking at whatever these fae creatures are.

"Let me handle this." His voice is tight with stress.

I want to. I want to trust him wholeheartedly. In my stomach, though, an acid pit of anxiety gurgles.

When he tried to sweet talk that ice troll outside of Sean and Shannon's place, it didn't exactly go according to plan. And yes, he's come of age now and has powers he didn't have then, like his voice changing to mimic other voices and sounds, which he showed off at the party last night, to much applause from the gnomes.

But he can't sense what I can.

And I don't know what I'd do if I lost him now, not after rescuing him from Nightglade's prison and helping him regain his mental and physical health.

It's this thought, the absolute terror of losing Quince, that's on my mind when my fists flame.

"Eevee, no!"

Keeping my eyes shut, I half-run, half-fly toward that being of wicked malice and allow myself a grim smile. Sensing anything other than animals is very new, obviously, and it's hard for me to pick up any emotions from our attackers, but this particular fae creature is so surprised I can sense it like a sudden flash in my brain.

I race closer to the creature. When I'm near, I raise my fists, ready to punch. The flames crackle across my knuckles, as if they were excited for some action. I throw a right hook and connect with air.

Braying donkey laughs surround me.

"Eevee, you need to stop, I–"

"This one was sneaking up on you, Quince!" I jab at it, sense it jump just beyond my reach, and grimace in frustration. My grin, small as it had been, is gone.

"Sneaking up on you! You need to stop!"

"Seriously, can you guys say anything original?" I ask through gritted teeth.

I don't think I need to repeat what they say. (It was what I said.)

My fists are flying now, sweat beading on my brow. I wish I could open my eyes! But after seeing how one look at them weakened Jaila to the point of collapse, I can't risk it.

Then again, maybe a small peek would be okay. Jaila had stared at them head-on; looking at them through a small crack in my eyelids might mean the effect is lessened, right? Besides, I wouldn't look directly at them, of course. And I'll need to make it quick, just enough to see what keeps dodging my punches.

"She doesn't know what she's doing, she's scared," I hear Quince explaining, the charm he's imbuing in the words making his voice thick and fuzzy. Like he's embarrassed for how I'm acting and is trying to do damage control for my actions.

I scowl, not that he can see me. "Yeah, I'm scared. I don't want to end up in a helpless, shaky pile on the ground, like Jaila. No offense, Jaila!" I call behind me. Her lack of response worries me, but I file that thought away for the moment. "I don't understand why you're not letting me help you, Quince." My fists crackle as I raise them, and I risk a quick peek at these fachan.

My eyes snap open and closed in a hundredth of a millisecond. Open and shut.

But what I saw in that time...

A single, beady black eye in the middle of each of their foreheads, four eyes total.

One arm sticking out of each of their chests, covered in wiry black hair and muscular enough to win a bodybuilding competition, muscles upon muscles. In each of their hands is a club covered in spikes. They obviously don't care too much about cleaning their weapons, because each of the clubs has brownish-colored patches I can only assume are dried blood they didn't bother to clean off before ambushing us.

Their short torsos are planted atop trunklike legs—more specifically, leg, for like the eyes and arms, they each only have one. But the one leg is enough. They hop about with surprising speed and agility. And they are currently hopping around Quince, focused on what he's whispering to them.

They also don't seem to care much for fashion. Their clothes are rudimentary; kilts cover each of their legs to the knees, and sleeveless tops with holes in the necks and chests cover their stomachs and backs in a thin, almost see-through material.

In place of hair, black feathers burst from their heads in wild disarray.

My blood runs cold and I shiver, the flames on my hands extinguishing as quickly as they appeared.

Even the briefest glance has affected me like a sucker punch to the gut.

Quince and Jaila told me not to look. Why do I always have to look?

The fight has left me, and I feel like I'm one strong gust away from falling over next to Jaila.

"She wants to fight," one of the fachan says. It's the first time they've said anything original that I could hear, and it sends shivers down my spine. I've lost my focus on the scene now, so I can't tell which one it is that spoke, but I'd bet my money it was the one with wicked malice in his heart.

No, I don't want to fight anymore. I open my mouth to protest, but my vocal chords aren't obeying my brain.

"She won't, I promise," Quince replies quickly, too quickly.

The fachan laugh.

"We don't think he will be too angry with us."

He who?

"We want a fight."

No, please.

"You don't want to fight." Quince's voice is commanding, and though his words are meant for the fachan, I find myself agreeing wholeheartedly with him. He's right, I don't want to fight.

"We don't want to fight," they repeat.

"You'll leave us now."

"No," growls the one, who must be their leader, even as the others repeat Quince.

"No?" they question.

"Yes!" Quince insists. "You'll leave now and forget you ever ran into us."

But he's lost the leader, and the leader has the upper hand now. Literally, since he only has the one.

"We fight!" he roars.

"Come on flames," I whisper, keeping my eyes shut like I should have before. But the flames don't appear. My whole body is limp and heavy; all I want to do is collapse next to Jaila and give up.

There's a sickening thud, and Quince grunts. "Eevee," he chokes out. "I'm so sorry. Get out of here, now!"

Funnily enough, that's exactly what he needed to say to me to get me to stay and fight. Either he wants me to stay and fight and he knows me well enough to realize the contrarian part of my brain hates doing what I'm told, or he wants me to run.

I'm going to assume he wants me to stay.

Flames or not, I rush forward. Stupid? Yes, definitely.

But I'm not letting these four fachan bully Quince.

I let out a scream. It's mostly a scream of terror, but I hope the fachan are intimidated regardless.

Their donkey-braying laughter would indicate they are not, in fact, intimidated, but I can't worry about that now.

My fist connects with a silky, feathery mass. For a split second I think I've finally hit one of the fachan, but then Quince says, "Ow, Eevee!" so I guess I didn't.

"Sorry," I say, turning so my back is to Quince's. "I assume we're surrounded?"

Quince responds with a whimper of pain as he collapses backward onto me, so I'll have to assume I'm correct.

We're a pile of feathers and wings and, shoot, do I smell smoke?

"Sorrysorrysorry," I cry, beating at Quince. Opening my eyes a sliver to look down at him, I realize my hands are flaming again, which would explain the smoke, so they are less than helpful when it comes to putting out the fiery feathers. They're actually making more flames, so with another "Sorry!" I flop on top of Quince's flaming wings, pinning him to the ground and smothering the fire in the process.

One benefit to our current predicament: the fachan have stopped attacking us for the time being because they're laughing so hard.

"GrrrooffffmmEevvvrrr," Quince says beneath me, which I take to mean, "Get off me, Eevee, and go fight those fachan," except obviously some of that message has gone unsaid.

"Okay," I say, heartened by the flames crackling at my knuckles. I hop to my feet and rush forward. This time, my fist connects with the rock solid mass of one of the fachan's stomachs.

"Wow, you guys don't skimp on the ab

workouts, huh?"

He grunts in response, then a whooshing sound to my right sends alarm bells to every single one of my nerves. I duck, just in time to feel the turbulence of air as the spiky club passes over my head.

I forgot to account for my wings, though, and a searing pain lances through my right wing and shoulder as one of the spikes tears through the edge of the wing.

The flames flicker and I will them to stay, raising my now shaking fists. "Is that all you've got?" I taunt, my mind racing. How are we going to get out of this?

Short answer: we can't.

Slightly longer answer: it's really hard to think clearly when your wing's been sliced with a spiked club and you can't look at your attackers without collapsing in a heap like Jaila (sorry Jaila, we'll figure out how to get you out of here once we've defeated the fachan, one step at a time, you understand).

Fingers reeking of rotting meat wrap around my throat and lift me into the air, giving me a nice whiff of the sharp tang of armpit sweat. I gag between the force of the fingers and the force of the armpit smell, stars dancing before my eyelids, which I refuse to open even now. I claw at the hand, my fingers slick with sweat, the meager flames at my fingertips as harmful as a birthday candle against the fachan's tough skin.

"Annoying flame fist," he grunts, his fingers tightening so the jagged, probably dirty, ends of his fingernails cut into my neck. "But if you think it's enough to defeat us, you're wrong."

I want to answer, but I can't. I can barely breathe. I scrabble at the hand slowly squeezing the life out of me. Only now do I think of the ring Shannon had slipped to me in the Snake & Stone. But my arms don't want to work with my brain, my fingers fumbling outside my pocket in vain.

Behind me, I hear a scuffle and repeated thuds, followed by an unmistakable cry of pain from Quince.

I hate that I helped Quince heal during our weeks with the gnomes, only to lead him into danger again. I know he realized the risks, and we decided together it was worth it to find the Eldest and learn more about the crowns and the coronation, but to die in the pursuit of that knowledge? So much unfulfilled, unknown, about what will happen to his parents, or Aspen, or the entirety of Elfaeme if Nightglade's power continues to grow. I also hate that Jaila, who has lived so much of her life shuffled from one place to another, never at home anywhere, will die without finding the home she wants.

Donkey brays float in and out of my ears, like a bad radio connection.

Words are becoming
   hard
 to string
   together.
 Is that
     a horn
   I hear?

We're Dying to be Saved

"Folk, to me!"

I hear the sounds of stamping hooves surrounding us.

"We want a fight!" I hear the leader announcing to the new arrivals. His grip slackens on my neck enough that I can breathe.

"You'll get one," someone answers grimly.

The warm, musty smell of horses fills my nose as the fachan drops me, assumedly to run toward the newest entertainment.

I don't dare open my eyes. Even though searing pain slices through my wing with every movement, I stumble around until I feel someone take hold of my arm.

Flames crackle and, without thinking, I punch my assailant in the gut.

"Oof! Eevee, it's me!"

I crack open one of my eyes and look up into the face of my birth father.

"A-Aspen? What? How?"

"Questions later. Here." He hands me what looks like a pair of sunglasses with neon green frames. When I raise an eyebrow at him instead of instantly putting them on, he adds, "They protect against the fachan's power. If you look at them too long without these on, it'll give you a heart attack. Literally."

"You don't have to tell me twice." I slide the shades on and open my eyes fully for the first time in minutes.

An odd sight assails me. Fae on horseback, all with neon-framed sunglasses, cantering circles around the four fachan, who are each brandishing their single fists uselessly.

"You want a fight?" asks one of the fae. He removes his helmet to reveal red hair and a freckled face I recognize instantly. The leader of the fachan hops toward him with a malevolent grimace, his bicep flexing.

"You're friends with the Seelie King?" I ask Aspen.

"And Queen," he answers, indicating another figure on horseback, whose auburn hair flows behind her as she and another fae hold two sides of a weighted net between them. With his attention on Oakspirit, the leader of the fachan doesn't notice the two coming up behind him until it's too late and he's tangled in the weighted net, struggling futilely to escape.

Once the leader is incapacitated, it's quick work for the Seelie to round up the final three fachan, especially with Quince using his ability to charm with words.

King Oakspirit nods his thanks to Quince, who replies with a stiff bow. The King and Queen trot over to where Aspen and I stand. "It appears we've arrived just in time," the King says mildly as they approach. "Is there a reason you and your friends walked right into fachan territory?"

Queen Hibiscus is less amused, her mouth pursed. She taps her pointed chin, her gaze unwavering as she stares at me. "You, Evelyn, are lucky. I do not like you. You insulted us in our own court, when we were offering you hospitality. You dared to question how we treat our humans, when all we do is find ones whose lives are lacking in quality, and allow them to stay with us, fed and housed, for completing simple tasks."

"To be clear, my stance on keeping humans as pets is the same as when we last met," I reply. "And I also don't like you."

"But," she continues through gritted teeth I think are meant to be a smile, "my brother insists that our friendship with your father supersedes any animosity I have for you."

I glance over at Oakspirit and catch him staring avidly at me. When he sees me looking back, he grins, his golden yellow eyes crinkling. *What is your connection to Aspen?* I wonder, breaking eye contact with Oakspirit to search for Aspen, who is no longer next to me. I see him chatting with a couple of Seelie fae, all three of them still wearing their protective sunglasses. The last time we saw each other, we had our first fight. And even though I said some awful things to him, he still called in a favor with the Seelie King and Queen to personally search for me.

It's…nice, I decide. To know that he cares about me enough to do this. He and I haven't had a chance to bond much, and the time we did spend together after the Winter Solstice Festival was stressful, not to mention he was grieving and closed off to me emotionally. But maybe this is his way of showing me I matter to him. A kernel of hope grows in my chest. I have a wonderful father already with Todd. How great would it be to have another father figure in my life, who is fae like me?

"We had to delay a soirée to come find you," the Queen adds, interrupting my rumination on the possibility of a father/daughter bond between Aspen and I. "And we'll have to delay it another day to complete the return journey."

I'm about to ask why they don't just realm-hop to Earth and then back to Seelie territory, and then I remember the rulers of Elfaeme are unable to leave.

"Oh, I'm so sorry," I say, not feeling sorry in the slightest.

Quince joins us, holding up a half-conscious Jaila.

"You've found our little Unseelie guest!" King Oakspirit exclaims when he sees who's with Quince. "She's been missing for months now. We had assumed the worst. My dear sister, delaying the soirée may have been worth it after all."

"Indeed." The Queen smiles for the first time, but there's no warmth in it.

"You will join us on our return journey," King Oakspirit commands. "At least for one night."

I bite back my refusal at a look from Quince, and instead nod tersely to King Oakspirit.

Two horses are brought over to us, and Quince helps Jaila onto the smaller one, a pretty dappled horse. When she's securely settled in the saddle, he turns, clasping at his ribs with a grimace.

"Are you okay?" I mouth to him.

He shakes his head and shrugs, and I want to ask him more, but Aspen comes over.

"The party's already starting to move," he says.

Quince and I climb onto the other horse that had been brought over for us, a majestic roan, while Aspen and a few Seelie fae take to the air. As we start moving, Jaila slumps forward in her saddle, a miserable expression on her pale face. Did looking at the fachan have any lasting impact on her heart?

Aspen dives down to fly next to us, the orange

butterfly markings on his arms striking in the early afternoon light. But now that the shock of the fachan attack is wearing off, leaving me with a painful ache in my wing, I realize he looks worse than I've ever seen him. Those first few days after Maeve had been turned to stone, he had looked near death himself, partly from whatever torture he had been subjected to, and partly because of the shock of Maeve's transformation. It's one thing to hear about the curse of the revoked crown, to hear Maeve's powers are waning, and another thing entirely to see the final result of the curse.

But flying next to me and Quince now, the arms he holds out in front of himself like Peter Pan are skinny, his cheeks sunken, as though he hasn't eaten in a while. He turns his head to peer behind us, and the sun catches flecks of gray in his blond hair I hadn't noticed before. And maybe I'm over-analyzing it, but his wings, a glossy green like a hummingbird's, seem to be flapping sluggishly.

Quince engages Aspen in a conversation about the Curious Caverns, which, it turns out, Aspen has visited. I have a hard time concentrating on their conversation. Instead, I watch the landscape transition from snowy to autumn-colored as we move out of Unseelie lands and into the In Between over the course of the afternoon. The Seelie fae pass the time with music. Flute song and voices rise through the air, as though the party has not a care in the world. By the time the sun touches the horizon, turning the clouds shades of pink and orange, the air has lost the bite of an

October night and instead is balmy, a sure sign we're at the edges of Seelie lands once more.

"—moves slowly there," Aspen explains to Quince.

The expression on Quince's, at least, the half of his face I can see from my spot sitting behind him, goes from puzzled to horrified.

"What is it?" I ask.

Horns sound from in front of the group. "The Queen requests we stop for the night!" calls a pompous voice I recognize. How had I not noticed Kieran, personal attendant to the King and Queen, before now? They are on a horse of their own, behind the King and Queen, their green, scaly arms waving to the company to halt.

We slow and begin to set up camp for the night to the sound of music, which has only increased in volume as more fae, who had not been playing while riding, take out various instruments: lyres, more flutes, even a bagpipe.

"Since we cannot have a soirée this evening, we shall have a jubilee instead!" King Oakspirit announces over the music to cheers. Even Kieran claps their hands and does a shimmy.

"With how much sound they're making, what's the likelihood we'll be attacked tonight?" I ask Quince in a low voice.

"Nonexistent," Aspen answers before Quince can. "We're in Seelie territory now. The King and Queen reign supreme here. No Unseelie creature wandering this valley would dare to attack." He grabs a few buckets off one of the horses, and gives me a deadly serious look. "Eevee. Sometime tonight, we need to talk." He flies toward the burbling brook that snakes its way through the valley without waiting for an answer.

"I hate when someone says 'we need to talk' and leaves me in suspense," I grumble.

Quince tugs at one of his horns, his eyes on the night sky. "Yeah, same," he says distantly.

I pull his hand down and twine my fingers with his. "What was it you wanted to tell me earlier?"

"Ahem."

I roll my eyes. Even their throat-clearing sounds huffy. "Yes, Kieran?"

"King Oakspirit requires your presence," they proclaim, their nose scrunching as though they can't imagine why.

I can't either. When I ask Kieran why the King would want to see me, they raise an eyebrow. "That's for the King to say."

"So you don't know," I answer, grinning at the way Kieran's face pinches. "There's only one way to find out, I guess. Lead us to him!"

Kieran shakes their head. "Only you. Not him."

Quince's grip tightens and he scowls at Kieran. "Why?" he asks suspiciously.

"I think we've already established I don't know why." Kieran sticks their scrunched-up nose in the air. They beckon for me to follow. "The King does not like to be kept waiting."

I turn to Quince. "I should find out what this is about."

"But–" Quince stops before he can say anymore, but I see it in his eyes. He doesn't trust the Seelie King. He's worried.

I fly upward a few inches, which is so much better than going on tiptoe, and kiss the tip of Quince's nose. "I'll be back soon."

"You better be." He traces the orange flowers that decorate the skin on my temples, something he's done a lot in the last few weeks.

Kieran coughs. "It's not like you're going into battle."

"An audience with King Oakspirit, battle, same difference," I say with a wink at Quince, then follow the prickly Kieran to where King Oakspirit's tent has been set up for the night.

I Still Don't Want to Be a Puppet

King Oakspirit's tent is huge. Kieran knocks on the tent flap, which I think they do more out of habit than anything else, because knocking on a tent flap doesn't make much of a sound, and clears their throat. "Evelyn Aspen-daughter to see the King!"

"Yes, yes, let's not waste time on pleasantries, Kieran!" I hear King Oakspirit call from within. Kieran's face pinches. They turn on their heels and leave me to lift the flap and enter alone.

A bed roll is set up in the corner, and the King himself sits on a stump. It's surprisingly bare in here. I had thought with all the horses and human servants they had brought with, he'd have all the comforts of his palace while camping out in the wilderness.

He catches me looking at his bedroll and his freckled face breaks into a playful smile.

I tug at the bottom of my shirt and look away, focusing instead on the rich, green color of the tent canvas. Such a pretty color, really.

"Why did you ask me to meet with you, Dáire?" I ask, using the name he told me to call him when he first introduced himself to me, rather than his official title of King Oakspirit.

"Why indeed, E?" He smooths the front of his dusky blue tunic.

"Folsom," I blurt out upon hearing the nickname. The name I had told Folsom to call me during my first visit to Elfaeme. "What has he got to do with you?"

Dáire laughs. "Oh, him. He is an interesting one, you know? We're somewhat related."

I splutter in disbelief. Folsom, related to the Seelie King and Queen? When he looked down on Quince for having parents from both Courts?

"It's a distant relation," Dáire amends, chuckling. "He never fit in at our Court, so he tried his fortune with the Unseelie, which he felt more affinity with, and fell in love with the Queen."

"Ew, what?"

"Oh, don't mistake the meaning behind my words. He was devoted to her, but I don't mean romantic love. Why, E, is romantic love on your mind?" He cocks his head, contemplating me with those golden yellow eyes of his, such a strange color compared to the rest of his complexion.

I wonder what it is he sees when he looks at me? A disheveled mess, most likely, after a night of partying with the gnomes followed by an attack from those awful fachan.

"Not exactly," I manage to say, my cheeks suddenly feeling like they're on fire instead of my fists. "Not with, you know…" I gesture vaguely to indicate everything.

Dáire's expression grows somber. "The turmoil in the Unseelie Court. Yes. Many in Elfaeme have been watching the events carefully. Some folk, like FREEDOM, are intentionally causing more havoc, rather than watching to see what happens next." Twin lines appear between his eyebrows as he frowns. "It's caused quite the imbalance. Even our soirées have lacked their luster of late."

"Oh, no, not the soirées," I say sarcastically.

His mouth quirks up in the left corner. "You may laugh, but it is who we are. The soirées are one way in which we express our gratitude for each other, for the land we call our own. We love to celebrate this life we are given, make the most of every moment."

I'm silent, considering this perspective. As an outsider, visiting the Seelie Court had been a bit of a shock. While the wild fae of Sweetbriar Wood, the fae I'm at least partly related to, love to dance and sing, the Seelie take celebrating to excess, at least for me. But I'm not Seelie, I'm a blend of wild and Unseelie, and I think it's starting to show. I love my freedom, like the wild fae do. It's why they refused to have any crowns made for themselves. And the Unseelie? Well, it's hard to think of the Unseelie without thinking of Nightglade's cruelty, of the fae who delight in torture and killing. But there are also Unseelie fae like Sean and Shannon, who are both fiercely loyal and frustratingly chaotic. Quince, being Seelie and Unseelie, has that loyalty, but also a passion for life which is addicting. It's impossible to refuse him when he gets that big smile on his face and says, "I have an idea of what we can do."

So maybe this is the key to understanding King Oakspirit and Queen Hibiscus. They don't insist on daily parties to live excessively. They are always seeking an outlet to express their joy.

Out loud, I say, "Have you considered other ways to celebrate?"

His golden eyes pierce me with their intensity. "Like what?"

I'm suddenly flustered. "Oh—well. I don't know."

For some reason, I think, not of the fae, but of my family, the Ackers. My parents encouraged us to pursue our passions. It's why Jess gets access to as many animal books and documentaries she can consume. Why dad takes Greg out hiking to look at birds, why mom has helped Amelia learn more about social media marketing for sharing her poetry and short stories. And why they got a membership to the Great Lakes Aquarium to take my littlest brother, six-year-old

Charlie, to see the fish as often as he wants.

My heart squeezes. I miss them so much. They're the ones who encouraged me to read Shakespeare. I had seen a production of *Twelfth Night* when I was in middle school, and the language appealed to me in a way more contemporary writing never had. So they bought me all of Shakespeare's works. Dad would stay up late with me, helping me read and understand the passages. And any time mom saw something Shakespeare related, she'd bring it home for me. Though I think she still kind of regrets getting me that Shakespearean Insults calendar.

"Actually," I say slowly. "If you do the soirées to celebrate life, why don't you celebrate each other, too? Like, aren't there any fae in your Court who are especially passionate about, I don't know, music? Instead of an enormous party, you could have a concert, where fae who'd like to participate sign up. And you could still have food and beverages after, of course. Or," I continue, warming up to the idea, "I'm sure there are some who are accomplished artists, right? Why not do an art exhibition? Or have a night of reading poetry? Taking turns performing scenes from plays? Or–"

Dáire holds up a hand. "I think I'm getting the idea." He places one finger gently on the cleft in his chin. "Yes. You may be on to something. But right now, the main concern we have is with the situation in the Unseelie Court. Do you remember our offer?"

I pick at the hangnail on my thumb, avoiding

236

his eyes. "Yes."

How could I forget? When I had naïvely thought the curse of the revoked crown could be broken with the help of other crown-wearers, the Seelie King and Queen, I had sought out their help. They offered it on one condition. Dáire—King Oakspirit—had said, "*…in exchange for our help to attempt breaking the curse of the revoked crown, not to mention trying to aid you in saving your loved ones from Nightglade's clutches, all we ask in return is to let us advise you when you ascend to the Unseelie throne.*"

In other words: yes, they were willing to help, if I chose to become their puppet in the Unseelie Court.

"The situation has changed," he says, drawing his shoulders back. "The curse of the revoked crown has not only been invoked, but completed. There is a vacancy in the Unseelie Court, and the Unseelie Queen's crown is rejecting any attempt at filling it." He whirls to face me. "Why?"

"I don't know." I step back from the forcefulness of his question.

"Don't you?" The smile on his face is as cryptic as his words. "Have you considered that the crown is rejecting any suitors Nightglade puts forward because the fae it's looking for is not attending the coronation ceremony?"

My lips feel numb. "What do you mean, Dáire?"

"It's not all duty and obligation, you know." He steps toward me, lowering his voice. "When you are one of the crowned rulers, you're connected to Elfaeme in a way only a few have ever been."

"Y–you're implying the crown is waiting for *me*?"

"Who else?" he asks, gazing down at me. "You are the daughter of the previous Queen. The crowns do not always select a successor based on lineage, but they often do. My sister and I inherited our crowns from our parents. And Maeve inherited her crown from her father."

The world spins and I feel like I might throw up. "So, what's the offer this time?" I ask. "You escort me to the Unseelie Court's next coronation ceremony so the crown has a chance to choose me? And then, as payment for your help, you…*advise* me?"

Like I don't know what he means by *advise*. He and his sister, Queen Hibiscus, want to have influence over the Unseelie Court.

"And what about the King's crown?" I add. "Nightglade still has claim to it."

"One problem at a time." His words are honey, but even though the situation has changed, I still don't want to take the Unseelie Queen's crown with strings attached.

If I do decide to wear the Queen's crown like Maeve, I want it to be on my own terms.

"'Hide not thy poison with such sugar'd words,'" I murmur, then meet his gaze defiantly.

There's a gleam in his eyes, an air of curiosity across his face. "You are full of surprises, E. I, too, enjoy Shakespeare. Perhaps sometime, when this is all behind us, we could discuss his work." He returns to the stump and sits, resting one foot on the opposite knee. "I can't say I'm not disappointed you won't accept my offer. I think it could be a beautiful partnership." His eyes linger on my face. "However, if that is your final decision…"

"It is." I cross my arms.

"Then I am sorry. It appears I have said too much unto a heart of stone."

I straighten. "*Twelfth Night.*"

He bows, inclining his head. "One of my favorites."

"Mine, too." I shift my feet, feeling awkward. "If that's all…"

"It is." He waves for me to exit. As the tent flap closes behind me, I hear him say, "For now."

Fireside Chat

I try to ignore the way my stomach rumbles as the food in my hand goes cold. Instead, I focus on the crackling flames of the campfire in front of me, and watch the jubilee, which is in full swing. Shifting the plate of food from my hands to my lap results in a grumbling twinge from my right wing. It stings where the Seelie medic had placed some kind of paste on the wound, but it already feels a lot better than before.

In many ways, this fire is much like the innumerable campfires I had sat next to growing up, either in the backyard or out camping at different state parks in Minnesota. One similarity between the fae and human realm is the insatiable hunger of fire in both. I glance down at the food in my hand, the conversation with King Oakspirit on repeat in my head.

A shadowy figure with green feathered wings sits down next to me on the log, and for a minute, neither of us say anything.

"Aren't you going to eat your food?"

"I ate enough Seelie food when I visited their court last year." I push the food around on the wooden plate.

Aspen nudges my shoulder with his own. "You know, I admire your sense of justice, I really do."

His face crinkles in a smile at the sideways glance I give him. "Quince told me about how upset it made you, seeing how humans are treated as glorified pets in the Seelie Court. But if you want the Seelie to change their attitudes toward humans, refusing to eat the food they provide you isn't going to sway them. If anything, it'll make them think there's something wrong with how their servants prepared the food, and–"

"Servants," I say with a snort.

But his words have the desired effect because I take one bite and then another. Even cold, the vegetable pot pie is delicious, each bite full of herbed vegetables covered in a delicate cream sauce. I taste onion, peas, carrots, and even peppery radish.

"This is delicious," I proclaim loudly. "Probably the best veggie pot pie I've ever had, and that includes my dad's."

Aspen doesn't startle at that, exactly, but he tenses up like a rabbit trying not to be spotted by a predator. "My adoptive dad's," I clarify. Then, in a whisper, I ask, "Too much?"

"Maybe."

I think about what he said as I gobble up the rest of the pie. If I want to change the Seelie's attitude toward humans, I'll have to spend a lot more of my time in Elfaeme than I had originally planned. My old goal to become a vet tech one day seems gray and distant, as likely to happen as winning the lottery. And, I reflect while I chew on another bite, maybe that's okay. The vet tech future was the goal I had made for myself before I knew I was fae.

For the first time since Nightglade started the current mess we're in, I seriously consider the empty seat at the Unseelie Court. And not just as a problem that needs to be solved by someone other than Nightglade, but as a possibility for myself to claim. King Oakspirit's freckled face floats across my vision. I know he'd help, using whatever means he could, to ensure I get a chance to be crowned Unseelie Queen. But if I ever decide to put myself in the running for one of the Unseelie crowns, I want to do it on my own terms, not on anyone else's.

Having a position of power like that would mean I'd have some sway in Elfaeme, and I could use that influence to make some changes, especially in the areas of fae/human relations and Seelie/Unseelie cooperation.

Of course, unless Nightglade up and kicks the bucket randomly, my co-ruler would be my birth mom's ex-husband who turned her to stone and has been manipulative, vindictive, and generally awful to me. Plus, he's shown no inclination to alter his stance on Seelie/Unseelie relations, and he cares even less about humans than the Seelie do. The Seelie may keep humans as "pets" in a sick, twisted way of "helping" humans who they deem to have substandard lives on Earth (which, as far as I can tell, includes most humans they come across), but at least they don't trick humans with the intent to kill, like many Unseelie and a smattering of wild fae do. And they have outreach programs on Earth, where fae volunteer to live there for a time and help with conservation efforts. That's a program I can support. It's one Nightglade currently refuses to partake in, however. No Unseelie fae is part of it. Yet.

And, as though I need any more reasons to dislike Nightglade, he's well aware that many of his subjects trick and kill humans, but he chooses to ignore it.

I finish another bite of the pot pie, biting into the savory-sweetness of a sweet potato, lost in thought. No. If any real change is going to happen in Elfaeme, there needs to be a difference in leadership, starting at the Unseelie Court.

"You're right."

I blink at Aspen, confused. I'm right about what? Had I done that thing where I speak my thoughts out loud instead of in my head? Or is he referring to our last conversation before I left the hotel, where I accused him of not being ready to be a father?

"Right about…"

"Change. It needs to happen." He stares into the fire, his elbows resting idly on his knees. "But fae change gradually. When you live at least a couple thousand years, on average, well…" He trails off, shrugging. "You tend to get stuck in your ways. Maeve, she–" He stops and I hold my breath.

Is he actually, for once, going to talk about my birth mother with me? I don't dare say anything, but I feel the wooden fork I'm holding dig into my fingers.

"By the time I met her, she had started to develop different thoughts and ideas about humans and other fae. Nightglade, her husband and co-ruler, had not."

I scoff. Of course he hadn't. He's an unyielding, self-absorbed, power-hungry jerk.

"After a while, it became obvious to her that he was not ever going to change." Aspen's face darkens, the flickering red light of the fire reflecting in his eyes. "Especially after he was crowned as Unseelie King."

I wonder why becoming Unseelie King would make a difference, but I don't dare interrupt.

"Maeve had eyes and ears working for her throughout the Unseelie Court, always on the lookout for corruption and treason."

Like Folsom, I think.

"Imagine her surprise when her most loyal spy…"

Yep. Definitely Folsom.

"…came to her and told her he'd heard a conversation between Nightglade and their advisor, Banethistle."

I'm gripping the fork so hard I know it'll leave a bruise, but I don't care. Of course Banethistle was involved somehow. I'd known him as Mr. Abscons, the evil substitute librarian at Duluth High, but after Sean and Shannon came to school with me and he fled at the sight of them (which, I still don't know what Sean and Shannon did to him to elicit such a response, but that's a question for another time), we found out that he'd been spying on me for Nightglade for months.

"What did Nightglade say to Banethistle?"

Aspen lets out an angry breath. "They were discussing his recent kingship. Toasting to it, in fact. They were…quite drunk, according to Maeve's spy. Banethistle made a crude joke about Nightglade producing heirs with Maeve, and he responded…" His hands clench into fists. "He responded that while it may happen, he had only married Maeve in the hope that when her mother died he could be considered as a candidate for Unseelie King."

I frown, confused. "But don't the crowns choose the next ruler? That's why Nightglade has been trying and failing to find a co-ruler, and three fae have died because the crown rejected them. How would marrying Maeve help him with that?"

"The crowns do choose, yes. But, you mean six fae."

I squint at Aspen. "No, I mean three. Two—

Ilinor and Banethistle–and the third, whoever that was, right after we got Quince out of the Iron Prison. Then we stayed with the gnomes for a few weeks and–"

"Eevee." In the firelight, his face looks haggard, like he's been awake for weeks. "Quince and I chatted about this on the way here. I thought you were listening, too."

I shake my head and gesture toward my wing. "I was a little out of it after the fachan attack. What do you mean, six fae?"

He slouches forward, as though he's borne the weight of the world and it's become too much. "You three thought you stayed a few weeks with the gnomes. But time moves slower in gnomish territory. The gnomes like it that way. It keeps their projects, the things they build, from deteriorating, so they can enjoy their creations for a long time."

I can't move. This isn't possible. If there have been six failed coronations, that means…oh, fudge. Panic rises in my throat. My thoughts are fragmented. Six deaths. Four to go, unless one of Nightglade's next attempts succeeds. My family. They must be so worried. I missed graduation. Did Cam and Maggie think I was dead?

"I know it's a lot to take in," Aspen says. "When Olearia finally told me you had gone to see the gnomes, we began calling on all the gnomes we were familiar with, of course. But we had no way of knowing which family of gnomes you had gone to see, whether you had traveled to the northern gnomes, or the ones in the south. I kept your sister, Amelia, updated on our search for you. So at least someone from your adopted family knew what was going on. And Sean and Shannon, Quince's cousins, frequently see Cam and Maggie, so they kept the two of them in the loop."

"I appreciate that," I whisper. At least, I think I whisper it out loud, but I'm not sure. My head is buzzing. But Aspen isn't done.

"And the whole time we were searching, we also had an eye on the goings-on at the Unseelie Court, thanks to some well-placed informants." He exhales noisily through pursed lips. "It's, frankly, a mess. Everyone in the Court is terrified. Either that Nightglade will choose them or someone they know as the next coronation victim, or that he'll turn on them and banish them from Court. They're all walking on eggshells, and Nightglade's behavior is growing more erratic with each failed new moon ceremony."

"Why doesn't he marry someone?" I ask, though my stomach churns at the thought of anyone having to marry a steadily crazier Nightglade. "Isn't that why he married Maeve? To have a better chance at getting the Unseelie King's crown? I still don't understand how that would've helped his chances."

"Ah." Though he doesn't have glasses, or a college degree as far as I'm aware, Aspen reminds me strongly of a college professor. "I was getting to that. Yes. Those interested in becoming a ruler of either Court can do certain things to influence that choice. For example, scholars who have studied the crowns since their making have found a trend. Historically, the crowns of both courts tend to stay within a family, like with King Oakspirit and Queen Hibiscus."

"King Oakspirit told me as much when we met earlier." I shudder. "And just because they tend to stay within a family doesn't mean they will." I think of the memory Jaila shared with me of Ilinor's ill-fated, unsuccessful coronation.

"No. Not always." By the grimace on his face, I imagine Aspen is thinking of the first coronation ceremony, too. "But familial relation isn't the only factor. The crowns also choose based on the motivations of the fae who wants to rule and the favor that fae has at his or her respective Court."

"So, by marrying himself to the Unseelie Queen and building up a loyal following at Court…" I say slowly, "Nightglade was trying to stack things in his favor for being selected as the next Unseelie King."

Aspen nods. "And he was successful. When Maeve's mother died, the crown chose Nightglade as Unseelie King. Maeve told me that at first she was thrilled to have her partner rule the Unseelie Court side-by-side with her. But when her spy told her of Nightglade's true feelings and motivations, she was devastated. Before that, she really had loved him, or, at least, she loved the part of himself he let her see. When she confronted him about it, the mask came off and he revealed his true intentions to her in private."

"She should've left him right then," I grumble. "I would've."

"Would you?" His mouth quirks up in an almost-smile. "I think she wanted to. But she felt trapped. In many ways, it was too late. They had been married for decades, the crown had already chosen him as Unseelie King, and the court loved him. Don't let his current erratic behavior fool you, Eevee. He was charming, suave, decisive, and clever, with just enough of a hint of cruelty to endear him to those in the Court with darker interests and ambitions. He had a loyal following. Outright resistance to him at that time would not only have been futile, but also fatal. Even if it was led by the Queen."

"So what changed?" I watch as he shifts, crossing his arms and legs, then it dawns on me. "Wait. You? You're what changed for her?" I set down the plate and fork I'd been holding on the ground near my feet and rub my arms, willing the goosebumps to go away.

"Not right away," he admits. "But yes, eventually."

"How did that happen?" I try to keep my voice casual, but I'm intensely curious, a sharp pang filling my chest. As a child, I'd make up stories in my head about my birth parents. Like who they were, what hobbies they liked to do in their free time, their habits and quirks, and how they met. Now, finally, I might have a real story to replace all my made up ones.

Granted, when I was imagining all of those scenarios, I never once thought "I wonder if my birth parents were even human." Fae children are remarkably similar to human ones, at least until they officially grow into their powers when they turn eighteen. And before that happened, I'd always assumed I had lucked out when it came to my hearing. Okay, there was a brief fantasy I had when I was, oh, nine or so? that both my birth parents were ninjas, which would explain my good hearing and seemingly natural talent for going unnoticed when I really concentrated. But then Cam and I did some research on ninjas and came to the disappointing conclusion that, while cool, it was highly unlikely my birth parents actually were ninjas.

But hey–while they may not be ninjas, they turned out to be fae, and one of them was even Queen of the Unseelie Court for centuries, so at least there's that.

Next to me, Aspen's face has grown soft.

"I was part of a–er–group of fae who often did covert missions. Only one changed my life. I had been sent to the Unseelie Court to investigate some odd goings-on we thought may be originating from there. Shadows were darker all over Elfaeme, but especially those in the part of the Sweetbriar Wood nearest Unseelie territory. It wasn't noticeable to most except the oldest fae, but it was enough of a shift to cause concern. I was one of several fae from this–group–who attended a new moon gala at the Unseelie Court. This would've been, oh, nearly a hundred years ago, now…"

He drifts off, a smile on his face.

I hardly dare to breathe. "And then?"

The twinkle in his eye as he looks at me has a

sadness to it. "Oh, I'm sure you want me to say it was love at first sight for us. But, no. She arrested me and some of my companions. We–er–weren't invited, you see. We'd gone in disguise."

Something I've observed about the fae: they love their disguises. Maybe it's because they can't lie with their words, so they delight in deceiving with their appearance.

"What happened after she arrested you? You must've had some reason for her to let you go, right?"

He shakes his head, a wry expression on his face. "Let us go? While her husband was using our capture to further solidify his influence at Court? No. She held us in prison for years. She would come and visit me, though. I tried every time to charm her. But she always saw my true self. It took her a long time to trust me, and me her. It didn't help that she thought we were part of FREEDOM." His hands, which had been clenched in his lap, twist together, the long fingers interlacing. "FREEDOM had been causing problems for both of the Courts, and at the time, it was primarily made up of wild fae."

"But...you weren't...?" I ask him, watching his face carefully for any sign of confirmation.

"I was." His tone is bland, matter-of-fact. At the look of disgust on my face (which, between you and me, any person or fae should have a look of disgust on their face when finding out one of their birth parents was in a radical fae group determined to "Reclaim the Earth and End the Dominion of Men"), he chuckles.

"As a spy, Evelyn. For the…group I was a part of back then. It's part of my powers. I have a charm ability, similar to your friend Quince. But mine is more subtle, which works well for subterfuge."

"Still, ick. You were part of FREEDOM."

"Yes." He sighs. "Ick. Not my most pleasant job."

In my head, though, I'm thinking how ninjas were kind of like spies, and having a birth father who was a fae spy might be partway to fulfilling my nine-year-old self's dream.

"Did you have a cool spy name?" I ask. "Like Double Oh Seven?"

His brow furrows. "Double Oh Seven? What kind of a spy name is that?"

Ah, right. He'd spent most of his life in the fae realm, and then in hiding in the fae realm, and then when he was in the human realm he mostly hung out in hotels and watched home improvement shows. "Never mind."

"My inner circle referred to me as Many Faces, since my ability makes me somewhat of a social chameleon."

A jolt runs through me. Many Faces. *Find the Fae of Many Faces. Only the Fae of Many Faces has seen the Eldest in the last hundred years.* Those were the words Carl's grandfather had whispered to us, along with the only directions he could remember, to go over the river and through the woods. *If you can't find the Eldest with the verses, you could try and find the Fae of Many Faces instead.*

"You look taken aback," Aspen observes. "Is it the name? I always thought it a little much, myself, but…"

"No, it's not that." Six deaths. But maybe we can end it there. "You can help us."

His face brightens. "I can? How?"

Quince and Jaila appear from the direction of the tents and sit down on the log next to Aspen, though one glance at the sheepish look on Quince's face tells me they've been listening to the conversation. I wonder how much they heard?

"The Fae of Many Faces," Jaila says musingly, giving Aspen a sidelong glance. "The name makes sense to me."

I remember how Jaila had been suspicious of Aspen, mentioning something strange about his face. I hadn't understood, then. But maybe, like Maeve, I see Aspen for who he is, not who he wants others to see.

Quince tugs at one of his horns nervously. "We need to speak to the Eldest."

"The Eldest?" Aspen slouches, his shoulders tucking inward. Is that a flicker of fear I see cross his face? "Why do you need to speak to the Eldest?"

"Only the Eldest knows information about the crowns and the coronation ceremonies which has otherwise been lost to time." Quince eyes Aspen, taking in his agitated appearance.

"I suppose that means you need me to lead you to the Eldest," Aspen says miserably.

The Eldest

As it turns out, the directions given to us by Carl's grandfather were accurate. We did go over a river and through some woods.

Then over more rivers and through more woods.

And it was nowhere near where the gnomes had deposited us in the Unseelie territory.

So, they were accurate-ish.

When I try and point this out to Quince, he kind of grunts and gives me a queasy smile. For some reason, both he and Aspen seem nervous to meet the Eldest, which makes me curious what they're not telling me.

Jaila isn't nervous, though. If anything, she's much more relaxed now than she was at the jubilee last night. She went to bed early just to avoid any more questions from the King and Queen and other Seelie fae like "When are you going to return to Court? We miss you so!" and "Why would you ever want to leave?" and "What can you tell us about your father?"

The last question especially turned her face into a thundercloud.

Ahead of us on the path, Aspen stretches. "Not far now. Why don't we take a break? I'll need to blindfold you for this next part. The Eldest takes their privacy quite seriously."

We follow him to a valley nestled in the trees. Aspen has led us from the edges of the Seelie lands, where we'd had the jubilee last night, to three different moonstones, a few of which were by rivers we had to fly over, and one which we accessed through the woods. Each moonstone took us from one part of Elfaeme to another like we were four balls in a pinball machine, transporting us from Seelie land to the In Between, the In Between to Unseelie territory, and finally back to the In Between, which is where I hope we'll stay because three times traveling by moonstone in one day is three times too many.

Jaila heads to the river and starts skipping rocks. I sit next to Quince, who is laying on his side, taking slow, deep breaths.

"It feels like the moment at the top of a roller coaster, doesn't it?" I ask, dropping my chin in my hands, which are propped on my knees in front of me.

Quince cracks an eye open, squinting from the light of the sun directly above us. "How so?"

"Like we're at the top of a precipice, and about to plunge downward." I chew at the inside of my cheek. "The Eldest, Quince. Talking to them will change everything for us. We might finally learn what we need to know to thwart Nightglade and stop his monthly homicides."

"I suppose." He closes the eye he had cracked open, his chest filling with another deep breath.

My eyebrows knit together, and I poke the side of his leg with my foot. "What's up?"

Jaila whoops and does a cartwheel. "That one skipped sixteen times!"

Quince keeps his eyes closed. "Eevee, hypothetically, what would you do if you were given the choice to save your family, but it meant you were risking a lot of other things?"

My foot, which had been bouncing thanks to the extra strong camp coffee the Seelie had made this morning, stills. Is Quince questioning the decision he had made, to stay with his family at the Winter Solstice Festival, rather than escape with me and Aspen?

"I'm not sure." I lay down on my side next to him and rest my head in the crook of my elbow, staring at him. I've missed being able to be this close to Quince. It feels like something we almost had was taken away from us before it could truly blossom, but here, on the ground next to this river somewhere in the In

Between, I sense the petals opening once more. He's engaging with me again, and not just for light-hearted conversation. It makes my heart sing.

When he cracks open his eye again, I realize I haven't answered his question yet. I consider it, then say, "I guess I'd risk the other things to save my family. Depending on what those were."

Quince exhales, though he still looks troubled. "I knew you'd understand loyalty to family."

"Why do you ask?"

He takes my hand in his, rubbing his thumb across my palm. "I'm risking a lot right now."

"What, holding hands with your partner while her birth father stares at you menacingly?" I joke.

From his spot atop a small mound near the river, Aspen's expression had been more pensive than menacing, though there had definitely been…something in it. Some caution when he looked at Quince. He looks away when Quince glances over at him, though.

"No, I think this is pretty low-risk." Quince brings my hand to his mouth and kisses it, and my stomach does a swoop like I really am on a roller coaster right now.

"All right, enough of that." Aspen stands and rummages around in the pack around his waist. He adamantly insists it's not a fanny pack. "I've got your blindfolds here. Let's finish this journey while there's still light to travel by."

I cross my eyes at Quince, pulling a goofy face I

usually reserve for my brothers, and am rewarded with a smile.

It doesn't quite reach his eyes, but it's close.

Aspen wraps black blindfolds around each of our heads. "I shouldn't have to warn you not to peek, but I'm going to say it anyway. Don't peek. Not if you value your life. Here." He places a rope in my hands, and I feel a tug as he passes the rest of the length to Quince and Jaila.

We walk. Aspen, as our leader, is careful to mention whenever there are rocks or roots on the path, so we make good time. For a while, the only sounds aside from Aspen's occasional warnings are chirps and croaks from various insects and frogs.

The rope I'm holding loses its tension. It takes a few seconds for this fact to reach my brain, though, so about the time I'm thinking, "Huh, that's funny," I'm running into Aspen's back. Quince smashes into me, and I lurch forward once more when Jaila crashes into him.

Now all I hear is laughter. Mine, a mischievous cackle, Quince's belly laugh, Jaila's twittering, and Aspen's reedy chuckle.

"I suppose this is my fault. I should have warned you I was stopping, Eevee."

Somehow we manage to extricate ourselves and stand up while blindfolded and holding the rope. It reminds me a little of some team bonding activities my homeroom teachers used to have us do with our peers on the first day of school.

"I wanted to pause here, because we're at the threshold. Before we cross it, you need to know the Eldest only accepts visits from those with pure intentions. I know what mine is. But you need to think long and carefully about what yours might be, and focus on that."

He pauses, and I focus on my intention. I want to prevent any more deaths. I want to learn what the Eldest knows about the coronation ceremonies so the Courts in Elfaeme can be in balance once more.

I wonder what Jaila and Quince's intentions are?

"Ready?" Aspen asks after giving us a couple of minutes to contemplate our intentions. We all must nod because he says, "Okay. Here we go then."

We shuffle forward. If I've crossed the threshold yet, I can't tell.

Aspen lets out a shaky breath. "We're in," he whispers. "You can take off your blindfolds."

I rip my blindfold off, accidentally pulling some of my hair out with it, and wince. "Ow…wow."

We're in a dense grove of trees. Above us fly what look like luminescent butterflies.

"Pixies," Jaila whispers after removing her blindfold. "Only found in certain pockets of Elfaeme."

On the ground in the middle of the grove is a stone pedestal topped with a crescent moon. Dangling off each side of the crescent moon are what look like two glass lanterns, one, the lower of the two, gleaming with a steady silver light. The other radiates a warm golden glow.

No fae in sight, though.

This grove is one of those places where you feel immediately at peace. I had visited a few places like that when camping with my family. It's a sense of deep connection, of belonging.

It strikes me at this moment. I've felt that connection here, in Elfaeme, but I've *also* felt it on Earth.

I belong here.

And I belong on Earth.

I may be a fae by blood, but I'm a human in how I was raised.

How can I ensure Earth and Elfaeme, and my friends and family from both, remain a part of my life?

"It's all about balance."

My eyes widen. The words sound like they come from all around and also within my head, a quiet, ponderous voice.

"Eldest." Aspen bows, so Quince, Jaila, and I quickly follow suit.

The pixies chitter, then swirl in a cloud above a spot at the edge of the grove. A shape shimmers, then materializes, beneath the pixies.

The Eldest does not look how I expect.

I mean, everyone's been calling them the Eldest, right? So in my head I had taken what Olearia looks like, with her lined, wrinkled face, age spots on the back of her hands, and creaky way of walking, and multiplied it by a hundred.

But the Eldest looks young, no older than
Aspen, with an unlined face which regards our group of
four thoughtfully. Who am I to judge by looks, though?
I've long given up guessing the age of any fae I meet.
They have two legs and look vaguely humanoid, as
though they thought about having human features and
then partway through decided they'd try something
different. Their face, arms, and legs are all the color of
tree bark shadowed by a canopy of leaves. Brown, but
dappled with gray.

They approach us, walking so smoothly it's like
they're floating, and as they get nearer I realize the gray
areas are actually scales of a burnished nickel color.

Their eyes are on Aspen, who stays hunched in
a bow.

"My prediction was right, I see." The Eldest
stops before Aspen, reaching down to place a hand on
his shoulder, which starts to quake. They turn their gaze
to me. "Your mother is gone," they say gently.

It is like they saw into my head, to the
unanswered questions floating in there, and found my
most secret one. "Forever?" I whisper, glancing up at
them where they tower over us, the height of a young
apple tree.

They cock their head, their eyes searching mine.
"Forever is a concept I have yet to experience."

Their eyes are the only part of them which seem
old. As I return the Eldest's gaze, it's like looking into
the eyes of someone who has lived a thousand lifetimes,
twin pools with layers of blue ice, but hints of depths

beyond imagining below.

"I have lived a long time, but even I do not know what forever truly is. Is your mother gone forever?"

Aspen sobs quietly beside me.

"Perhaps in the way she used to be," the Eldest finishes. They remove their hand from Aspen's shoulder and a pensive line appears on their brow. "Until I live forever, I cannot answer that."

The pixies swirl and some alight in the treetops. Jaila lifts her head to watch the Eldest amble away until they stand in front of the pedestal.

"Balance," the Eldest murmurs, gazing at the two lanterns, one gold, one silver. They beckon us over. Aspen and Quince straighten. Aspen's face is shiny with tears which he doesn't bother to wipe away.

"You see this?" they say, gesturing at the lanterns. The fabric of their clothes, what looks like black silk, billows with the movement. "Too much weight one way or another, and one of the lanterns would crash and break." They place a hand and press down on the edge of the crescent moon nearest the silver lantern, which dips even closer to the ground. When they lift their hand, the sculpture returns to normal. "If one crashes and breaks, what then?" Turning to Quince, they raise a questioning eyebrow.

The light of the two lanterns reflects in Quince's dark eyes. "Then the whole thing is imbalanced," he answers after a pause.

"And?"

"And…" Quince's brow furrows. "And it'll never be the same?"

"No, it wouldn't." The Eldest watches us with an air of someone waiting.

"The other lantern would break, too." Jaila fidgets with her braid, which has lost most of the flowers that Carl had braided into it. "If the heavier side suddenly loses the weight of the lantern, the structure would tilt the other way."

The Eldest inclines their head, a hint of a smile on their face. "Both would break." They look directly at Quince, and their smile fades. Quince blinks and glances away, flushing.

"Like the crowns," I breathe.

I'm pierced by their ancient gaze again, but their face relaxes. "Yes, like the crowns."

Aspen looks as though he could use a chair to sit on or a stiff drink or both. "Hold on." His voice is croaky. "If I understand this correctly, you're implying if Nightglade fails…" The Eldest hums an agreement and Aspen blanches.

"If Nightglade fails, then the Seelie crowns return to dust, too?" I ask, dread seeping into my body like molten lead.

From what I understand, the crowns help keep the power between the Courts in check. Without them, everything I know and love about Elfaeme could be gone forever.

"Two lanterns," the Eldest says. They're staring at Quince, who's looking back like a deer caught in headlights, his eyes wide. "Not unlike four crowns. Take away even one, and the balance is irrevocably changed. It cannot be done."

Quince trembles, and I take his hand, which is cold and clammy in mine.

I think we've learned enough to convince the Seelie to help us without any deals.

They don't know their own crowns are on the line.

Aspen bows again. "Eldest. As always, your insight is valuable."

The Eldest smiles, revealing sharp, pointed teeth. "But not my predictions."

A pixie lands on the Eldest's head, burrowing into their tawny feathers they have instead of hair.

"It is not your fault you can see the future so clearly," Aspen chokes out. He turns away, hiding his face in his hands.

"Only pieces," the Eldest says, their shoulders drooping under the weight of Aspen's despair. "And even then, not always as clearly as you may think. I am sorry, in your case, I was correct that the next time you would visit me it would be without Maeve."

"True." Aspen lowers his hand, and looks straight at me. I'm struck by how much emotion is in his face. Grief, of course, that's been there since I saved him from the Winter Solstice Festival. But also pride, and a cautious, questioning love. "You didn't mention my next visit would be with my daughter and her friends."

Jaila's nose scrunches. "Friend is a strong word. Unlikely allies, maybe. If it hadn't been for–" She cuts herself off, shrugging. "Well. You're okay, I guess. Better than I had thought at first."

"A ringing endorsement," I reply, holding back a laugh.

The Eldest sighs. "Maintaining this form is exhausting. I have not done this in nearly a century. But there is something else I had meant to share before you go." They raise a hand to their head and scratch it, dislodging the pixie which had taken up residence. "Blood. Contracts. Ah."

Those blue eyes search each of our faces and land on mine.

"Blood?" I squeak.

"Your human parents," they say. "Yes, I remember now. Your parents knew the risks of adopting a fae child. They signed the adoption papers, then lost all memory of your true origins. Until you told them yourself, I imagine?"

I swallow hard. "Yes."

"This of course upset the original contract. But there's a way to break it."

Hope surges in my heart. To be able to return home, to actually talk to my parents about my life instead of avoiding any topic of my true identity to prevent a blank memory spiral? "How?" I ask, hardly able to breathe.

"I already answered how."

They reach down to touch my chin, their

fingers hot like coals, but not burning.

And at their touch, I understand. But my hope fractures and breaks into a million pieces.

Blood. Contracts.

I had burned the adoption papers my parents had given me.

A tiny thread of hope burns in me. There has to be some way to get another copy, right? Maggie would know, and if she doesn't, she'd know how to find out.

The Eldest straightens, and I notice how in the dappled sunlight the edges of their body are blurred.

"I need a rest." They yawn widely. "My golden bed is calling."

They shimmer and dissolve.

Quince

The Eldest's words play on repeat in my head as I walk behind Eevee and Aspen, Jaila striding silently on my left, lost in thought. We left the Eldest's grove the way we came: blindfolded until Aspen deemed us far enough away. Now, I'm not sure where we're going. This works for me; I have so many thoughts swirling around my head that I don't know what to do with them, except transform them into haiku. I want the Eldest's words to be different than what they were, to be helpful, to be what Nightglade wants, but no matter how much I play with enjambment and line length, the meaning is the same.

Each Court must have two
crowns to be fully balanced,
never ruled by one.

It is not the information that Nightglade hopes to hear.

And I am screwed.

Besides, we found out another delightful bit of information about the crowns, which I can hear Eevee and Aspen discussing, their heads bent together, her chaotically adorable short hair next to his shoulder so they're almost touching. The way they both walk with almost a hop to their step…my chest squeezes. It is unmistakable that they are father and daughter, and I know how much Eevee would like hearing that, after spending so much of her life looking for parts of herself in others. I should tell her later.

"…need to share this news with Oakspirit and Hibiscus…" Aspen murmurs.

"You really don't think they know?"

I tune them out, chewing on my lip. Ever since the Eldest told us that someone had to successfully take the second Unseelie Crown, and soon, or all crowns would return to dust, a gaping hole of terror has been forming in my chest, chilling me from the inside out.

Nightglade wanted me to learn of a way to keep the crown all to himself, so he can be Unseelie King without a Queen.

That's what he had told me, after depositing me

back in my cell.

For a crazy moment, as his slate gray eyes had stared into mine through the iron bars, I had thought he wanted me to seek out the Eldest so he could stop killing fae on a monthly basis, especially after the death of his most trusted member in the Unseelie Court. But no. He had crooked a finger and beckoned me forward. Unwillingly, I had obeyed, until mere inches separated our faces between the bars.

"I do not trust anyone to rule the Unseelie Court with me," he had admitted in a low tone that seemed to indicate I was meant to appreciate being his confidante.

I had not.

Evil fae ruler translation of the above sentence: "I want to rule the Unseelie Court alone."

"You will let your…" his lip had curled up in a sneer of disgust, "partner rescue you. Sooner or later, she will. With the right nudge, she will come here and save you from me. When she does, you will encourage her to find the Eldest. And then you will return to me at once to share what you learn from them."

He hadn't left me much choice but to agree.

And now I am wishing past Quince had more of a backbone, or more common sense to realize he was entering into a no-win situation.

Present Quince has a choice to make (okay, I'm done talking about myself in the third person).

Aspen will be leaving us soon to go warn the Seelie King and Queen. Should I stay with Eevee and

Jaila and help them decide what to do with this information? Or should I sneak off when they're not paying attention to me and return to Nightglade?

If I stay, I'll be breaking my promise to Nightglade. And breaking a promise to the Unseelie King…my whole body shudders and the hole of terror in my chest grows larger. My father had warned me, when I was little, about making and breaking promises to those who wear the crowns. But when the time had come, and someone wearing the crown had offered me a deal, had I thought of his advice?

Well, yes, I had, but I had also immediately disregarded it because I had wanted him to continue living to give me more advice in the future.

Somewhere behind that gaping hole of terror, my heart constricts. I watch the way Eevee's almost translucent orange wings flutter and flap as she talks, the tear in her right wing barely visible now that it's mostly healed. All I want to do is find somewhere private, away from Aspen and Jaila, where I can wrap my arms around Eevee and hold her tight, never letting go, and breathe in her smell of sweet flowers and vanilla. All I want to do is forget, for a brief time, that I'm betraying my friends because I made a deal with the Unseelie King.

She turns and smiles at me, her whole face lighting up, and I force myself to smile back at her. Hopefully she doesn't notice the ice-cold terror now consuming my entire body.

I have to leave Eevee, and soon.

I Miss My Chance for an Autograph

Glancing back at Quince, worry gnaws at my heart. I know something is bothering him. He's been unusually quiet ever since our meeting with the Eldest.

The Eldest was not what I expected, to say the least.

"I should leave soon," Aspen says, his thumb tapping a rhythm on his index finger.

He's been both distant and overly energetic, like he knows he's being distant so he's trying to make up for it with loads of energy. We've talked a lot about the crowns since leaving the Eldest, but neither of us have touched on the other pieces of information we learned.

Like the one about Maeve's condition being irreversible.

I had hoped the Eldest would have a different answer for us, for Aspen's sake more than my own. But having an answer, even if it isn't the one I had hoped for, is better than not having an answer at all. Now, when all this business with the crowns is over, we can work on saying goodbye to Maeve properly.

"Did you want to come with me?" Aspen asks us. The hopeful look in his eyes when he meets my gaze is hard to bear. A tugging sensation in my chest encourages me to accept his invitation. What else can Jaila, Quince, and I do anyway? Being with the Seelie may be our best chance of surviving long enough to stop Nightglade and find an Unseelie fae that the crown would deem worthy.

The thought flits across my mind again—I could take the unclaimed crown. But just because I could try, doesn't mean I want to. Who else would be crazy enough to decide on a whim to be the next ruler of the Unseelie Court, I wonder?

"What is it humans are saying these days? Hard pass?" Jaila snorts. "I never fit in with the Seelie. I'm not going back there willingly."

Aspen regards her with almost fatherly concern, and a stab of jealousy hits me. "Do you have anywhere safe to go, where Nightglade can't find you? I fear if you get captured, he'll be willing to see if his second daughter isn't more worthy of the crown than his first."

Jaila shudders. "I have a few places in mind. I

can stay hidden if I need to."

"Quince, Eevee?" he asks. Quince startles at the sound of his name.

"What do you think, Quince?" I ask. "Should we go with Aspen to the Seelie Court, warn them that their crowns are in danger if the Unseelie Court doesn't find a new ruler?"

He looks at me, an odd expression on his face. "I have something else I need to do." I raise an eyebrow, but he shakes his head at my silent question. "I can't go to the Seelie Court. But you should, Eevee. It'd be safer for you there."

Aspen frowns at Quince, his eyes narrowing. "Something else?"

Quince's gaze darts nervously between my face and Aspen's. Whatever he sees in either of our faces, he decides the ground is safer to look at. "Yeah. Something else."

"I've been in the cloak-and-dagger game for centuries, Quince," Aspen says, his voice harder than I've heard it before. "There's something you're not telling us."

Thinking back on Quince's quieter, more closed-off behavior, a part of me agrees with Aspen. But this is Quince. He wouldn't hide anything from me, would he?

The face Quince turns to us is pale. "I promise you, my intentions are pure. I wouldn't have been able to join you to see the Eldest if they weren't, right?"

This gives Aspen pause. "I…suppose that's

true," he admits slowly.

"Aspen, I trust Quince with my life." I take Quince's hand in my own. "If he has something else to do that's not at the Seelie Court," I give Quince a searching look, then turn to face Aspen, "then I want to stay with him."

"Eevee, no, you should go with Aspen." Quince, if possible, looks more miserable, which only adds fuel to my stubbornness.

"No, Quince, whatever you need to do, we'll do it together. Jaila?"

Jaila shrugs. "Better than attending another soirée."

Aspen bites at his lip, worry clouding his face. "The last time you and I parted, I didn't know if I'd ever see you again, Eevee. You could've been anywhere in Elfaeme, or captured by Nightglade, or killed, or–"

I let go of Quince's hand and, for the first time since we've met, I hug my birth father.

My head fits right into the space between his shoulder and neck. The green feathers on his wings tickle the back of my hands as I wrap them around his waist.

For a second, he stands as stiff as a petrified piece of wood in my embrace, but then he softens and his arms circle me. He tilts his head so his cheek presses into my temple.

"I don't know if I'll ever be able to let go of Maeve," he says, his arms tightening around my shoulders. "But I want to make one thing clear. I am so grateful to have you. She lives on in you, Eevee. And my heart is happy to see it."

We stay in this embrace for a minute, and in that time, my breath slows. He's warm, and smells like fresh cut cedar. My birth father.

When he pulls away, he blinks away the tears in his eyes and smiles down at me. "Let's make a plan to meet up somewhere after the next new moon, at least. Let's see…today is Monday, which means the next new moon is tomorrow."

"Should we plan to meet at the Reflecting Pool on Wednesday, then?"

He nods. "That would work. At sunset?"

After going over final details of our plan to meet, Aspen looks a little less worried. His mouth thins when he looks at Quince, though.

"Stay away from the Unseelie Court. This will be Nightglade's seventh attempt to bend the Unseelie Queen's crown to take a fae of his choosing. We still have time to come up with a plan to overthrow him and ensure the crowns have a proper chance to choose new Unseelie rulers. There's no need to be hasty."

Jaila's the quickest to react to what Aspen just said. "Overthrow Nightglade?"

She looks almost eager at the thought.

Aspen coughs. "Well. Yes. Er, forget I said that. There are a lot of threads to figure out, can't reveal too much. It's a delicate business."

I fight back a laugh. "It's been a while since you've been in the spy business, hasn't it, Aspen?"

His expression grows grim. "It has. And these are dangerous times. Nightglade has never been a benevolent ruler, and his recent decisions are causing more strife across Elfaeme than I think he realizes or cares about. My point is, you should stay away from the Unseelie Court. It isn't safe."

Quince doesn't answer. His face is similar to what my dad's looks like after getting off a spinny ride with my brothers, so I say, "We'll do our best to stay out of trouble."

Though Aspen doesn't look convinced (which, he shouldn't; our track record of staying out of trouble is not great), he's back to tapping his thumb on his index finger.

"King Oakspirit and Queen Hibiscus need to know what the Eldest told us about the crowns," I say gently, feeling my expression soften at his reluctance to leave me. "You're the best one to tell them. They trust you."

He squares his shoulders. "Wednesday then?"

"At the Reflecting Pool," I confirm. "Wouldn't miss it."

We say our goodbyes, and he realm-hops, his body disappearing from view.

"Before we make any decisions about what we're doing between now and Wednesday, I need to eat," Jaila announces.

"I remember seeing a raspberry patch near the path a little ways down the path," Quince says, with a little too much cheer in his voice. I shoot him a "what's going on" look, but he shakes his head at me.

"I was going to suggest phasing to the human world for fast food, but you're right, Elfaeme raspberries are better. Race you!"

Jaila runs off along the path, and with a quick grin at Quince, I follow suit, but take to the air instead. The chilly late afternoon air brushes my face and whips my hair into a frenzy, but I don't care. Like usual, flying reminds me how much I love Elfaeme. How light and free I feel when I'm here.

Small pixies launch themselves from the tree branches around me and fly alongside me and Quince, darting in and around our arms and flipping midair, filling the air with their tinkling laughter. They must have followed us from the Eldest's grove. One bops me on the nose, making me laugh. They're like glowing butterflies with the energy of tiny squirrels, and I love it so much. I look at Quince, wanting to share this delightful moment with him, but his gaze is trained on the ground, his expression grim.

A pixie lands on my head, tangling its limbs in my already knotted hair, just like the other pixie had done with the Eldest, and I giggle. "Quince, a little help?"

A ghost of a smile is better than nothing, right? At least it's something. He flies over and gently extricates the pixie from my hair, while it chitters at him irritably.

"They're so ridiculous. I can see why the Eldest likes to live in a pixie grove," I say conversationally. "I think I'd laugh every day if I lived with the pixies."

He chuckles, and if it's a little more hollow-sounding than usual, I find I'm grateful for even this shadow of Quince's usual humor.

"I'd laugh every day just being with you, Eevee."

We find the raspberry patch after ten minutes of hard flying and running. Quince and I touch down next to Jaila, who's already elbow-deep in the brambles, seemingly unconcerned by the thorns. Nearby, a creek trickles merrily over a rocky bed. The early afternoon is cool after a warm spring day, the environs now transitioning to the vibrant colors of fall, and a few tendrils of fog settle amongst the dewy grasses.

Talking and laughing with Jaila, who's growing on me, despite our rocky beginning, my hands slowly fill with the ripe berries. Quince plucks a few and eats them distractedly, only occasionally joining in with our conversation. I make a mental note to ask him what's bothering him. I'd think it was a symptom of his time in the Iron Prison—there's no way his mental health didn't suffer from his months of imprisonment—but there's been a noticeable difference in his mood since we met with the Eldest earlier. He's constantly looking over his shoulder, as though expecting to be attacked at any moment. And his energy levels have been low. Usually I have to work to keep up with him when we fly, since he's had years of practice over my sporadic months. But when we were flying down the path after Jaila, he was often the one catching up to me, not the other way around, even with my right wing twinging from the fachan's attack yesterday. Seelie medicine helped a lot, but didn't completely heal it.

A hand reaches for the same raspberry I'm about to pluck, snatching it out from beneath my fingers.

"Hey!"

My eyes follow the hand to the arm it's connected to, all the way to the body, a thrill of fear coursing through me like a shockwave.

The fae takes the raspberry and tosses it into the air, catching it in his mouth. He grins, twirls, his silky black horse's tail billowing behind him with the movement, and bows.

"How now, spirit!" he exclaims with a horsey smile. "Whither wander you?" He blinks questioning eyes at me, and a memory tugs at my brain, but I can't place it. Why do those words sound familiar?

His gold eyes, luminescent even with the overcast day, capture my attention as I gaze up at him. My fear recedes, replaced by curiosity.

Quince steps next to me, arms crossed. "Púca."

The fae gives another flourishing bow, his trumpeting laughter echoing around us. "Well met! I am that merry wanderer of the night."

"It's daytime still," Jaila points out, wiping the raspberry juice from her mouth with the back of her hands. "In case you hadn't noticed."

"Púca," I mutter. "Merry wanderer of the night. Where have I…?" Then it dawns on me. "Púca. Puck."

He winks, and I feel my jaw drop. "Puck? Seriously? *The* Puck?"

"There are a number of púca." Quince stands stiffly next to me, an unimpressed look on his face.

"Ah, you speak the truth. However, while there are many who can claim to be *a* púca, I am indeed *the* púca." He transforms from his humanoid shape into a glossy black horse with golden eyes, and tosses his mane, trotting around us and nuzzling playfully at my elbow. "You think Shakespeare came up with all those lines on his own?"

My heart races. "You knew Shakespeare?"

If it's possible to fangirl as a fae, I'm doing it. This púca claims to be *the* Puck. The inspiration behind the character in *A Midsummer Night's Dream*.

Would it be weird to ask for his autograph?

"I've never met a púca." Jaila pats his head and runs her fingers through his mane. "Being able to change your shape would be so cool."

As if to win to more cool points, Puck turns and dashes away, then circles back to us and transforms mid-step into a wolf. With the next step, he's a rabbit with a twitchy nose.

"Aww!" Jaila bends down and picks him up.

"Why are you here?" Quince asks while Jaila tickles his chin.

He opens a golden eye. "Right to the point, I see."

"Does he have to have a reason?" I mentally kick myself for not having a pen or paper on me.

"I neither reason have nor reason need, as often reason and I do not get along." He transforms into the shape of a cat, with dusty fur a lot like Scamp's. "But your friend is right indeed. I am here for a purpose, even if that purpose doesn't have a specific reason."

Hopping out of Jaila's arms, he transforms midair and lands as a horse-tailed humanoid once more.

"All I have come to say, dear travelers, is you may want to resume raspberry picking another day. A gwyllyon is nearby and heading this way."

He points at the fog on the ground, which is thicker than before.

If Quince's face is any indication of mine, we're both as white as sheets. Our last encounter with a gwyllyon didn't go well, and it was only because of Scamp we made it out of her endless fog at all.

At the mention of the gwyllyon, Jaila's face doesn't go pale, but she does lift a trembling hand to adjust a few strands of her silvery blonde hair which had escaped from her braid, tucking them behind her ear.

I bet she's wondering what the likelihood is that the gwyllyon making its way toward us is her mother. Fae who have lost their lovers and succumb to the ultimate grief, have the potential to turn into a gwyllyon, though it's rare. It happened to Jaila's mother, though, who was Ilinor's mother as well. I think she felt that giving Nightglade two daughters was more than enough to keep him by her side, but he rejected her.

She left her youngest daughter, Jaila, at the Seelie Court, as far from Nightglade as she could manage while still keeping Jaila in Elfaeme. I don't know why she didn't bring Ilinor as well. I've never asked Jaila, and she's never offered that information. If I were to guess, I'd say Ilinor was already being fostered somewhere by the time Jaila's mother ran from the Unseelie Court with an infant Jaila in tow. Nightglade certainly couldn't have had Ilinor at the Unseelie Court, not when he had to maintain the illusion of a steadfast ruler who had been betrayed by his Queen.

Of course, Nightglade didn't know then that his Queen had left because she was pregnant with me. He just knew that she had chosen someone else over him, after working so long to keep her in his control.

It must have been infuriating.

"So, you see, while I have not reason, I have purpose. Shall we away?" Puck asks, bringing me out of my speculation. He's reverted back to his horse form, his front hooves pawing the dirt path impatiently.

"I really would rather avoid seeing another gwyllyon," I admit.

Quince has moved to the edge of the fog, kicking at tendrils around his feet before lifting a few feet in the air. "Thanks for the warning."

Jaila stares at the fog, her gaze intent, as if searching for something. "...could work," I hear her mutter. "She doesn't know. If she knew…"

"Jaila?" I ask. The fog swirls around her calves, concealing her leather-clad feet. "We should listen to

Puck and get away from here before the gwyllyon arrives."

It's like she doesn't hear me. She continues muttering under her breath. "I mean, it's only an idea, and it's risky, she might not..."

I scramble backward, running into Quince. Puck trots behind us, snorting at the fog. "Jaila, we need to go now!"

She turns to me, a crazed light in her eyes. "My father has used and abused too many fae. It's about time he learns that's not okay."

Without another word, she runs headlong into the fog.

"No!" I shout. Stupid, impetuous fae. She annoys me, I don't fully trust her, but even still, I don't want her to wander forever in the gwyllyon's fog.

Quince grabs at my wrist. "Eevee, she's gone."

Puck nods his horse head up and down in agreement. "She's gone to her fate, whatever it may be. Like the fog, her future is clouded. But yours is not. If you don't move, you will be lost forever."

I let Quince drag me away from the fog, but I keep my eyes on it as I retreat, looking for any sign of Jaila's green eyes, her skinny frame, her long-sleeved green shirt and leggings, but see nothing.

My foot connects with Quince's on my final step back. "Oh, I'm so sorry, Quince, I–"

He grips my elbow, his fingers digging into my skin. "We're surrounded," he whispers, his breath warm on my ear.

I frown. "What?" A quick tap into the ever-present murmerings of animal emotions and thoughts is fruitless. There's nothing more than the usual: a few birds, squirrels, even a toad and a pixie. Which means it isn't wild animals surrounding us.

"Try anything, and your lives are forfeit!" a gruff voice calls.

"Why didn't you warn us of this, too?" Quince demands of Puck, who transforms into a humanoid again with a look of exaggerated surprise on his face.

"Why, my dear young one, if this shadow hath offended, think but this and all is mended. I promised you I had purpose but lacked in reason. I am an honest Puck, and I stand by my statement."

Quince grinds his teeth. "Nothing is mended, Puck! You saved us from one danger but led us straight into another! Why?"

Puck's grin is the definition of mischievous. "Why not?"

He jumps into the air, becoming a raven with silky black feathers and bright, beady eyes, and caws with laughter as he flies away.

About a dozen fae step out of the woods surrounding the path, all of them armed. Some point arrows or spears at us. All have suspicion written on their faces.

One fae steps forward. A goblin, based on the bat-like ears and short stature, though he wears a curly white wig and has penciled in eyebrows, giving him a permanent look of astonishment. "You're being detained by FREEDOM's fourth cohort, travelers. Escape or fight, and this won't be pleasant. Cooperate, and you will be escorted peacefully to the nearest barracks, where you will work to help us achieve FREEDOM's glorious goals."

It's stupid, but I feel my gaze sliding from the ridiculous-looking goblin into the sky, where Puck's raven form is retreating, and I can't help thinking how I missed my chance to get an autograph.

FREEDOM's Newest Recruits

"Detained for what purpose?" Quince asks the goblin with the curly wig. "Since when is FREEDOM in the business of capturing fellow fae?"

The goblin turns up his snout to look at him. "For your information, we have been in this business for months."

I grimace at Quince. Of course FREEDOM had to pick up their activity during the months we spent with the gnomes.

"We won't tie you up so long as you don't fight." The goblin glances down at my fiery fists.

I lean closer to Quince, my fists crackling merrily. "We can take them, right?"

"I dunno." He rubs the back of his head, scanning the dozen fae surrounding us. "It's two against twelve, Eevee."

To say I'm dumbfounded is an understatement. Even my flames fizzle out. What happened to the thing Quince needed to do? These twelve FREEDOM fae are an obstacle to him accomplishing whatever the thing is. And yet, he doesn't want us to fight our way out of it? Only half of the fae here are winged. And if we realm-hop, we'd lose them in a flash.

Seeing the desire to flee on my face, the goblin holds up a greasy hand with perfectly manicured nails, filed to points. "You should know, my friend Leaf here, a wild fae through and through–"

"And proud of it!" Leaf interrupts.

"Yes, and proud of it," the goblin repeats. "Anyway. Leaf has an anti-phasing device. It isn't as strong as the shields around the Courts, but it does keep fae from phasing in or out of Elfaeme within a thirty foot radius of him. Go on." He claps delightedly. "Try it. I do so love when our new recruits attempt phasing to escape."

The Courts operate opposite to this device, I think, eyeing Leaf for any hint of what the device may look like. Fae from either Court can't realm-hop directly into the Courts, but they can realm-hop out of them. Usually, to visit one Court or the other, they have to travel the long way, or find a moonstone close enough to where they want to go.

Actually, what the device reminds me of is Sean

and Shannon's home security system. I have no idea where they purchased it, or who they purchased it from, only that it may have cost them a literal arm and a leg. But it was effective. It had made it impossible for me to realm-hop into their house, and the consequences of trying had been less than pleasant. I clutch at my stomach at the memory. Maybe realm-hopping right now wouldn't be the best idea.

Leaf, who looks like the mossy side of a deciduous tree, places his hands on the space where his hips would be if he had them. His torso is all one width, very much like a tree trunk. "You'll listen to Mort, now. We don't have much time until the next new moon, and we need to train as many of the new recruits as we can."

I feel Quince's arm brush mine, his skin cool from the evening air. "You've said 'recruits' a few times now. What do you mean?" he asks.

"We're recruiting," Mort answers, brandishing his spear for emphasis. "Any fae we can find are added to our cause."

FREEDOM. Fae Reclaiming the Earth, End Dominion of Men. My heart beats wildly. Are we going to be forced to help FREEDOM fight for more control over Earth? I'd risk realm-hopping to avoid that fate.

"We see this upheaval in the Unseelie Court for the opportunity it is," Leaf explains. "A chance for us to unbalance the leadership in Elfaeme. With no one to take the Queen's crown in the Unseelie Court, our intelligence tells us Nightglade will also lose his crown."

Leaf's dark eyes burn with frenetic energy. "He only has a few more chances left. Then, with no one on the throne in the Unseelie Court, we can move in, take control."

"Gain more influence in Elfaeme so we can recruit more fae to join us," Mort adds. He grins. "Just think of it, folk. No one on the throne!"

An excited murmuring erupts around us, but it's drowned out by the buzzing in my ears.

"No one on the throne?" I say in horror. After everything the Eldest told us, to imagine anyone working to throw off the balance of Elfaeme to such an extreme…well. It's terrifying.

"No one," the wild fae, Leaf, confirms. His face shines with fanaticism. "So, until the time runs out, we're wrangling anyone we can find to help us."

I'm beginning to realize they don't care if their recruits join on a voluntary basis. FREEDOM is snatching any fae who might be easy prey and forcing them to fight alongside them at the Unseelie Court every new moon.

Mort nods apologetically at me and Quince, his perfectly coiffed curls bouncing. "Nothing against you two on an individual level, of course. Once you see the bigger picture, you'll see FREEDOM was right all along and you'll be glad we made you join us. This is the best course for regaining fae power for the fae. Next step will be to use that power to do the same thing in the Seelie Court."

I rub my temples, the Eldest's warning about

how the four crowns' fates are tied together echoing in my head. I can't share that with FREEDOM, though. It would only add fuel to the fire and make them more eager to prevent any coronation from happening in the Unseelie Court. "Elfaeme is a reflection of Earth, a kind of shadow realm, right? Haven't you thought about what would happen if you messed with that?"

Mort's face grows stormy. "I don't engage with non-believers." He stomps away, followed by the other fae in the cohort, leaving us with Leaf and his anti-phasing device for company.

Leaf shrugs. "You'll come around to our way of thinking." The smile splitting his face reveals mossy teeth. And I don't mean dirty teeth in need of a good tooth-brushing (though, running my tongue along my teeth, I could really go for a toothbrush and some extra strong mint toothpaste right about now). His teeth are literally covered with some kind of moss. My point? Leaf definitely has plant matter growing on his teeth.

Quince's shoulders scrunch upward in a small shrug. "Let's wait for a better opportunity to escape," he mutters as we walk, Leaf trailing behind us.

We travel the slow way across Elfaeme. Apparently the members of FREEDOM refuse to realm-hop unless absolutely necessary, claiming that traveling to Earth is too painful. It reminds them of their failure to reclaim it for the fae, according to Leaf. "Not to mention," Leaf adds, "my device doesn't discriminate, and we don't want to split up our cohort."

Next to me, Quince has been quiet since we

decided not to fight FREEDOM. Oddly, he seems okay with our capture, though I worry he's maybe repressing memories of being imprisoned in order to deal with our current situation.

He takes my hand absentmindedly and smiles when I look up at him. "At least we're together, right?"

I squeeze his hand. Above us, a winged Seelie fae, who's been keeping an eye on the group from above, calls down. "I see the FREEDOM marker ahead. And Snowtwist is already there with someone!"

There's a ripple of talk and activity at this announcement and we pick up the pace. I keep Quince's hand in mine. I think of how, this time, we're going to our fate together, rather than separated. And even though we're on our way to wherever FREEDOM is training fae who've been recruited against their will, I feel an odd sense of comfort knowing this time, Quince is by my side.

"–a mistake, I didn't mean to kill him!"

"What's going on?" I ask, craning my neck. I'm not short, as far as fae go, but I can't see around the folk in front of us to know what's happening.

"Not sure," Quince frowns, eyeing the front of the group. "Some kind of argument between what's his name–Snowtwist? And Mort."

I take a chance and fly a few inches off the ground. Not enough to get in trouble, Mort's warning about what they'd do to us if we tried to fly away is fresh in my mind, but enough to get a better look at the situation.

It's a good thing Quince has my hand, because I drop the couple of inches and stumble, my knees suddenly weak.

"What is it?" Quince's face is creased, his dark eyes brimming with concern. "Who's been killed?" At the look on my face, his face falls. "Is it someone we know?"

The rest of the group comes to a stop near Snowtwist and Mort, who are both gesturing violently.

"–obviously a security risk, but you know our policy, and you broke it!" Spit flies from Mort's mouth.

"I broke it to keep us safe!" Snowtwist bellows back. His eyes dart around, looking for support from any of his fellow FREEDOM folk, then settle on Mort again. His posture is defiant: white, glittering shoulders drawn back, head held high. I see why he's called Snowtwist. He has a frosty demeanor, and the white, glittery skin isn't confined to his shoulders. Like a tornado, it twists around his arms and neck, with a splash of it on his face. The rest of his skin is the color of a midnight sky, which makes his red eyes all the more startling.

"You broke it to keep yourself safe," Mort accuses in a dangerously low voice. "To keep your place at the Unseelie Court." He shakes his head in disgust, then adjusts his wig, while the whispers amongst the rest of our captors intensify. "You've grown soft, Snow, with your cushy life at Court. It's been too long since you've had to rough it with the rest of us."

Snowtwist is quiet, but his defiant posture

remains unchanged. "My outlook hasn't shifted with my life at Court," he finally says, his upper lip curled. "I want the same thing you all do. This," he indicates the body at his feet, "was an accident, plain and simple. I meant to rough him up a bit, sure, but I never meant for him to die."

"Him who, Eevee?" Quince asks out of the corner of his mouth, his grip on my hand like a tightening clamp.

I debate how to answer. Quince doesn't exactly care for the dead fae, but a picture is coming into focus in my mind of what this fae had been doing to help us without any expectation of thanks, all for the love of his former Queen.

Mort and Snowtwist must come to some kind of understanding, because Mort waves to the company to keep going. "Leave the body," he says with a glare at Snowtwist before stomping to the front of the group, his curly-haired wig askew.

"Wait!" I call, tugging my hand out of Quince's grasp and dashing forward. I'm blocked by two burly fae who turn and crack their knuckles.

"Give us a reason," the one on the left warns with a sneer.

"We don't need one," the one on the right adds, twisting his neck to crack that, too. "But we like to offer that option to those lookin' for trouble."

"I'll carry the body," I say hastily, holding my hands up to show I mean no trouble. "Until you make camp. Then my friend and I will bury him."

"He was a back-stabbing, slippery fellow in life." Snowtwist, who had noticed the holdup, had made his way over, standing with his arms crossed next to the neck-cracker on the right.

"I know that." Desperation fills me. How do I explain to them I need to do this for my birth mother? It's the least she'd want me to do, given what I'm beginning to realize about Snowtwist's victim.

Snowtwist eyes me with those unsettling red eyes. "He didn't deserve death, but he also doesn't deserve a proper burial. You know what he would've done if he'd discovered my ties to FREEDOM?" He laughs. "Of course you do. And you would have approved, I'm sure. You crown enthusiasts are all the same. I shouldn't have expected anything less from the daughter of a former crown-wearer." At the look on my face, his grin turns wicked. "Oh, I'd recognize your face anywhere, daughter of Maeve. I long served in the Court with her as my Queen. And yes, even then, I was working for FREEDOM."

"What's the holdup?" Mort asks, frowning at Snowtwist. "We need to keep moving, or we risk being found by the you-know-what. You know they like to catch us unawares."

Jabbing a finger at me, Snowtwist snorts. "This one thinks she's all high-and-mighty, and can make requests of us like she isn't a lowly recruit."

Mort raises a penciled eyebrow, looking from me to Snowtwist.

"I want to carry the body until you make camp

for the night," I explain as calmly as I can. "And then bury him. That's all."

It's a long shot, but I study Mort's face as he thinks. He doesn't outright refuse, which I take as a hopeful sign.

"Fine," Mort says. "You can do that if you wish. On one condition." He leans over and whispers in my ear. "You accept that, if any suspicion of his death comes on us, you truthfully say you didn't see any of us kill him. You don't say a word about the conversation you heard between myself and Snowtwist. Agreed?"

"Agreed," I reply without hesitation.

Quince silently approaches as Mort shouts for the company to keep moving. His cheeks are flushed. "Why would you do that for…*him*?"

I bend to pick up the small, froggy fae. The one who kept an eye out for any sign of me in Elfaeme when Maeve and Aspen didn't dare. The one who frustrated me, who was certainly not always kind, but who was loyal to his Queen, my birth mother, until his death.

Quince eyes me questioningly as I straighten, and the betrayal in his eyes hurts, even though I know, once I explain, he'll understand.

"Let me tell you what I've figured out about Folsom."

Saying Goodbye

Folsom's weight in my arms is next to nothing. It's like holding a green, frog-faced feather. In death, Folsom's face is relaxed, all of the anxiety and weight of duty lifted from it. Quince lifts Folsom's gnarled staff from where it had lain discarded on the ground and frowns down at it, shifting it from one hand to the other as I tell him all I've pieced together about Folsom. I finish, and we walk for a while longer in silence. When I look up at Quince, his expression is dazed.

"I can't believe…I spent so long hating him, thinking he was just like the other Unseelie fae who follow Nightglade." He shifts, looking uncomfortable.

"There were many times I wanted him to suffer."

"He wasn't perfect," I say, cradling the old fae and looking at him. "He shouldn't have said you were…" I can't bring myself to repeat Folsom's words when he met Quince.

"A bastard son of an Unseelie traitor?" he finishes mildly. It's only because of how well I know Quince that I can hear the undercurrent of bitterness beneath the mild tone. "Technically true."

"But the way he said it…"

"Had to be believable, I guess," Quince says. "Or so he thought. He was a paranoid one in life, wasn't he? For good reason."

We both fall silent. The rest of the walk, I keep looking down at Folsom, unable to believe he's dead.

He had been doing so much for us, as a way to continue serving Maeve even after she had been turned to stone. Sending Jaila to find me. Using his connections in the Unseelie Court to ensure we'd be able to rescue Quince. And trying to find any Unseelie willing to challenge Nightglade.

Which is what I think he was doing when he approached Snowtwist, from what I've overheard the other FREEDOM fae muttering about to each other. Snowtwist had left the company a while ago, claiming the need to return to Court before he was missed. Who knew that a fellow Unseelie Court member would be Folsom's downfall? In his search for those willing to challenge Nightglade, he had learned too much about the FREEDOM infiltration of the Unseelie Court.

And now Quince and I know about it, too. I wonder how many of the fae at their reclamation barracks also know, or how many have changed their ways and joined FREEDOM?

We stop for a rest somewhere in the In Between. It isn't forested, like where I first met Folsom, but rolling plains as far as I can see. The sun is low in the sky now, and I slump to the ground, exhausted.

Quince kneels next to me.

The rest of the company takes their positions around us, but their faces are turned away, and I hear them laughing loudly amongst themselves.

Anger like a burning hot brand flares inside me. "How can Snowtwist have killed him?" I hiss to Quince. "I know he's small, but if they value fae life like they say they do—"

"They don't care much about anything besides themselves and their agenda," Quince whispers. "And Folsom knew too much." He wraps an arm around my shoulders, the weight settling the panicky fluttering my heart had been doing the last couple hours as we walked.

"If I were in charge—"

"You'd what?" he asks. "Stop them from meeting? I don't like their agenda, but does any ruler have the right to silence their people for thoughts and feelings?"

"No," I agree. "Of course not. But FREEDOM's been capturing fae. They *want* to do harm. They want to take the Earth away from the humans!"

"So maybe rather than tell them they're wrong, we show them another way?"

"How?" I ask hollowly.

He huffs out a laugh. "Beats me. If you figure it out, let me know." He lowers his voice. "That's a problem for another day, though. How are we going to get out of this?"

"I've been thinking about that," I say, keeping my voice barely above a whisper. "Back when we busted you out of the Iron Prison–"

At the mention of the Iron Prison, an odd look passes across Quince's face, like pain or torment, but then it's gone.

"What about it?" he asks, angling his face so he's looking down at Folsom. For all the FREEDOM folk know, we're saying a few words over our dead comrade's body.

"Sean and Shannon gave me a way to contact Scamp directly, no matter where I am."

"They did?"

"You sound surprised."

"Well…" He hesitates. "I am. Sir Cornelius is a notorious free agent, of course. But he hasn't knowingly worked with any Unseelie fae that I'm aware of. The fact he'd allow Sean and Shannon to set up such an arrangement is intriguing."

"Hey!" The gruff voice of the neck-cracker interrupts us and my shoulder immediately feels the loss of Quince's arm like an ache. "We're moving, rats.

Grab the baggage and get a move on.”

I gape at the face that looms above us, yellow eyes and tusks and hair coming out of his ears. “The baggage? You awful–”

“We’ll carry him,” Quince interrupts.

Neck-cracker grunts and takes up his position at the back of the company.

“Whatever it entails, that thing from my cousins, just do it,” Quince mutters in my ear. He stands and pulls me up next to him. With gentle hands, he takes Folsom from my arms and pulls the brown hood down over his blank face before turning and walking with the rest of the FREEDOM company surrounding him.

Walking alongside him, I grab the enhancer ring I’ve kept in my pocket this whole time and slip it onto my finger. *Scamp*, I think desperately. *Scamp, we’re separated from Aspen, and FREEDOM found us, and I don’t know what they’re doing with us or why, the only thing they’ve said is they plan to thwart the Unseelie crowning*. And then, feeling pathetic, I add, *I’m so scared. They have some kind of barracks they’re taking us to.*

I don’t know if it works. The ring is like a band of ice on my index finger, but that doesn’t necessarily mean the magic is working.

He’s dead, I think. *Folsom’s dead. I know you two didn’t get along at all*. That’s an understatement. *But he died trying to turn folk against Nightglade. He died because he learned too much about the wrong fae.*

As we walk, I continue thinking everything I

can about our surroundings, hoping that maybe one detail will be the hint Scamp needs to ascertain where we are.

Another hill. This one looks like my grandma's crooked nose. Oh, that probably doesn't help you.

Now we're passing through a field of purple wildflowers. Can you see purple?

There's three hills in a row we passed and they look like eggs. One has a stone on top.

I have no idea if the ring is working, but concentrating on my surroundings has calmed me in a way. And I haven't felt even a semblance of calm since FREEDOM captured us earlier.

The afternoon passes, and by nightfall my hope dies with the last ray of sunlight.

We're in the middle of an endless field, the soft grasses tickling my knees as I walk. Above us, the sky yawns wide, with sparkling stars as far as I can see. The sight is both familiar and foreign. Growing up, how many camping trips had I spent looking up at the stars while sitting at a campfire with my family? But here in Elfaeme, it's like everything has a sharper quality, both more real and more ethereal.

I focus on that beauty. Even while I'm a prisoner of FREEDOM, I still feel that flush of awe like a spreading warmth in my body when I remember that I'm *fae*. That this is my world, where I belong.

"We rest here for tonight!"

The order ripples through the band of FREEDOM members. In a stupor, I listen to their conversation.

"Any sight of the you-know-what?"

"None. Should be safe here for the night."

This is the second time they've mentioned this mysterious "you-know-what." With how much trepidation is in their voices, I kind of wish this thing would show up.

Quince sets Folsom's body on the ground, then kicks a toe at the dirt. "The ground is soft," he says.

He doesn't have to say any more. I fall to my knees next to Quince and we both start digging with our hands.

"What do they think they're doing?"

"Tryin' to dig their way to freedom?"

"You mean trying to dig their way away from FREEDOM, right?"

They laugh, pleased with themselves.

"Ah, let 'em be," I hear Leaf say. "Mort told 'em they could bury the slimy traitor. It's not hurting us any."

"Aww, they're burying their friend?" someone comments.

"How quaint."

I snap and stand to face them. "You know, he was a fae, like you. Aren't you all about helping fae? Or do you all have your heads so far up your own butts you can't unbend for long enough to help anyone other than yourselves?"

They don't offer to help us, but at least they shut up.

I glare at them, then rejoin Quince, who has already dug a hole a few inches deep. As soon as I turn my back, they burst into cackles.

"Ignore them," Quince says.

"I'm trying," I reply through gritted teeth.

My nails fill with dirt and my hands begin to ache but I keep going, working silently beside Quince, who's digging furiously, throwing handfuls of dirt to the side, where we have a pile going.

Despite the "fae first" attitude of FREEDOM, they have yet to feed us. After spending most of the afternoon and evening walking and now digging, I feel my energy flagging. Soon enough, though, the hole is deep enough and wide enough for us to lower him into it.

We cover up Folsom's body, but not until after I've laid his staff over him, folding his arms around it.

Quince takes me in his arms after it's done, and I'm surprised to find I'm shaking. "I didn't even like him." I smear my hand across my face, momentarily forgetting that it's covered in dirt.

"I know," Quince says, his breath fluttering the hair on my head. "But he loved Maeve. He was loyal to her, almost to a fault. It caused him a lot of strife and made enemies where maybe there wouldn't be any otherwise. But he was loyal, and died while carrying out his duty, which I think, for him, was an acceptable way to go."

I cry for Folsom, and, pitiful as it seems, for myself. Losing Folsom felt like losing an important thread to understanding Maeve. He knew more about her than almost anyone, except Aspen.

Aspen. I'm glad he departed before FREEDOM came upon us, but I wonder where he is and if he's doing okay. I'm barely holding it together after learning the curse of the revoked crown can't be reversed. I'm losing something I never really had–my birth mother in my life–but he's permanently losing the fae whose soul saw through his many faces to his real one.

The air around us remains fairly warm despite the night wearing on, and I pass this fact on to Scamp in my head, twisting the ice-cold ring around my finger. *Probably somewhere in Seelie territory now.*

And in my head, I feel an answering tug, a sensation of a question more than any actual words.

I sit up and gasp, breaking away from Quince.

"Whazzit?" he asks, his words blurring together sleepily. I hadn't even realized he'd fallen asleep holding me.

Gripping his hand, I send out another thought, this time twisting the ring again. I almost cry when I feel reassurance answering me, seeming closer than before.

"I think Scamp knows we need help," I whisper.

His hand tightens in mine. "Do you know when he'll be here? What can a cat do against a small army of fae?"

"He's a magical cat," I remind him.

"And we're still surrounded by nearly a dozen fae who have made it clear that in no uncertain terms are we to attempt to escape or they'll make us suffer."

"I–" I frown, another image coming to me from Scamp. "I…oh no."

He'd sent an image of a wyvern with a saddle on its back, its wings outstretched and its mouth open wide.

Correction: a saddle with a very familiar-looking fae on it, and another flying alongside.

Suddenly the grumbling about the "you-know-what" makes a whole lot of sense.

"So that's how they've been helping?" I grumble. I describe the image to Quince.

He raises his eyebrows, but not in a questioning look. No, I doubt he'd be surprised by anything his cousins do at this point. "They're turning into quite the vigilantes, aren't they?"

"What do we do when they get here?" I ask.

"That depends on the manner of their arrival," Quince answers drily.

We lay back in the grasses, our fingers intertwined, gazing up at the night sky. It would almost be peaceful, if it weren't for the fact that we are surrounded by fae who captured us and would torture us if we step even one toe out of line.

I must drift off, because suddenly a jolt shoots through me and I jerk upright. My back is damp from laying in the grass, and a jumble of sounds attacks my ears.

"They're back!"

"It's the 'you-know-what!'"

"Take cover!"

"Positions, everyone! Don't forget the new plan!"

In the air, there's a piercing shriek, and against the starry night sky, a dark shape descends on the FREEDOM camp.

Watching Shannon fight from the back of Fearghas with Sean flying at his side is exhilarating, and I'm immediately filled with a desire to be up there with them, wreaking havoc.

Because that's exactly what they're doing, I realize. They aren't attacking so much as causing chaos. Fearghas swoops down, blasting fire at equipment and scraping its claws along weaponry, breaking the spears in half as easily as a hot knife cutting butter. FREEDOM members launch volleys of arrows as Leaf sprays thorns into the air from his hands, but the wyvern evades it all with ease. Sean and Shannon work together to protect each other and their wyvern, holding up shimmering shields and taking turns throwing makeshift knives of ice. But their aim isn't to kill. Or, if it is, they're failing spectacularly.

One knife slices through the canvas side of a tent. Another spins through the air, finally embedding in a bag of food, sending the rations spilling everywhere, apples and crackers that crumble to dust.

With a move made fluid by practice, Sean sends out an ice knife connected to a rope. Its tip pierces an apple, and he pulls it back toward him. Shining the apple on his sleeve, he takes a bite and tosses it in the air. Fearghas snaps at it, swallowing it whole.

From a saddle bag, Shannon reaches in with a gloved hand and pulls out a handful of something, then drops it on the fae beneath him.

The fae react with disgust, scrabbling away from the projectiles, scratching at their skin wherever the marble-like objects had touched.

"Fae charms," I breathe, recognizing Maggie and Cam's handiwork. So that's what they've been up to with Sean and Shannon. Thwarting FREEDOM's plans all these months.

I tear my attention away from Sean and Shannon's antics, a grin made wide by hope on my face, only to have my heart stop.

Quince isn't by my side.

A quick glance around quiets my panic at the thought that he's been snatched by one of the FREEDOM members in all the confusion. But, no, they're all so distracted by Sean and Shannon, they've completely forgotten about their prisoners.

Lucky for me.

So where's Quince?

Frantic now, I rush away from the camp, the morning dew soaking my shoes. I scan the ground, then my eyes move skyward.

There. Flying away. Without me.

What the hell?

Anger and confusion cloud my vision, but I

blink it away and launch myself after him.

He's had years of practice flying, whereas I only learned last year, but he doesn't know how stubborn us Ackers can be.

I beat my wings furiously, blood pumping loudly in my ears. The intense activity on so little food and sleep makes me dizzy, but I still fly after Quince, unable to answer the question burning in my brain, needing an answer only he can give me. He told me he loved me not long ago, when we were safe with the gnomes. Can his feelings have changed, after I didn't say it back? Why else would he leave without me?

Little by little, I feel myself losing altitude, but his figure grows closer until I'm within shouting distance. Or, I would be, if I could shout. My breathing is ragged, a copper taste coating my mouth and throat.

Just a little closer, I tell myself.

"Quince!" I croak.

He looks over his shoulder. We make eye contact. I feel the moment his gaze connects with mine. We're not close enough for me to see his features, but his gaze spears me.

Then he turns around and puts forth a burst of speed.

"No!"

At my side, my fists burst into flame, but I don't bother putting them out. Not yet. I can feel my wings shaking and I know they won't last me much longer, but I zero in on Quince's back and force myself forward. Inch by inch, I gain on him, until I can reach out a hand–no longer flaming, all my energy sent to my wings–and grab at one of his wings.

"Eevee, what the–" He jerks back at my grip, and then we're both plummeting to the field below.

"Why did you leave without me?" I shout as the wind whistles past my ears.

"Let go of my wing!"

I repeat my question, my grip tightening on the silky feathers.

"We're going to crash! Let go!"

"Answer me then," I say. "With the truth!"

I don't tell him that I'm planning to let go at the last minute rather than letting us crash. I'd like to think he trusts me enough not to have us both plummet to our deaths simply to get an answer to a question, but desperate times and all that.

The ground looms ever closer.

Right before I decide to let go, he yells, "Fine!"

I release his wing, and we both hover, panting, eventually lowering ourselves to the ground. I refuse to let him out of my sight. And maybe my crossed arms and angry expression don't totally cover up the hurt I feel inside, because I see his features lose their harsh edges when he looks at me.

"So?"

He runs his hand through his dark brown, nearly black hair, ruffling it even more than the wind had, then tugs on one of his horns. I wait, keeping my arms crossed.

"There's something I have to do."

"Okay." My voice is flat, right? And definitely doesn't sound wounded at all.

He comes toward me and I take a step back. Lowering his hands, he sighs. "I…it's better if you weren't with me."

Each word pierces my body as easily as Sean's ice knife pierced that apple. Seven words, seven stabs, mostly centered on my chest. Ouch.

But I didn't chase him down to hear a non-answer. "What exactly is it you need to do that's better without me?"

It's his turn to step back. He recoils from me, as if my words maimed him as much as his did me. "I didn't say what I had to do would be better without you. I said it would be better if you weren't with me."

"Why?" I throw out the word like a weapon, unyielding steel in my tone.

"I can't tell you why. Eevee, please trust me. If I could tell you, I would."

"You almost sound believable."

He paces back and forth in front of me. "You're infuriating sometimes, you know that?" He doesn't sound angry, though. He sounds exhausted.

"It comes with being an Acker. I was raised to tell the truth. And you're not telling me everything."

"No, I'm not."

Suddenly, he's so close, his face above mine, our bodies inches apart. I can smell him, fresh water and heady pine, and the inches between us are not enough and too much all at once.

"I have something I need to do back at the Unseelie Court," he says quietly. "Even saying that much to you is a risk." His hands on my shoulders are heavy, his gaze as he looks at me even more so. "But that's where I'm going. I've put it off for too long. Bringing you with me is not something I'm willing to risk. I don't know what I'd do if–"

"Quince." The anger that came from being left behind is sapped out of me at his words. He isn't leaving me behind willingly. He's telling me he loves me in everything but his words, and I almost find myself telling him what I've kept from him, that I love him too, but instead, I open my mouth and say, "Whatever you need to do, I'm coming with you."

"But–"

I pull his face toward mine, my lips finding his. I plant kisses as light as butterflies against his mouth, his cheeks, his nose. "I'm coming with you," I repeat in a whisper.

He closes his eyes and swallows, his expression pained. "I don't suppose there's any way I can convince you not to?"

"No."

His arms encircle my waist and he buries his face in my shoulder.

"This is probably the worst plan ever," he says in a muffled voice.

"I'm with you, though." I lean until my head rests on his and I breathe in, feeling an odd combination of terrified for what's to come and at peace in this particular moment. "Whatever you have to do at the Unseelie Court, I'm not letting you face it alone."

"It has to do with Nightglade." The terror in his voice is palpable, but I laugh anyway, the sound brittle.

"Of course it has to do with Nightglade," I tell him when he looks at me with surprise. "Who else at the Unseelie Court do we know who's giving us this much trouble?"

"Going back there will most certainly be a trap. But I need to go anyway."

"You're not doing this alone." I keep my voice firm, even though the memories of the Iron Prison with its dank cells filled with tortured prisoners won't leave my head.

"You're infuriating," he says again. But this time, he says it with a smile in his voice. "I'm walking headlong into a trap, and you're just like, hi, yeah, remember me? I'm Evelyn Gray Acker, I'm coming with you?"

"Two heads are better than one," I retort. "You'll need someone to help you get out of the trap you're walking into."

He lifts his head from my shoulder, and the intensity of the look he gives me sends a curl of heat through my body.

"I hope you're right. Because I can't see a way out of this trap."

"I'm always right," I say primly.

Lowering his face until I feel the heat of his lips

on mine, he says, "I've never hoped for anything more." He plants a quick kiss on the corner of my mouth, then gathers himself. Proffering an arm to me, his mouth quirks up in an effort to regain his usual light-hearted demeanor. "Coming?" he asks. "We have a couple realm-hops to do between now and our imminent trap."

I take his arm, and he tucks my hand to his side. "To imminent traps!" I declare.

Quince eyes me, worry wrinkling his brow, but nods.

We step, and our surroundings fade around us as we make our way to a certain trap.

It's a Trap, Alright

It's one thing to sneak into the Unseelie castle.

It's quite another to enter it openly, knowing Nightglade is there somewhere, probably still awake despite the late hour. After all, he's got a lot of planning to do before his next monthly murder (I have little hope that this month's new moon will be any different than the last six). I didn't check the time to see how long I had slept before Sean and Shannon appeared at the FREEDOM camp, but it can't have been long, meaning we have hours to go until dawn. And the day of the new moon.

Quince and I walk through the town which surrounds the castle, the will-o'-the-wisps lighting the streets with a dreamy glow.

I'm not sure if it's my hand or Quince's which is sweating profusely, but it's probably mine.

On the one hand, I trust Quince.

On the other, I don't trust Nightglade.

When we reach the castle doors, they are flanked by two guards I don't recognize. Nena and Ash must have the night off, or are positioned elsewhere.

Quince slips and stumbles up the cold stone steps, scrabbling to pull himself upright, which is when I notice his whole body is trembling uncontrollably.

"Eevee, whatever happens, please know I love you."

I freeze to the spot, my eyes widening.

Before I can formulate an answer, because yes, Quince, I love you too, I hadn't expected to declare it in front of Unseelie guards, though, he continues. "I just…I wanted you to know, in case–"

"The King has been expecting you," the guard to our left says.

"Excuse you, we're kind of having a moment," I reply.

Quince grabs both my hands in his, the look in his eyes earnest. But also fearful. "You can still get out of here, you don't need to be here, I'm not sure it's safe, I–"

I open my mouth to answer, then frown, and glance to the guard. "What do you mean, the King has been expecting us?"

"Him, at any rate," the second guard nods at

Quince. "Though he'll be delighted to know who he brought with him."

"Took you long enough to complete your mission for the King," the first guard says with a shake of his head.

Quince's…mission for the King?

The world falls out from beneath me, then fills with a roaring, blind anger. Anger at Nightglade, because I'm sure he forced Quince into this mission, whatever it is, but anger at Quince, too, for accepting it.

"How could you?" I say around the hot, angry tears trying to drown me.

Two hands clutch at my arms and drag me away from Quince, who is being hauled away by the other guard. I recognize immediately where my guard is taking me. To the Iron Prison. But Quince's guard is bringing him somewhere else.

To Nightglade.

Darkness consumes my every thought until it's like a vacuum in my head and all I can think is that this whole time, even when I thought Jaila and I had succeeded in rescuing him, he had really been doing Nightglade's bidding. Nightglade had known I was going to rescue Quince, wanted me to rescue Quince, but for what purpose?

The guard throws me in an empty cell in the Iron Prison haphazardly so that I crash against the wall, my skin numbing and my stomach clenching in an effort not to throw up from the iron embedded in the stone.

I'm left alone, accompanied only by the rage and sense of betrayal, which stalk around my mind like predators.

Look how gullible you were, Eevee.

How could Quince do this to me?

The dirt beneath my face muddies with my tears.

"How quaint," a soft voice whispers from outside my cell. "Do you cry for him, or for yourself?"

I sit upright, forcing myself to look up at the face of the Unseelie King.

"Both," I snarl.

"Such an emotional one, you are," he muses, his gray eyes glinting. "It must be your human upbringing." His lip curls. "Disgusting."

"Did you imprison me for the sole purpose of insulting me? Because that's kind of lame, even for you," I shoot back.

He chuckles, and my skin prickles like it's being stabbed with needles. "You should know, I didn't force your mate into anything he didn't want to do. He agreed to retrieve some information for me. In fact," his smile could freeze ice, "he is waiting for me right now."

As Nightglade turns to go, I blurt out, "What are you going to do with me?"

"Do?" He pauses, the dark cloak billowing around his body, then leaves without answering.

This is it. I'm going to rot in prison forever.

I'll never see my family or friends again. There's a small comfort in knowing my mom and dad will never know what happened to me, the fae magic will cloud their memories. But what will Aspen think on Wednesday when I don't show up at the Reflecting Pool?

My heart feels like it's been crushed flat.

I don't know how many minutes pass before I sense a presence in front of my cell. I look up through the frayed edges of my hair, which is long enough now to get in my eyes if I don't style it right. And I haven't exactly had the time to style it lately.

"What?" I ask Nightglade shortly. I'm in prison already, there's not much worse he can do to me.

"I've just come from a visit with your mate. His information was…disappointing."

"Why are you telling me this?" I ask, tucking my knees up to my chest and wrapping my arms around them tight, anchoring me. I feel like I'm floating above the cell, above the Eevee who looks so tiny on the packed dirt, above Nightglade who stands so rigidly he could be a statue like Maeve.

"I've thought of something to do with you," he replies.

This catches my attention, and not in a good way. More in a I-feel-like-I've-been-plunged-in-a-pool-of-ice-water way. "What?"

"Why, I can't think of anyone more worthy to try on the crown tomorrow than Maeve's daughter, can you? If it fails again…" His face is blank, expressionless. "Well. Then I'm rid of you. If it succeeds, then you can be Queen from prison."

Quince

I said it's a trap
but the depth of betrayal?
Immeasurable.

Guilt courses through me as I pace the room where Nightglade and I had struck our initial deal. He had joined me here not long after the guard had deposited me without a backward glance.

When I told him what the Eldest had said, *"Two lanterns. Not unlike four crowns. Take away even one, and the balance is irrevocably changed. It cannot be done,"* I thought I was going to die right then and there.

But he didn't kill me. He didn't laugh, he didn't

even throw a chair in anger or anything.

He simply walked out, leaving me to my self-loathing.

Eevee is somewhere nearby, in the Iron Prison.

God, Eevee.

I told her everything I could, I warned her that we were walking into a trap, but now she knows the depth of my betrayal.

She knows now that I had been gathering information about the coronation ceremonies for Nightglade. She knows that even her rescue of me was only possible because Nightglade had allowed it, not just because of Folsom and his connections.

She will never trust me again.

I wouldn't trust myself again if I were her.

At least I told her I love her. Before I saw the pain of being stabbed in the back take all the light out of her usually vibrant eyes.

Because in the end, I did not have the strength to tell her not to come with me, even though I know Nightglade. I know how cruel he is, how he encouraged that cruelty in his followers. Being crueler than most is how Banethistle got Nightglade to notice him, and how he became Nightglade's most loyal supporter.

His cruelty extended to others in the Unseelie Court he deemed potential rivals, which included my father. My parents had been living two lives. One, at their respective Courts. My mother at the Seelie Court, my father with the Unseelie. Their second life had been in a home in the In Between. I don't remember the home, and when I had asked my parents about it, curious to visit it, they had said it'd been destroyed. Banethistle found out about my father's second life, about his wife from the rival Court, and he had not hesitated to pass on this information to Nightglade, who had immediately banished my father. My mother, who had refused to live without my father, and whose secret life had been exposed in the process, had made the decision for the three of us that we would live amongst the humans instead, only returning to Elfaeme for visits.

Which is why, at the age of four, I had moved from the In Between to Duluth, Minnesota, and learned to hide among humans.

I suppose in some twisted way, I have Banethistle to thank for Eevee and I meeting. But I refuse to give him any kind of credit.

And now she's a prisoner in the Iron Prison, just like I had been. It is…less than ideal.

Coughing, I groan inwardly at myself. Less than ideal, Quince? Really? Yes, the possibility of the one you love rotting away in prison the rest of her long life is certainly less than ideal.

"Your turn."

"Oh, you," I say, lifting my gaze to stare daggers at the goblin with the snoutlike mouth who has been outside the room, guarding the door. His face leers at me around the door, which he's cracked open. Then his words sink in, and I frown. "What do you mean, my turn?"

"Nightglade has finished…talking with your mate. He wants me to bring you to him."

I fly toward him across the small space of the room. "What do you mean, talking with her?" I ask, barely able to move my mouth because of how tight my jaw suddenly is.

His laugh is like nails on a chalkboard to my ears. "Oh, she's alive."

"That's not what I asked."

His red-rimmed eyes darken. "Well that's all I'm gon' tell ya, see?"

With more force than is necessary, he shoves the door open further, so it bangs against the wall. "Come here. The King is not patient."

"What has he done to her?" I ask, feeling faint, but planting my feet.

The goblin grabs my arm and rips me away from the door. "Nothing you need to know about. Now, let's go get you glamoured up. Nightglade has plans," he grins, revealing teeth that are perfectly, unnervingly straight, "for when your mate sees you next."

Trepidation pours into me, filling me until it's the only emotion I have room for.

Whatever Nightglade's plan for me is, I can guarantee it will be cruel. After all, I had disappointed him greatly when I had relayed what the Eldest had said.

It's worse than I thought.

The Morning of the New Moon

I'm dragged from the Iron Prison at the crack
of dawn. "Time to prepare for tonight's festivities,"
says the guard, a grasshopper-looking fae with a
lopsided smile on her bug-face like she'd been hit with a
shovel sometime in her youth and it had healed poorly.
"Your presence is required."

Remain silent, I tell myself. *Don't let them get to you.
They're just doing Nightglade's bidding.*

But the way the guard gleefully ties my hands
behind my back, so tight they already feel like the
circulation's being cut off, I suspect she enjoys cruelty
as much as her King.

The halls of the Unseelie castle are bustling with

movement, but I notice the way most keep their heads down, only darting quick looks here and there. They're nervous. This is the seventh month in a row they've prepared for a new moon coronation ceremony.

Will it be their last?

I stumble behind the guard, my fingertips numb. If only I could get my hands to light on fire, but the bindings make that impossible. Even if I could, where would I go? I'm in the heart of the Unseelie kingdom, my birth father won't even know to look for me until tomorrow, when I don't meet him at the Reflecting Pool, and the one who I thought loved me has betrayed me.

The awful part? I love Quince, even now. Even after knowing he had been searching out the Eldest for Nightglade, and not to help the rest of us defeat Nightglade, like I'd thought.

Am I weak for loving him still?

The morning light assails my eyes and I instinctively move to shield them, then remember my hands are bound behind my back. I consider trying to realm-hop, now that I'm away from the Iron Prison, but my energy is low after a sleepless night and when I step, all that happens is I move one step closer to my destiny. My doom.

"The King!" someone calls from across the clearing.

All bow toward a banner as it unfurls from the branches of two enormous pines behind a raised platform. The goosebumps stand at attention on my arms. It's the same platform I saw in the memory Jaila shared with me. But all the blood has been washed from it, leaving no evidence of the six fae who have died so far in Nightglade's twisted pursuit of a fae worthy of the Unseelie Queen's crown. The wooden planks have a freshly scrubbed appearance, all traces of blood bleached away. On the banner, some painter has taken the time to paint an enormous picture of Nightglade striking a heroic pose.

"Now!" I hear.

"Not again." The guard who has led me out here groans. "Every damn new moon, another random assortment of FREEDOM fae tries to attack."

"Should I sound the alarm?" asks another guard with a plumage of white wings. I recognize her as Nena, the guard who had been stationed in front of the Unseelie castle when Jaila and I had snuck inside the Iron Prison to bust Quince out.

A stray question pops in my head. Have she and Ash made copies of Cam's portrait of them yet? Have they shown it to their friends? How funny would it be if Cam gained fame in Elfaeme for their artwork?

"I already did." Ash shifts a spiked wooden club from one hand to the other. "We'll have backup soon. In the meantime…shall we?"

My focus turns inward, centered on the point in the small of my back where the guard has tied my hands. If I can't realm-hop out of here, maybe I can loosen the binding just enough.

Pandemonium breaks out. My guard seems to

have forgotten about me, or decided I won't be able to go anywhere fast with my hands tied behind my back. I watch as she dashes into the fray on her insectoid, jointed legs, with Nena, Ash, and other armed Unseelie guards, all shouting "For the King!"

I inch backward, but even as cautiously as I'm going, I still trip over a rock and fall onto my wings. My elbows scream at the awkward angle and the spot on my right wing where the fachan had attacked spasms. Falling had an unintended effect, though. I groan and roll onto my side, noting how the sensation of pins and needles has infused my hands from wrists to fingertips. The rope, tied tight to prevent me from activating my fire, has loosened the tiniest amount. But it might be enough.

Panting, I struggle to my feet, which is a lot harder without the use of hands, and back up from the fighting in the middle of the snow-covered clearing. Flakes of snow drift down on the frenzy, but even without the guards' backup appearing yet, I can tell this is a losing battle for FREEDOM. Pity. A part of me kind of hoped they'd succeed where I have failed spectacularly in stopping Nightglade.

Of course, then I'd have to deal with getting the crowns back from FREEDOM before the time ran out, but that would be a problem for another day that won't happen.

FREEDOM, or rather, the ten or so members of FREEDOM who had attacked the clearing, are falling back. Many have blood dripping from their faces and one even holds his own dismembered arm in the opposite hand.

The edge of the platform hits me in the back beneath my wings and I wince.

"I'm going to get so many splinters from this."

With that cheerful thought in mind, I set to work rubbing the rope around my hands against the rough edges of the wooden platform.

My goal isn't to fray the rope completely. That would take longer than I have. But if I can loosen my binding, I'll be able to ignite my fists.

What then?

I haven't thought that far in advance.

Sweat breaks out on my brow as I scrape my bindings up and down against the platform.

Then…the slightest give, more pins and needles rushes into my hands.

I take that burst of feeling and imagine the flames crackling across my knuckles and to my wrists.

The smell of burning rope, cloth, and skin reaches my nose and I realize I'm screaming, not like anyone can hear me over the chaos.

My fists may be fire resistant, but the rest of me isn't.

I feel the ropes crumble away and I breathe through the pain searing across my lower back. Okay, Eevee, what next?

I turn and spot the banner of Nightglade in all its garish glory, look down at the fire still crackling across my knuckles, then back up at the banner.

It may be stupid, but what else do I have to lose?

I skirt around the platform, my stomach twisting when I think of Ilinor bent over it, blood pooling around her lifeless body, and stand at the base of the banner, looking up at it.

A painted Nightglade stares down at me, his gray eyes, even in painted form, filled with pride.

My hands flare and I touch my palms to the banner.

Flames hiss and sizzle, as Nightglade's painted likeness goes up in smoke. Literally.

A dark pleasure settles in my chest. "Take that," I say.

Merciless, lifeless laughter echoes throughout the whole clearing.

My skin immediately feels like someone is scraping it with tons of tiny razors, or like someone sprayed me with thousands of drops of acid.

Looking away from the burning banner, I see all of Nightglade's guards have clapped their hands over their ears.

The remaining FREEDOM fae are all collapsing on the ground, mouths open in silent screams.

Oh. I bring a trembling hand to my mouth. So is mine.

I bring a trembling hand. Wait, no, I already did that.

Shaking my head to clear it only makes the

world spin, everything blurs and divides until I'm looking at two clearings, two sets of FREEDOM fae, two sets of Unseelie guards.

Two Nightglades strolling into the fray, heads thrown back, mouths wide open, purple and black and green magic whirling in them like swirling voids.

Both Nightglades make it to the center of the clearing and close their mouths. The abhorrent laughter fades, and the two Nightglades merge into one, as do the rest of the fae in the clearing, but Nightglade is different somehow. He looks larger, more menacing. More like an evil King than ever before.

"You've failed. Again." His voice is forbidding, even though, compared to the horrendous sound of the laughter, it's as quiet as a whisper. "Nothing will stop the coronation ceremony."

At his gesture, the Unseelie guards who had been covering their ears lower their hands and reach toward the members of FREEDOM still in the clearing. I count six, which means four either escaped or were killed.

The FREEDOM fae are led away from the clearing at spearpoint, looking disoriented as they stagger and lurch out of sight.

Nightglade's face finds mine, then looks at the charred banner behind me. I glance over my shoulder to see the top edges still wreathed in flames. Most of it has become a pile of ash on the ground, gray blanketing the white snow.

When I look back at Nightglade, it isn't the

richness of his velvety robe that catches my attention, or the simple, gold circlet on his head, indicating his royal status. The Unseelie King's crown will replace it during the ceremony tonight.

No. Instead, what I notice is the look of pure hatred in his eyes when he looks at me.

Is it me he sees? Or Maeve?

Or both?

The grasshopper-like guard who had led me out here kneels at Nightglade's feet. "My King, I have failed you. I ignored my duty to the prisoner to fight those FREEDOM fae. My life is yours to do with as you will."

Nightglade doesn't take his gaze from me.

"Make sure all the rebellion is stamped out of our special prisoner before the coronation ceremony this evening."

She raises a gleeful face to Nightglade, her lopsided smile wide. "With pleasure."

Another Month, Another Attempted Coronation

The scent of pine sap permeates my nostrils. I blink groggily, the events of the morning like a hazy dream.

My right elbow throbs when I use it to push myself up. The thin fabric of the shirt and pants they've dressed me in don't do much to keep out the cold; even with my Unseelie blood, I feel winter's sting on my skin. I grimace, dried drool and blood cracking on my cheeks with the movement. I don't want to open my eyes, because when I do, I'll know exactly how much time is left before Nightglade and the loyal fae of his Court complete the new moon ritual and place the

Unseelie Queen's crown on my head.

Cracking one eye open the barest slit, I force down the moan wanting to escape my lips. Sundown. Red rays of the last light of day burn through the boughs of the pine trees. The scene is beautiful, picturesque, and utterly at odds with what I know is to come next: either my death, or my forced Queenship, followed immediately by imprisonment.

"Eevee."

Wrath, confusion, hurt, and betrayal all burn through my veins and numb the pain. I turn toward the sound of the whisper. The cage I'm in, so much like the cages I saw at the Winter Solstice Festival half a year ago, sways beneath me with the movement.

And all my harsh words fizzle in puffs of smoke.

"Oh, Quince." My hands fly to my mouth, covering the cry of horror. "What has he done to you?"

Quince's face is a mottled mess of purple bruises, his eyes barely visible because of how puffy his cheeks have become. The front of his clothes are stained with blood, as I'm sure mine are, too. But his wings, they—

I can't bring myself to look at the space where they used to be.

Dry heaving only reminds my brain of every single place Nightglade's thugs, led by my favorite grasshopper-like guard, kicked and punched me in the torso after I had burned his banner this morning.

Which, in comparison, is nothing.

"He didn't like what I told him."

Quince clutches his arms across his stomach, his whole body shaking. Now I see that any part of his skin not colored by bruising is deathly pale and shiny with sweat.

"I did what he asked." Quince talks so quietly, his face turned to the ground, I wonder if he's talking to me anymore at all. "I did what he asked. But it wasn't enough. He let my parents go, like he promised, but he made them stay until…" He gulps and shudders. "Made them stay until his–" His face spasms in pain. "Until they saw my wings–" Growling in frustration, he buries his head in his hands.

I'm seized with hatred so strong I can taste it like molten metal in my mouth. Or maybe that's the blood. I spit and heave. When I'm finally able to speak, I don't know what to say.

Quince is watching me, still trembling. "Eevee, I'm sorry. You have no idea how sorry I am. I just wanted to save my parents, they'd suffered enough, and Nightglade, he made it sound like all I needed to do was go find out some information about the coronation and bring it to him and that'd be it. He never mentioned anything about capturing you or using you as his next coronation victim." His dark eyes, as they meet mine, are totally devoid of any of their previous sparkle, and that, more than anything else, breaks my heart like a rock shattering glass. He continues, his voice cracking with emotion. "I swear I didn't know. I thought he'd want to avoid using you in the ceremony since you look so much like Maeve and would only remind him of his failures. I miscalculated, and–" He groans, his strength spent on whispered words.

"You don't need to apologize." And he doesn't. Seeing him caged and wingless brings a new clarity to me. We all make choices, and each choice has consequences. Quince chose to find that information for Nightglade on the promise of his parents' safety. Had I been in his place, I probably would have made the same choice to save my mom and dad, too. Not Maeve and Aspen, as much as I owe to them for ensuring I grow up away from Nightglade and the politics of Elfaeme, but my adopted parents, with all their human affection and anxiety and insistence we do things together as the Ackers, like camping in tents for days in order to "bond." Thinking of them is so painful it takes my breath away. All I want, more than anything in the world, is to hug Todd and Penny Acker one last time. Because soon, in less time than I'm comfortable with, I'll die or be imprisoned seemingly forever, for longer than their lifetimes at least.

Quince is unresponsive, his knuckles white against the dark fabric of his shirt.

"Seriously, Quince. You don't have to apologize. I was mad at you when I found out, but mostly because I was hurt, and–"

"Yes, I do have to apologize." His shoulders hunch forward. "Because if given the choice, I'd do it again."

I reach out, careful not to let my arm touch the

iron bars. Quince hesitates, then reaches a hand out, too, and our fingertips brush.

"You made your choice. And your parents…?"

"Safe." Relief permeates every fiber of his being. "Nightglade finally let them go this morning."

The thought crosses my mind, briefly, that his parents wouldn't have wanted their only son to make this kind of sacrifice for them. Yet I can see why he did. After so many years of protecting him through personal sacrifices of their own, he only wanted to do the same in return.

Pressing our fingertips together, we watch silently as below us the forest clearing fills with fae. Their footsteps are soft on the powdery, snow-covered pine needles, and their voices hush as they look up at our two cages. I can practically hear their thoughts: *So, Maeve's daughter is to be this month's sacrifice.* Or perhaps there are some who hold out hope that this month will succeed where others had not, and they think: *Maeve's daughter, will she be our Queen?*

Some fae, wearing robes of midnight blue dotted with silvery stars, circle below us. The song I remember hearing from the memory Jaila shared with me floats through the air as first one of the robed fae, and then another, sings it.

> "When day turns to night
> and the new moon's time is ending,
> place the crowns on the heads
> of the new Unseelie sovereign.

Thus the Unseelie will be protected,
thus their new leaders will be filled
with power to use for the good of their folk
as the crowns' purpose is willed."

Quince's fingers drop from mine and he huddles, curled up on his side in the center of his cage. He looks so small without his big, feathery wings with their glossy black feathers. I loved to run my fingers through those feathers, and I feel a pang of loss for him so sharp it's like a dozen papercuts across my heart. He'll never experience the rush of wind through his wings anymore, nor the intimacy of someone's fingers combing through them.

"When Elfaeme stood on the brink of devastation,
three fae united to create the crowns.
Two for Seelie, two for Unseelie,
and two for the wild fae, which they drowned.

The Seelie crowns choose their leaders
at the height of the moon's luminescence
and the Unseelie crowns select theirs
when the moon hides her face.

So the cycles continue:
leaders are chosen, and cast down
by the crowns, whose sole purpose
is to protect their own."

Fear freezes me in place. The cage is lowering. I want to call out to Quince, but my vocal cords don't cooperate. They're frozen, too, and all I can do is look at Quince's bloodied, wingless back as I'm lowered inch by inch to my fate below. How do I say goodbye to the one who so happily showed me around Elfaeme, who took on my quest as if it were his own, who saw me for who I was right from the beginning and loved me for it, imperfections and impatience and Shakespeare obsession and all?

I suppose Shakespeare does have words of farewell I can use for this moment. My lips form Juliet's words to Romeo, though no sound escapes them. "Good night, good night! Parting is such sweet sorrow." The last time I had referenced this quote with Quince was in a text, when I was being overly dramatic. Now, though, I feel it keenly.

And then my cage lowers some more and my view of Quince is gone. I stand, my knees creaking, and my legs shaking with fear and adrenaline. But I stay upright, my chin held high.

"The wild fae, who chose long ago
to throw their crowns in the deeps of the sea
show allegiance to both courts and none at all.
Their freedom comes with a fee."

Shuddering to a halt, the cage hits the ground, puffs of powdery snow wafting up around me in a cold, crystalline circle. I pitch forward, and my hands grip the iron bars. I immediately let go, my body suffused with waves of revulsion. My palms tingle like I'd slept all night on them, both numb and stinging at the same time.

> "Four crowns remain, forged of silver and gold,
> imbued with the need to defend,
> they will choose leaders from the fae who dare
> to place them upon their heads."

The singers start again with "When day turns to night…" and I clench my hands to my side to stop their quaking. I meet the eyes of one of the robed fae, raising my chin defiantly again until she looks away and continues to sing, guilt swimming in her brown eyes. I know I look like Maeve, the Unseelie Queen she remembers, in the shape of my cheeks and the tilt of my eyes. The only pronounced difference between our faces are the markings on our temples. Where the flowers on Maeve's temples were blood red, mine are a fiery orange. I look at the robed fae as they sing, hoping viciously that all of them, as they gaze upon me, are reminded of the Queen who they drove from her own court because they couldn't stand up to their King and his obsession for Unseelie power.

They finish the song a second time. I had never heard the song in full before, just the bits and pieces from Jaila's memory. Though thinking of the memory Jaila shared makes me think of Jaila herself. At least

Jaila had the sense to get the heck out of Dodge while she had the chance. Maybe she somehow escaped the gwyllyon's fog and is back in New Zealand. For someone who's spent most of her short life in one Court or another, she seemed to talk fondly of New Zealand.

After two more rounds of the song, the robed fae stop their circling and part to allow Nightglade to step forward.

He's dressed head to toe in clothing of the deepest black studded with diamonds, like someone had taken the night sky and transformed it into garments. On his head is the Unseelie King's crown. The other, the Queen's crown, the one I remember from Jaila's memory, lies on the same pillow of midnight blue. This time, though, it's not the same bearer who brings the crown forward, and I wonder what happened to the fae who had skin like a twilit sky, if he was one of the victims from the months we were with the gnomes of Curious Caverns. This evening, the crown rests in the talon-tipped hands of a fae I've seen in my nightmares since last fall, confirming what I've always suspected about that night Quince and I had been "saved" from fae attackers by Nightglade.

The Unseelie King himself had set up the ambush so he could come in and "save the day." An early, manipulative ploy to get on my good side when he thought there was a chance I may be his legitimate daughter.

Anger seethes in my gut.

The fae bows to Nightglade, his dragonfly wings trembling in the air behind him like he can barely contain his excitement.

"My lord…" His voice is thin. Last fall, he didn't talk at all during the ambush. Now I see why. I don't think I would've been as intimidated by him if he had started talking. "The Unseelie Queen's crown is ready for a new wearer." His glowing orbs of eyes glance over at me and I grip my arm where his talon had ripped my skin, leaving a long, jagged scar as a reminder of that night. At the hungry, predatory look in his eyes, I drop my hand and scowl at him, which only makes him smile wider, revealing needle-like teeth.

The entire crowd drops to their knees. "The time has come. The crown will choose. The time has come. The crown will choose." They chant over and over, their voices throbbing in my ears.

Nightglade lifts the crown from its pillow and holds it aloft. The silver gleams like moonlight on this moonless night, but as beautiful as it is, I eye it with growing unease. So far it's claimed the lives of six fae, starting with Ilinor in January, deeming none of them worthy to take on the role of ruling the Unseelie Court with Nightglade. And did he stop, take time to think of another strategy? No. Each new moon, he chose another to sacrifice. Because no one, whether it be his own daughter, his most trusted advisor, or the daughter of his ex-wife, is safe. You're in his life until he can use your death for something better. My odds are not great.

"I'm sorry."

I look up to see Quince, his face screwed up in pain, gazing down at me, tears in his eyes.

All that we've worked for: finding my birth parents, thwarting Nightglade, it's all led to this moment. And there's no going back.

"I know," I mouth up at him.

The lock on my cage opens with a clunk and talon fingers grips my arm with steely strength, yanking me out onto the snowy ground. Pine needles dig into my bare feet, but I hardly feel the cold when my whole body is numb with fear. Tendrils of mist curl around my ankles as I stride forward, refusing to give anyone, especially Nightglade, the satisfaction of seeing me dragged toward him.

"The time has come. The crown will choose." The chanting grows to a feverish pitch as the distance between myself and Nightglade shortens. Two more steps and I'll be at the base of the platform, directly beneath the crown he holds aloft. Exactly where I had seen Ilinor's body lay lifeless upon it.

"Eevee!" A voice calls above the chanting, from somewhere in the back of the clearing. A few of the fae falter, sitting upright from their prostrate positions to glance around.

My heart quickens and warmth floods my limbs. I can't believe it. I had told them to stay away, but...

"E!" Another voice shouts from the far left, somewhere in the trees, and tears fill my eyes. Cam and Maggie are here somewhere, somehow.

At the sensation of delight in my mind, I

understand how they found me. Scamp must have followed Quince and I as we escaped from FREEDOM and alerted Sean and Shannon we had gone to the Unseelie castle.

Now the chanting completely stalls. Nightglade's face hardens in fury. As the crowd looks around for the source of the voices, Nightglade lowers the crown, tucking it to his chest, and strides away from the platform, a wolf on the hunt.

The vice-like grip on my arm tightens. "Get away from her, filthy human."

A voice I've longed to hear for months whispers in my ear. "Cover your ears. No time to explain."

"Ames…"

Talon fingers pulls me away from my sister, who holds up her phone, makes eye contact with me, and shouts, "NOW!"

In the process of clapping my hands to my ears, I destabilize talon fingers, who still holds my arm tight, and we both stumble.

From three locations around the clearing, the ringing of bells resonates, and I'm immediately grateful for Amelia's warning, because even with my hands covering my ears, I have an intense urge to rip my ears off at the sound. The crowd descends into chaos; fae run every which way, hands clutched over their ears a second too late.

The bells keep ringing. Amelia holds her phone out toward the panicking fae, a look of determination on her round-cheeked face and satisfaction glinting in her eyes.

Keeping my hands over my ears, I wrench myself away from talon fingers, who is writhing on the ground next to me, moaning, his dragonfly wings trembling. The contents of his pockets, some money, black objects that look disturbingly like dead flies, and the keys to the cages, empty out around his thrashing body.

I stumble toward Amelia. "What now?" I ask loudly, hardly able to hear myself over the bells and pandemonium.

She nods to something behind me and I turn. Out of the forest strides an enormous wyvern, at least the size of a Clydesdale, if a Clydesdale also had a ten-foot-long tail attached to it. I hadn't realized how big Fearghas had grown when I saw him flying last night. Riding atop him are Sean and Shannon, their ears covered with protective ear muffs. They wave, and seeing Shannon's cheerful face and Sean's feral-yet-comforting grin lifts my spirits more than I thought possible after the last few hours.

Fearghas either doesn't care or doesn't notice the fae flying and running around him as he makes his way toward me. I admire his single-mindedness, until...

"Look out!" I shout, terror streaking through me.

Sean and Shannon's faces crease with confusion. Shannon indicates his ear muffs and shrugs, mouthing, "What?"

But it's too late. It's the night of the new moon, and Nightglade is still the King of the Unseelie, which means his power is strong tonight, as is his connection with the Unseelie lands. With a dismissive wave of an arm, Nightglade calls on the power of the trees, bending them to his will so their branches stretch and grow with lightning speed, wrapping around Sean, Shannon, and Fearghas until they are enveloped in layer upon layer of sap-covered pine boughs.

A shout of surprise distracts me from the sinking horror I feel at seeing Sean and Shannon so easily captured. I sneak a glance in Amelia's direction and my heart sinks even further, the little bit of hope I'd had at the sight of their appearance now completely extinguished. Pine branches are wrapped around her legs, holding her tight to the spot, and are creeping up her torso. The wispy mist of a few minutes ago is now a pool of fog at our feet.

"Stop the bells." Nightglade's voice is calm yet strained, and I think, "Good." At least I know the sound of the bells is affecting him, if only slightly.

Amelia shakes her head, her brown curls flying every which way, and the branches around her abdomen tighten. Her eyes well with tears.

"Now, if you won't do it when I ask, then I'll have to take matters into my own hands, like I did with the other two."

The other two?

Oh no.

I can't see them, but I think of the voices calling

my names. I hadn't believed it when I heard them, but Cam and Maggie are here. After I told them to stay away. What brought them back?

"My friends," I croak. "What did you do to them?"

"Oh, they're not dead yet," he says over his shoulder. "I just destroyed their damned contraptions and made sure they have a good view of you for the coronation."

He looms over Amelia, slipping the phone from her grasp and throwing it up in the air. Tree branches shoot out and spear it to smithereens, sending shattered bits of her phone raining down on her head.

With a lazy twirl of his fingers, Nightglade wraps the rest of Amelia's body with branches until all that's showing are her wide, doe-like eyes.

"Eevee, run!" Quince shouts from above.

But what's the point?

I sink to the ground, the cold fog swirling around me at the sudden movement.

What's the point?

Nightglade takes a deep breath, his cold eyes trained on me. "I'll deal with you later, Quincent Florentz. After you've witnessed this human-loving, bastard child of my traitorous wife put the crown on her own head."

"No!" Quince's cage rocks back and forth as he tries to get out. "Eevee, don't do it!"

Nightglade steps toward me, holding it out. "Be a good girl and put on your crown."

I raise my head and look, not to Nightglade, but to Amelia behind him. Her eyes are terrified and pleading. The only thought I can latch onto is that at least if I'm going to die, the last thing I'll see is my sister's eyes. And isn't that selfish of me? I should be worried about what will happen to Amelia after I die.

But as I stand and reach for the crown, something makes me pause. Amelia's eyes are harder to see than before. Aren't they?

I squint. It's like…

And then, understanding dawns on me.

It's like they're getting lost in the fog.

The Gwyllyon's Revenge

A gut-wrenching, heart-breaking wail pierces the night, announcing the gwyllyon's approach.

Every fae in the clearing, even Nightglade, freezes in horror.

I'm unable to look away from Nightglade's face. His stern appearance has sagged at the sound of the gwyllyon's cry. The Unseelie Queen's crown drops from his hands, but he doesn't seem to have noticed. He plays with one of his many rings, a silver piece with a sapphire.

The gwyllyon wails again, her cry sounding closer than before.

My brain is as foggy as this clearing. Maybe this is how it ends, with the whole Unseelie Court getting lost in the fog together, fated to wander the misty paths forever.

She arrives, exactly as I remember her. Do all gwyllyon look alike, or is this the same one?

Her empty eye sockets are trained on Nightglade.

She lifts a skeletal arm, pointing her bony index finger at Nightglade. Mouth open wide in a perpetual shriek of heartache, she advances on him, floating above the snowy ground, her gauzy garments fluttering in a ghostly breeze.

For the first time, I hear words in her howling.

"You! You took everything from me!"

Nightglade commands the trees like before, branches shooting toward the gwyllyon, but she turns as insubstantial as the fog which announced her arrival and re-materializes, looking angrier than ever.

He throws his head back, his arms out wide, and pulls more and more from the trees around us, until all the fae who are left in the clearing are pressed to the frigid ground in an attempt to escape getting whipped by the branches.

It does nothing.

Finally, the gwyllyon reaches him, her empty eye sockets trained on one of the ringed fingers on his left hand.

He stops drawing on his power to the land, his face ashen, and the branches recede. When he glances at the hand her face is pointed toward, he looks as though he might faint.

I never thought I'd see the Unseelie King look scared. But now, he's terrified.

He cowers before her, stuffing his left hand in his robe to keep it out of her sight. "We can fix this," he says, in a voice unusually meek for him. "You–you can come back to Court. We'll find a way to fix this state you're in, and you can live here at my side–"

"Too late!" she yowls. "Too late! Too late!"

Her words dissolve into a howl of anger, and noxious yellow gas streams out of her mouth, settling into a toxic cloud around the Unseelie King.

Then, the fog grows so thick I can't even see the hand I hold in front of my face.

This is it. We'll be stuck in the fog forever.

I sink to my knees, hot tears dripping from my chin into the snow.

The New Unseelie King and Queen

The fog clears.

And beneath the light of the stars, over a snowy landscape in a pine forest, all the fae gathered here tonight gasp as one.

Nightglade is gone.

In the place where he had cowered, where the gwyllyon had faced him, pointing her moss-covered, skeletal finger in accusation, is nothing more than a pile of his clothing, a few sparkling pieces of jewelry he'd been wearing, and the crown of the Unseelie King, which sits atop it all with a reddish glow around it, the Queen's crown nearby where it had dropped from his hands, also glowing.

Huh, glowing crowns. That's new. I can't take my eyes off of them, the way the light pulses. What does it mean if the crowns glow?

Jaila darts forward to the pile of clothes on the ground, either unperturbed by the crowns or choosing to ignore them, and I catch a glint of silver and sapphire as she pockets one of the rings Nightglade had been wearing.

She stands and catches my eye, and I understand. She came with the gwyllyon. Her mother. Jaila had risked getting lost in her mother's endless fog of despair, on the off chance she could convince the gwyllyon to come after Nightglade directly.

But…why isn't anyone yelling at her for riffling in the former Unseelie King's clothes? Yes, he's her father–or *was* her father–but that doesn't necessarily give her the right to paw through his final wardrobe.

Her wink tells me all I need to know. *'My invisibility isn't all or nothing. I can choose who sees me and who doesn't.'* She's made herself visible only to me.

With a wave goodbye, she dashes away into the trees, deftly avoiding any of the fae gathered around, until the dark of the night swallows her up.

And then the collective silence is broken by none other than a human.

Maggie drops out of the tree she had been trapped in by Nightglade, and saunters forward. Without any magic to make her invisible to the eye, the crowd watches as she bends down to meet my eyes.

"You okay, E?"

I nod, but I'm not sure if I'm okay or numb. Nightglade's gone. Just like that.

She taps her chin, eyeing me. "No, you're not. But you will be."

Turning to the surrounding fae, she holds her cell phone held out like a sword. It doesn't work anymore, but they look wary of it anyway. "Alrighty then, anyone gonna tell me why the crowns are glowing?"

"They're floating, too!" Shannon shouts. For the first time since I've known him, there's more trepidation than glee in the way his words quiver.

Maybe that's because the crowns are…

I blink, rub my eyes, then look again. The crowns, Nightglades, and my mothers, the one that was supposed to be placed on my head before the gwyllyon intervened, float in the air, both glowing a luminous red.

"What's going on, Eevee?" Cam asks. I hadn't noticed them come up behind Maggie. Their eyes are wide, and I can see the glow from the crowns reflected in them.

"I dunno, maybe ask…" I pause, then bitter joy jolts through me. Quince! Oh, Quince. If only Nightglade had waited one more day to torture him, if only if only if only.

I fly up to where he's caged.

"You'll need this!" I look down to see Amelia lobbing the keys to the cages that talon fingers had used. He must have run off when Nightglade disappeared, or gotten lost in the gwyllyon's fog, because I don't see him. Good riddance. With a quick (albeit graceless) dive, I catch the keys, then fly the rest of the way to Quince, my heart alternating between gasps of joy and relief and sorrow.

His hand reaches through the bars to grab mine, and I clasp my fingers in his.

"We did it," I whisper.

He cracks a smile, his black eyes glittering with more mirth than I've seen in a long time. "Did we? I think if it weren't for Jaila's forethought to find her mother…"

The gwyllyon's pain and rage echo in my mind. Nightglade was the source of so much hurt. And ultimately, it was the one who he hurt most deeply who caused his timely end.

"Okay, so we had some help." My grin matches the one on his face. "Now let's unlock this cage and get you down from here."

"*Get* me down?" He raises an eyebrow. "I can get down myself."

"It's a twenty foot drop!" I protest. "And–with your wings–"

He turns, and forces me to see what my eyes have been avoiding since flying up here.

Except his wings are *there*.

"How?" I demand as he turns back around.

"Fae glamour." His demeanor suddenly resembles a thunderstorm. "Plus some well-worded, binding promises not to mention it."

"We did say we had family members with the ability," Shannon calls up to me. Below, both crowns are now hovering, circling around the heads of the leery fae, as if looking for prey.

"Are you going to unlock the cage now, or…?"

"Oh, right." I fit the keys in the lock, my fingertips numbing as they touch the iron. How did talon fingers handle this every time?

The door swings open and Quince flies out, tackling me midair. We plummet a few feet, and then we're soaring, higher and higher, spinning through the air, the wintery breeze like cold kisses on my skin. Quince's arms pull me to him until my face is pressed against his chest and all I smell is pine woods and mountain springs. It smells like home. For an adoptee, my idea of home has always been transient. I soar in the haze of his smell, his dark eyes grazing down my face and stopping at my mouth, and I think how in the end, it really is true, the cliché. Home is where your heart is.

My thoughts are interrupted by his lips on mine, sending electricity through my whole body, igniting my blood until I'm light-headed.

It's seconds, minutes, hours, days of bliss in one kiss. Time passes and stands still, all I feel are his lips on mine, his arms around my waist and in my hair.

He stops and I open my eyes to see him smiling at me.

"What?"

"I'm so glad I saw you, back in the Duluth High

office with Jeeves–"

"Mr. Jives."

"–last September. You've made my life better, Evelyn Gray Acker."

I gesture down to the cage he'd been in, swinging from a branch far below. "One could argue I made it worse for a while."

"Hey." He places a finger under my chin. "Sometimes things have to get worse before they get better. And if it weren't for what you helped set in motion, Nightglade would still be here. Now, the Unseelie Court can reset and Elfaeme can work on rebalancing itself."

My mind fills in what he doesn't say aloud: now, fae like him, who are of both Courts and neither, will have more of a voice in the places they call home, whether that be in the Seelie or Unseelie Courts or with the wild fae. Or in the human realm.

His eyes are hopeful as he looks down at me, and I don't hesitate at all or hide behind Shakespeare's words when I blurt out, "I love you."

He freezes. Only his wings behind him move, beating languidly in the air to keep us hovering in place. Under the intensity of his gaze, I find myself babbling. "I should've said it sooner, I should've said it when you said it to me last night, but I was afraid, it was easier to hide my feelings, to focus on other things, but I wish–"

Leaning closer until his mouth is almost touching mine, he says in a low, gravelly voice, "You have no idea how much I needed to hear that."

And then the little space that was left between us is gone.

"Whenever you're done making out, something weird's going on down here!" Maggie's voice floats upward, thin and wispy on the wind.

"Do we have to go down yet?" I whisper to Quince.

He dips us so we're upside-down, facing the ground, a dizzying hundred or so feet in the air, and dropping fast. A shriek escapes my lips before I remember I have wings and can prevent myself from crashing if I need to, but I cling to Quince anyway, relishing in our closeness that, until the gwyllyon came and took care of Nightglade, I thought I'd never experience again. The scene on the ground has changed since we left the land behind to kiss mid-air (something that's become a bit of a tradition for us, not that I'm complaining). The crowd of fae, which had previously been a disordered mass of confusion in the wake of Nightglade's sudden disappearance, has formed itself into a circle around two fae who are cast in the glow of the crowns. Quince halts our freefall, turning us upright, and we exchange a look.

"We should maybe see what that's all about."

Reluctantly, he separates himself from me and we fly the rest of the way down, hand in hand.

Maggie and Cam's faces are both lined with anxiety from where they stand, just outside the circle. Maggie's mouth is turned down, and Cam's hands are shoved in the front pocket of their hoodie.

When we land, I see why.

The two fae in the center of the circle, the ones bathed in the red glow of the crowns, are Sean and Shannon.

There's a hush in the crowd as they all watch the crowns. Sean and Shannon, for some reason, are ignoring the crowns floating above their heads, their eyes instead locked on each other's. Some kind of intense telepathic discussion must be going on, because their stances are combative. Sean's arms are crossed firmly across his chest, Shannon's are on his hips.

"How long have they been like this?" I ask Cam out of the corner of my mouth.

"Not long." They breathe out slowly. "Any idea–" Their eyes widen and they point to Sean and Shannon.

I watch as Sean's arms unfold and he gives the tiniest of shrugs. "Fine. Why not?"

Shannon's smile is radiant. "Excellent."

In tandem, they reach up to grab the crowns floating above them, and without any pomp and circumstance, plunk them on their heads.

For the second time this evening, we all collectively gasp.

The glow intensifies, radiating out from Sean and Shannon in waves, faster and faster, until, all at once, it goes out and the clearing is plunged into darkness.

Panic grips my heart as I wait for my eyes to adjust. With the lack of any visuals, my brain kicks in and replays the memories Jaila shared with me. The blood trickling down Ilinor's head to pool around her cheeks, her lifeless eyes. The air around us is full of murmurs and buzzing whispers like insects.

And then a white light blazes from where Sean and Shannon are standing.

They're standing.

Not dead.

No blood to be seen.

The breath I didn't realize I was holding rushes out.

"Well, I'm not dead!" Shannon announces unnecessarily, raising his hand, which holds a shining ball of ice, above his head.

"Nor am I." Sean smoothes his shirt, though I didn't see any wrinkles that needed smoothing out.

"You know what this means?" Quince mutters. The look on his face is equal parts apprehension and amusement.

One of the robed fae strides forward. She pulls the hood back from her face and kneels in front of Sean and Shannon.

The entire crowd follows suit, even Maggie and Cam.

Even Quince and I.

"You may rise."

I've never heard Shannon's voice have such a regal air to it before. And yet, it fits him.

The fae who had knelt first turns to us. "The crowns have chosen, and the Unseelie Court has its new rulers. All hail King Shannon and Queen Sean!"

As one, the crowd shouts, "Hail!"

"Should we be worried at all?" I ask.

Quince regards his cousins. Shannon waves at the crowd merrily with his free hand, the other still holding the icy ball of light aloft. His King crown already sits at a jaunty angle on his head. Sean stands next to him, erect and dignified, his Queen crown sitting on his head so evenly it could be used as a straight edge.

"Maybe." Quince grins. "But I guarantee they'll keep the Unseelie Court on its toes."

I Get a New Job

The open courtyard in Sean and Shannon's revamped palace grounds is a masterpiece of artistic endeavor, but I have eyes only for one thing amidst the ice sculptures and twinkling lights, and that's the stone figure of my birth mother. A crew of fae had moved her out of the caves, where she had been stored after the first new moon ceremony this year, and into the open for all to see. It serves as a reminder to the Unseelie of what they had and then lost due to their inaction, Sean explained to me. By choosing to do nothing to oust Nightglade, they lost a beloved queen who had been forced to live the last couple of decades of her life in hiding, protected only by her trust in one fae: Folsom.

My gaze roams over the immobile figure of my birth mother, my already thin patience evaporating like a puddle on a summer's day.

Maeve's face is frozen in an expression of longing and torment, her mouth slightly open. Her last words to me play on repeat in my head.

"Don't. Don't say it."

I hadn't realized at the time what she had given up when she accepted the crown. Motherhood. A family of her own. Sean and Shannon wouldn't tell me what they had to give up when they became King and Queen. No one knows what Nightglade forfeited, though often my bitter thoughts suspect he gave up his heart, his ability to empathize with anyone. How else could he have willingly risked his own daughter's life?

The choice Maeve faced when she found out she was pregnant with me was an impossible one. She couldn't give up the crown. To do so would be to trigger the curse of the revoked crown, and so few fae had taken that risk, the lore was spotty about what would happen to her. She couldn't risk it, and Aspen didn't want her to risk it. But to keep me was also impossible. With Nightglade growing increasingly power-hungry and garnering loyalty with the factions of the Unseelie Court who frequently preyed on humans and any fae who were not affiliated with the Unseelie, she knew my life would always be at risk in the place she'd called home for centuries.

So they came up with a plan, her and Aspen,

and when she could no longer hide her pregnancy, they fled, with Folsom helping lay false trails and keep their location secret from everyone.

I sit at her feet and lean on her legs, resting my head against her thigh. The stone bites like ice against my cheek, but I leave it there.

Somehow, Aspen convinced Maeve to let humans adopt me. It'd be safest, he argued. Nightglade's power, like Maeve's, was connected to his Court. The further from it he went, the less he had. If he dared go to the human realm, he'd have no more power than the average fae does. Maeve knew her husband better than anyone. She knew he'd never give up the power the Unseelie Crown gave him, even temporarily.

But Maeve, she did give up that power. She chose to live in Seelie territory, knowing her magic there was limited. She chose to have me adopted by Todd and Penny Acker, so even my birth record would be human.

And in the end, before she turned to stone, she was no more magical than the average clod of dirt. She was simply Maeve: a fae who risked her life for love, who escaped her fate as long as she could.

Between Nightglade invoking the curse of the revoked crown and my reappearance at the moment's Maeve power was weakest, it was too much. Her guard came down. Not a lot, just the tiniest crack in her heart, the smallest of "what-ifs" whispered in her mind, but it was enough.

The curse took hold. She hoped for what the crown had taken from her, and it sensed her desire to be a mother, to have a family.

"I'm sorry," I say to her, looking up at her face, her outstretched arms. The Eldest hadn't thought there was any way to reverse the curse of the revoked crown. Hearing their words was like how I imagine it would feel if I had a piano dropped on me unexpectedly. "I wish we had more time. I wish I could have known you for centuries, like you knew your parents, and…" I swallow. "I wish we had that time to share our lives together. There's so many things I would've liked to do with you. It would have been wonderful to introduce you to my parents, so you could meet who raised me. Maybe you could've been a part of our family get-togethers. I know mom and dad would've done their best to make you feel welcome, just like they've been doing with Aspen." Despite everything, my lips part in a smile. "You should've seen the first time Aspen tried hot dish."

There's a part of me that still hopes, though. I stand, face-to-face with Maeve. We're almost the exact same height. "You never know," I whisper. "The Eldest could be wrong. Maybe there's something we can do. With the combined power of the Seelie and Unseelie Courts working together, I mean…"

"We were worried this is why you requested an audience."

I spin to face Sean. He's dressed in a tunic of black silk to match the streak of black in his hair, which is pinned back neatly from his face. His eyes, usually sharp ice, are blue like the sky around the sun, warm and yet difficult to look at directly. I stare at my feet instead.

"You can't reverse it?"

"There's only so much our magic can do." His voice is uncharacteristically gentle. "Even if Shannon and I joined with Oakspirit and Hibiscus to perform some kind of reversal spell. It still wouldn't be enough."

My whole body is shaky and unsteady as I step away from Maeve. "So that's that, then." I feel like I'm closing a door on a part of my life, a part full of what-ifs and possibilities, a part where Maeve is there, instead of here, forever immortalized in stone.

Saying goodbye to the possibilities and what-ifs is harder than I thought. Unbidden tears fall down my cheeks, trailing tracks down my neck.

"Come with me." Sean turns and heads toward the castle. "Shannon and I have something we wished to discuss with you while you're here."

Woodenly, I follow him. The interior is as different as night is to day compared to the last time I was here. Nightglade preferred decor that was black and white, with occasional glints of silver. Everywhere I look I see Sean and Shannon's influence. Bursts of color, tapestries of moments from Unseelie history adorn the walls. One in particular catches my eye. It depicts an army of fae facing what looks like a dragon. The dragon's fire glows in the light of the torches.

"There are dragons?" I ask. Wyverns are one

thing, but if I've been traipsing around the whole of Elfaeme with no thought of running into a dragon, well…

"That tapestry shows the battle between Tembyn the Insane and a coalition of fae—wild, Seelie, and Unseelie," Sean says over his shoulder, sounding like a museum employee giving a tour. "Usually dragons live peacefully with the fae, but Tembyn wanted to rule all of Elfaeme. In the face of that kind of threat, the fae banded together, using their combined magic to defeat him. This was over a thousand years ago now. Most dragons prefer to coexist with us in humanoid form. You've met one, you know. Or did you think the Eldest was just some run-of-the-mill fae?"

My mind reels, thinking over my interaction with the Eldest, rearranging it to fit this new information. The scales across their skin. The sharp teeth. The golden bed they said they were napping in.

The Eldest is a dragon.

"In here." Sean gestures to a doorway to a small room. It's brightly lit with glowing balls of ice forming a chandelier above a wooden table. Shannon sits in one of the plush chairs, a pair of reading glasses perched precariously on the tip of his nose as he reads over the papers in front of him.

"Ah." He sets his glasses down and looks up at us. "You're here. Lovely."

"Shannon, you look…"

"Exhausted?" Sean volunteers. "Like death?"

"Thank you for that," Shannon responds

mildly.

"Is being King really that stressful?"

"Being King isn't, no," he says, pushing his chair back until it balances on the back two legs. "Cleaning up Nightglade's mess, though, is another story."

"He had his hands in a lot of unsavory businesses," Sean explains grimly. "Outwardly, he made it look as if he merely was looking the other way when certain Unseelie would torture and kill humans. But it seems as if he was actually providing funding for some of these groups."

"They're less than pleased to hear that with a change of leadership their activities will no longer be tolerated, much less funded," Shannon adds.

"Which brings us to why we're glad you requested an audience." Sean seats himself next to Shannon and I'm pinned by their two sets of eyes.

"What is it?" I ask, slightly alarmed. If they ask me to help them fight these groups, I may have to remind them of how my fighting abilities really leave something to desire.

"We've been so busy dealing with these groups, we don't have the time to set up some of the other efforts we wanted to explore." Sean riffles through the pile of papers in front of Shannon and draws one out. "So we're recruiting some help."

He turns the document to face me. At the top, in bold letters, it says, "Now Hiring: Official Human/Fae Liaisons."

"Liaisons plural?"

"We already have some applicants, but yes, we're gathering a team. It's our hope you could be one of the leads. You are one of the only changelings of this generation, and your time among humans gives you a unique perspective."

"You'd be okay working with our cousin?" Shannon inquires. "We'd like to ask Quince as well."

"Oh no, more time with Quince?" I ask sarcastically. My heart is thumping wildly. After I'd changed my mind about being a vet tech, my future loomed, full of question marks. Preventing Nightglade from killing any more fae had consumed enough of my time that those question marks had been pushed aside, but lately they've taken up a lot of my thoughts.

"We'd pay you for your time, of course." Sean slides another paper toward me with a sum of money worth more than I'd ever make at Gramp's Diner in a year. My jaw drops.

"Is that enough for a monthly salary?" Shannon asks. "We want you to be fairly compensated for your time. Plus, you know Elfaeme has its own risks and dangers."

"Monthly?" I squeak. My mind swirls. With this kind of money, I'd be able to get my parents the camper they've always dreamed of but never bought. I could help my siblings pay for college if they want. Plus, as soon as I read the job title, I felt something click into place, my body fizzing with excitement and yet calm at the same time. Like this is what I had been waiting for.

Sean and Shannon regard me patiently.

"Let's talk logistics," I say, contentment suffusing my entire body. At their raised eyebrows, I add, "Yes, I'll do it."

Epilogue

Cold wind blows around my legs as the automatic doors open and I walk into the hotel. I tug my jacket around my waist and check my phone for the thousandth time today. No text from Maggie. Slipping the phone into my pocket, I worry at my bottom lip. She'd said she had something for me, but kept it super vague.

I find myself in front of the hotel room Aspen told me he'd be in. Without hesitation, I raise my hand to the door and knock. The bed creaks and I hear the muffled sounds of what is unmistakably a home improvement show of some kind.

"Eevee." Aspen opens the door and sweeps me

into a hug, all in one move. "Give me a moment."

He bustles back into the room, turning off the TV and pulling on some shoes. "Penny told me to bring some kind of appetizer if I could, so does this work?" He holds up a family size bag of chips.

A laugh bubbles up. "Sure, Aspen. Everyone loves chips. Let's pick up some dip on the way."

We settle into my parents' car. Our conversation is fluid, natural, with none of the tension we'd had earlier this year.

After a detour to pick up the dip, we pull up to my parents' house. Disappointment swirls in my gut when I think of the next few hours. Yet another family dinner where I have to watch what I say, because any mention of the fae messes with my parents' memories.

"You okay?" Aspen asks, the bag of chips and dip dangling from one hand as he joins me at the door.

"I wish I could tell them," I admit. "I hate hiding this big part of who I am from them, especially since–"

"I know." He touches my elbow, his eyes warm and understanding.

The sound of car tires crunching over gravel stops my hand as it reaches for the door handle. I swing around to see Cam parking their old, rusty van, with Maggie in the passenger seat.

"Mags!" I rush over and see her face breaking into a wide smile. She opens the car door and my words all come out in a rush. "You can't keep me in suspense like that! Is it…?"

She holds up a packet of paper. "It is!"

I grab it from her, anticipation thrumming in my veins. "Thank you so much for helping me with this. With spending half my time in Elfaeme lately, I couldn't have done this without you."

"I know, I'm the best."

Aspen joins us by Cam's van. He knows exactly what the envelope in my hand entails. "Should you do it now, before you go in?"

I'm gazing down at the packet of adoption information, a copy of the documents my parents had given me over a year ago. Maggie had helped me with the forms to request the information and kept an eye on the mail for me, so she could intercept the packet when it arrived. It had taken months, but finally, finally! It's here.

"Does anyone have anything sharp?" I ask, looking up from the envelope.

Cam holds up a hand. "I do." They open the trunk to their van with some difficulty, then rummage around. "Here." They slam the trunk shut and hold out a utility knife. "I use it for sharpening my pencils."

"Wait." Maggie intercepts the handoff, taking the knife and pulling out a mini bottle of hand sanitizer from her purse. She douses the knife in the hand sanitizer, then hands it to me. "No need to give yourself an infection in the pursuit of breaking fae charms."

I take the utility knife, freshly cleansed, and glance at Aspen. "It doesn't take a lot of blood, right?"

His eyes go hazy as he thinks back to his time

with Maeve. "I don't think so. But Maeve didn't use her blood magic around me much."

"We'll try a small prick, then."

In my heart, I gather all my intention, just like I did before seeing the Eldest. *Blood*, they had said. *Contracts.*

Please break the enchantment on my parents, please let this work.

I prick my index finger and let a single drop of blood fall on the envelope.

We watch as it shimmers, crimson against the gold. Then it glitters black and disappears. My head swirls and I sway on the spot.

"Did it work?" Cam asks, taking the knife from me gingerly while Maggie hands them the hand sanitizer.

"Only one way to find out." I stride toward the front door of my childhood home and enter.

The house is a chaotic blend of laughter and voices.

"Eevee, is that you?" I hear my dad shout. "About time! We're hungry!"

"I brought chips!" Aspen declares with pride, kicking off his shoes and ambling toward the kitchen.

"Put them on the counter," my mom advises him as he walks by. "Cam, Maggie, we're so happy you two could make it tonight!"

Greg and Charlie run up and give me a hug, then dash away as quickly as they came. Jess waves from her spot on the couch, where she sits next to

Quince, who is probably learning more than he ever needed to know about apes from her. Seeing the envelope in my hands, he raises an eyebrow. I shrug, crossing my fingers.

Amelia barrels down the stairs, followed by shoulders guy—Trent, I remind myself—and squeals when she sees the envelope. "It worked?!"

"We'll see," I say.

"See you later, bean," Trent says, bending down to give Amelia a quick squeeze.

"You're welcome to stay," mom calls from the kitchen.

"I got work, otherwise you know I'd never pass up some of Todd's cooking!" Trent shouts back.

In true Minnesotan fashion, it takes him another ten minutes to leave after he says goodbye to everyone.

"Hey, Sean and Shannon are here!" he shouts as he finally opens the door.

"You got here just in time to eat," Aspen says, his mouth already full of chips.

Looking at them, you'd never guess they were Unseelie royalty. They're both dressed in jeans and long-sleeved shirts. Shannon's hair is straight as a pin, and Sean's is tied back neatly from his face.

"Excellent," Shannon replies, stepping inside. "We're starving. Dealing with a minor FREEDOM uprising is hungry work, and—"

"Let's not talk shop here, Shannon," Sean says, his lips pressed into a tight smile.

"Right, right," Shannon agrees affably.

We all gather in the kitchen at my dad's insistence that we shouldn't let the food go cold. I barely pay attention to what I load on to my plate, my mind on what I'm about to say. When we're all seated, I take a breath. At my side, Quince reaches for my hand under the table and gives it a squeeze.

I wait for the right moment, and it finally comes in the form of my mom asking, "So, Eevee, how's your job been?"

Quince grips my hand tighter, sensing the thrill of nerves coursing through my body like wildfire. But now is not the time to lose my nerve.

"Actually," I clear my throat. "I've been meaning to talk to you about that. Here's the thing…"

And as I tell everyone at the table the story of my life over the past year–learning I was fae, searching Elfaeme for my birth parents, rescuing Aspen, thwarting Nightglade, and helping the newly crowned Queen Sean and King Shannon as their fae/human ambassador, I watch my parents' faces carefully for any sign of the fae enchantment's telltale signs.

Not once do their eyes go blank.

Fate of the Fae Artwork by Jessi Linn

Added for the 2nd Edition

Eevee and Jaila Spy on Aspen
(Chapter 6)

The Gnome Family: Urlin, Furla, and their children
Marpo, Julna, Gilvi, Lessi, Jolmi, and Molbi Pell
(Chapter 14)

Resting Before Seeing The Eldest
(Chapter 20)

Sean and Shannon (and Fearghas) Come to the Rescue
(Chapter 24)

Acknowledgments

Back in 2020, I had vowed to take a break from writing.

Eevee had other ideas.

I'm so grateful to have people in my life who have been with me on this journey, from the beginning, when the first concepts were being puzzled out, to the trilogy's completion.

First and foremost, I want to give a big thank you to my editor, Laura Cossette. Laura, if you happen to be reading this, never underestimate how much you mean to me. Your time and effort to help these books truly shine is so appreciated. Without you, these books would not be as wonderful as they are.

To my husband and kids: you all are my foundation and my cheer squad, and so many parts of this book would not have happened without your help. Thanks for letting me share my thoughts and ideas with you. And special thanks to my husband, who had to listen to me read multiple renditions of scenes until they were just right.

Like with *Finding Fae* and *A Twist of Fae*, I absolutely have to thank the real Sean and Shannon. Quince's cousins come to life on the page because of the inspiration you two gave me.

Finally, to my friends and family. I value your

presence in my life, and hope to continue bringing joy to yours. Thank you for all your continued enthusiasm and support.

About the Author

El Holly loves to write, especially books full of adventure and whimsy. When she isn't writing, teaching, or "mom-ing," you can find her sipping on coffee or taking her dog, Mack, on walks in Minnesota. Like Eevee, she is adopted. Unlike Eevee, her birth parents are not fae (that she knows of).

Follow the author for updates on new releases

Facebook:
http://www.facebook.com/elhollywrites

Website:
http://elhollywrites.com

Amazon Author Page:
http://www.amazon.com/author/elholly

Instagram:
http://www.instagram.com/elhollywrites

I'd love to hear from you!
eholly42@gmail.com

www.ingramcontent.com/pod-product-compliance
Lightning Source LLC
Chambersburg PA
CBHW032113310726
48972CB00001B/203